Miss Wildthyme and Friends Investigate

by Stuart Douglas, Cody Schell,
Jim Smith & Nick Wallace

Obverse Books 2010
Published by Obverse Books
info@obversebooks.co.uk
www.obverse books.co.uk

Cover Art by Bret Herholz
Iris Logo by Anthony Dry
Cover Design by Cody Schell

First Published May 2010

The Found World © Jim Smith
The Irredeemable Love © Nick Wallace
Elementary, My Dear Sheila © Cody Schell
The Shape of Things © Stuart Douglas

Iris Wildthyme and Panda © Paul Magrs
Manleigh Halt Irregulars © Stuart Douglas
Senor 105 © Cody schell

With thanks to Anthony Dry, Jay Eales and Paul Magrs

Stuart would like to thank Julie Douglas and George Mann.
Cody would like to thank Rudolfo, Alejandro and Aaron, or as they're better known, or as they're better known: El Santo, Blue Demon and Mil Mascaras. Also Stuart and Paul, or as they're better known: the Plaid Masked Man and the Marauding Mancunian.
Jim would like to thank Eddie Robson, Lance Parkin, Swyrie and Saliya Cooray, Mark Clapham and Mags Halliday.

The moral rights of the authors have been asserted.

All characters in this publication are fictitious and any resemblance to any persons, living or dead, is purely co-incidental.

All rights reserved. No part of this publication may be reproduced or transmitted in any form by any means, electronic or mechanical, including photocopying, recording or any information retrieval system, without prior permission, in writing, from the publisher.

This book is sold subject to the condition that it shall not, by the way of trade or otherwise, be lent, resold, hired out, or otherwise circulated without the author's prior consent in any form of binding or cover other than that in which it was published and without a similar condition including this condition being imposed on the subsequent publisher.

Printed in Great Britain by the MPG Books Group, Bodmin and King's Lynn

Also from Obverse Books

Iris Wildthyme and the Celestial Omnibus

The Panda Book of Horror

For Iris, Panda and Paul

Contents

The Found World - Jim Smith   009
The Irredeemable Love - Nick Wallace   055
Elementary, My Dear Sheila - Cody Schell   105
The Shape of Things - Stuart Douglas   155

The Found World
by Jim Smith

Prologue

How peculiar to be running from such savages, thought the tattooed man as he thrust a crowbar into the thin gap between the heavy, ornate doors. He cursed as he discovered that pushing hard against the end of the lever simply caused the soft wood of the doors to splinter and crumble at the edges. Behind him, he could hear the heavy slap of feet on the cold floor, his pursuers evidently approaching quickly.

He closed his eyes in concentration for a moment and his arms and hands began to shimmer. His slim fingers thickened as the smooth skin on his forearms became hard and knotted with muscle. He opened his eyes again and forced his hands - now twice their previous size – into the slight gap created by the crowbar in the rotten doors.

With a loud grunt he ripped the two doors apart and stepped quickly through. He was out of the City, at least. He still needed to get himself to a point some miles out in the desert before he could make a full escape, but for the first time in days he felt confident of getting his cargo safely away.

He slowed slightly in order to open the pouch in the front of his kilt. Inside, he could see the dull glow of the bottle. Short of a disaster, it seemed that everything was finally going to work out. He risked a glance back over his shoulder, just as one of his pursuers knelt and puffed air through the blowpipe in his hand. A ludicrous shot at this distance, the man thought, a heartbeat before he felt the sting of a dart in his leg and then a numbness spreading through his body.

He felt himself stumble and nearly fall. He could hear the guards close behind him now. He would have to risk a small jump now, there was no other choice. He concentrated...

...and reappeared, still stumbling, a few steps from the edge of a cliff. He had time to take in the existence of a fast-flowing river hundreds of metres below, before his momentum took him over the edge and he was falling, hands clasped protectively around the pouch, desperately trying to hold it closed.

Part One: 1916

1: Expedition

South America

Every day at about this time the sun, already bloated and orange from its exertions, sinks behind a vast, nameless plateau and the outcrop's rocky shape suddenly casts a long, wide shadow across the jungle. When that happens a strip of land stretching for miles to the east is plunged into sudden and almost total night.

At the furthest edge of that strip, as the shadow ends, a waterfall pools the river at its base and sends it onwards, widening and slowing as it hits the plain and begins to make its way to the ocean.

Sitting at this precise point in the jungle, on the eighteenth of September nineteen hundred and sixteen, was Edward A Malone, formerly of the London Daily Gazette. Behind him three massive Apatosauruses trooped calmly in a column, each with a large wooden box strapped, Howdah-like, to its back. Swaying gently from side to side as they passed, the mere sight of a species supposedly one hundred and fifty million years extinct would have been the most extraordinary experience most people ever had, never mind the fact they were being treated as common pack animals.

Malone, however, was sketching trees.

Not that he had lost the sense of wonder which had once propelled him into investigative writing, and thence onwards to Professor Challenger's second, valedictory expedition to South America. That trip had resulted in Malone's first contact with the extraordinary 'lost world' of ancient peoples and supposedly extinct species, the long, dark shadow of which Malone could see from his current position.

No, it was much simpler than that. It was that these strangely shaped trees growing in the centre of the river were quite unlike anything he had ever seen. This was his third visit to the plateau in less than five years and at that moment he was more interested in the unfamiliar trees than he was in the dinosaurs that he, like everyone on the short-staffed expedition, took turns at feeding, guarding and – when it was unfortunately necessary – mucking out.

Malone had never expected to return to the plateau. Challenger had slowly come to the conclusion that the tribespeople in particular should be left in peace, unmolested by the boisterous and crude interventions of twentieth century humanity. The irony of a man so prone to intervention, and so often perceived as crude, making such a pronouncement was not lost on the friends who had ventured to the plateau with him; but that very fact had convinced them it was the right thing to do. They had all agreed that they would never return to the Plateau and that they would keep its precise location a secret from all questioners. This, of course, was before the War, and thus before the government's quite extraordinary recent request.

Challenger's initial reaction had been to refuse even to consider the matter. He had reminded his friends, loudly and at length, of the problems that had arisen when he himself had brought a Pteradon back from the plateau. Over and over again, he had gone through the chain of reasoning which had led them to the conclusion that they should never return. He had, in short, fought tooth and nail to avoid acquiescing to the government's request for access to his 'lost world' and not, Malone was certain, for reasons of simple ego. This was a matter of principle.

But in the end there was more at stake than mere principle. There was the nation's interests to be considered as well.

Even so, it had taken extensive representations from Malone and their adventurous friend Lord John Roxton to get Challenger finally to agree to the government's request. When the Professor had at last been persuaded by a combination of rational argument and patriotic appeal, he had still been most insistent that the plateau's wildlife and indigenous peoples had to be preserved. Indeed, that his original intention that its very location should be kept secret still applied, even in the face of national security and potential international disaster.

It was because of this, combined with a sense of obligation and duty, that Roxton and Malone had agreed to undertake the errand to the plateau in Challenger's place. The Prime Minister's insistence that his own representative join the expedition was hardly unexpected, though whether it absolutely had to be a man of whom the Professor freely confessed a considerable dislike was more questionable.

The interloper was a thin, loquacious, mean-looking old man. Old enough for Malone, who was willing to take the Professor's judgement on trust, to be reluctantly but thoroughly impressed by the way he had handled the physical difficulties of the journey to, and across, South America. Roxton, however, had professed himself unmoved by their guest's exertions, opining in his clipped, Harrow tones that the man was 'essentially a bounder, whichever way you look at it.'

Roxton had taken particular exception to the man's insistence on being referred to as 'Sebe', pronounced 'Sabre' and his nearly explicit conceit that they were insufficiently important to be allowed to know his true name. Roxton was profoundly suspicious of the old man in any case, convinced that he knew 'Sabre' from somewhere and that, given time, he would remember exactly where that was.

Malone had initially tried to build bridges between the two men, mindful that the expedition was long, arduous and complex, but having failed time and again he had eventually given up. They had less time in the jungle, less time left to travel, than they had already expended on the expedition and it was no longer worth the effort. So he sat and drew these unlikely trees. Behind him Roxton shouted at Sabre, and Sabre bellowed at the Accala bearers, who were clearly doing the best possible job under the circumstances. Malone shut his ears to the noise and concentrated on the matter in hand. Which was when a naked, feral man crawled from the river directly in front of him.

The figure staggered through the last few feet of shallows, water streaming from his mouth and nose. He was tall and hairless, covered in tattoos or war paint of some kind, delicate abstract sigils in blue and orange that seemed to be carved into, not merely painted on, the flesh of his torso, his long spindly legs and his strange stubby arms. His eyes burned disdainfully, distant black coals in a face unlike any Malone had ever seen.

The naked man paused at the river's edge, looking around him in confusion, briefly uncomprehending. He stared at the jungle floor, as if expecting something to emerge from the ground beneath his feet. After a few moments, he dropped to his knees and began to dig into the thick mud with his fingers, pulling at the ground hurriedly, his head rocking from side to side with the urgency of his movements. His physicality was almost disturbing. His proportions were fractionally incorrect to Malone's artists eye. Imposed into Leonardo's drawing he would have been revealed for what he was; a physical freak. The way he *moved* was somehow wrong. He flowed and flickered like something from a dream.

Malone didn't know what to do. Should he call for Roxton or Sabre? Try to greet this strange creature in friendship? The decision was taken from him as the figure, tiring of its exertions, raised its head and saw Malone. The expression on its face reminded Malone of a big cat, a lion or a leopard, unexpectedly interrupted while at play: wary, dangerous, beyond human comprehension.

The creature stood still, rock steady, holding Malone's gaze with absolute calm. Then it broke eye contact and ran as if for its life, helter skelter away and up the river, diving into the water and swimming into the shadow of the plateau, into a darkness so complete that Malone's eyes were unable to adjust quickly enough, and he lost track of the figure in the gloom.

Unsure of quite what had just happened, unsure even that it had happened in the way he had perceived it, Malone stood there for a few moments, feeling as though he should be scratching his head.

Then, as the sun cleared the cover of a passing cloud, bright light pulsed briefly in the ground where the animal man had searched. Standing up, Malone made his way towards it. He stood for a moment; eyes fixed on where he was sure the light had come from until, briefly, it flared again.

Malone slid his hand, then his arm up to the elbow, into the soft ground beside the flash and touched a smooth object with the very tips of his forefinger. A bottle? A vase? A shard of pottery? He pushed his arm further into the squelching riverbank, right up to the shoulder, ruining his shirtsleeve in the process, and began to pull the object out of the ground.

2: Keeping The Spirits Up

Berwick Street, London W1

Iris Wildthyme was having fun. The party was swinging, her guests were happily singing and there had, she freely acknowledged, been a fair amount of drinking. She must have had a skinful herself, actually, in order to think this was a good idea. That was assuming she did think it was a good idea, of course. Which she must have done at some point. She couldn't exactly recall doing so, but it had to have been her. She was the only person around there who'd have any idea at all what the ritual was for. Ritual. Tsk. That was a daft name for it, obviously. Just some mumbo jumbo gloss that had been layered onto her parlour trick by someone in the bar: an invention of one of the gaggle of excited patrons singing noisily around the piano of Iris's bijou Soho cocktail lounge, *The Tradesman's Entrance*.

The piano had been Panda's idea. It was only a scraggy, battered upright and it wasn't entirely in tune, but it provided an atmosphere, and a kind of entertainment, entirely appropriate to early twentieth century Soho. Panda had surprised Iris by being able to bash out a fair few songs on it, including plenty that, strictly speaking, hadn't been written yet. That her bar had gained a reputation as a place where risqué, if sometimes incomprehensible, songs could be heard delighted her no end. She was also rather amused that her more chronistic patrons assumed that Panda was some kind of ventriloquist's doll worked from inside the piano itself. The Chinese whispers flying around the Soho small traders association that Iris Wildthyme, proprietor of that new bar on Berwick, had a twelve-inch pianist were something she was slightly less keen on. They were literally Chinese whispers too, started by that seemingly quiet Mr Hong from Lisle Street after she'd slapped him for taking liberties; and by "liberties" she meant "gin".

Her customers were a mixed bag most evenings, but the clientele was particularly odd tonight. There were a few people who hadn't been born yet and about as many that were, strictly speaking, already dead. Not that it stopped them dancing. Perhaps it was that which had brought this peculiar little trick to mind? She waved at her staff for another round of gin martinis with bruised cucumber and as little vermouth as possible.

Suitably replenished, she moved back towards the piano and listened to the singing patrons, waiting for a suitable point to join in.

In London's fair city, where the girls are so pretty,
I first set my eyes on sweet Molly Malone!
And now 'er ghost wheels her barrow,
from Eton to Harrow,
singing "Cockles and Mussels alive alive oh!"

Their singing reached a raucous, almost entirely atonal, fever pitch at this point, and the communal voice sledged roughly into the folk song's chorus, imbuing its easier-to-remember words with even more vigour and gusto. Just before the second bout of "Alive alive ohs!" began, Iris took a deep breath prior to joining in, only to be interrupted by a quiet cough that somehow cut through all the noise of the bar, silencing even the chorus. There was a girl in the doorway. She was pretty, dishevelled - indeed pretty dishevelled - and looked surprisingly strong. She was wearing a distinctly old-fashioned dress and an odd mop cap. She looked decidedly peeved.

'Ladies and gentlemen!' said Iris at the top of her voice. 'May I introduce the lady herself, Miss Molly Malone?' Applause followed and Iris bowed deeply, failing to notice that Molly failed to do the same. It was only in rising from her bow that Iris noticed the sheer level of irritation on the newcomer's face.

'Why are you singing my song?' she asked, with a face sufficiently thunder-filled that even Iris swallowed nervously.

'So why *did* you summon me?' Molly demanded to know. *The Tradesman's Entrance* had all but cleared now, leaving only Iris and Molly sitting at the bar, and Panda sweeping up the dancefloor, whistling jauntily. Iris explained that she hadn't meant to summon Molly at all but that yes, she did know that was the inevitable result of what she'd been doing. She'd just sort of forgotten. She shrugged. Anyway, wasn't Molly pleased to see her old pal Iris? So why didn't she just have a drink and forget all about it, because, well, wouldn't that be nice?

Molly frowned. 'It would be nice, if you hadn't dragged me here against my will, rather than inviting me like any good friend would do upon deciding to open a gin palace.'

She had a point and Iris was just about to explain when unexpectedly, she found herself asking exactly how the singing of an old folk song had dragged Molly to the bar? She felt awkward and slightly *off* asking it. The words didn't sound right and, anyway, she already knew the answer.

'It's perfectly simple,' said Molly with a pained expression, 'the why and the how, I mean. That's my song. I'm it. It's me...'

'Because you're an Incremental, yes darling, I know,' interrupted Iris, shirty because she knew she was in the wrong and unsettled because she still didn't know why she'd asked.

'Yes, an Incremental. A conceptual entity. Someone who gradually comes into existence because enough human beings refer to them as if they're real. Anyone sings my song anywhere in the world, a little bit of me goes with it and a little bit of the singing changes me. You know this.'

Iris nodded, then shuddered slightly. It was almost as if unknown eyes were raking across her. What was going on? She *did* know this, she went to speak but the disgruntled Molly continued -

'If you take that singing and my relationship to it and mix in someone,' her eyes darted at Iris, 'some*thing* with a brain like yours then it's not enough for me to feel it, or even be changed by it, I have to be a part of it. It happens to Clemmy too. We both hate it.'

'How is Clemmy?' asked Iris, thinking fondly of the brassy Spanish strumpet and wishing she was here to give the atmosphere a hefty boot up the posterior.

'Not good,' said Molly, her expression pouring cold water on Iris' briefly revived spirits, 'Those ghastly Californian puritans have been singing her song, bowdlerising the words no less, and it's changed her. Sometimes she's not the Clemmy we all love, she's actually rather shy and retiring. Her hair goes blonde and she gets all hoity toity.' For a moment Molly looked like she might actually start crying, 'I think I've lost my best friend,' she said.

The muggy feeling in Iris's head began lifting as she took another extensive hit of her drink and she shook her head to finally dispel it, then put her arm around Molly's shoulders.

'I'm sorry, duck,' she said as soothingly as she could, 'For that and, er, that other thing. Look, don't go off in a huff, stay here and we'll do something fun tomorrow. We could go and see the dinosaurs in Regent's Park?'

'Oh, I wouldn't want to do that,' said Molly, leaving Iris feeling as though she were banging her head against a wall.

'I actually feel sorry for those poor creatures,' Molly said, 'So did Clemmy. We have a sort of fellow feeling with them because we used to be the same.'

'They used to be fictional Spanish whores as well?' asked Iris, not entirely sure where this conversation was meant to be going. Molly narrowed her eyes at Iris and pouted.

'No! They used to be Incremental as well'

'Did they? How does that work, then?' said Iris, suddenly interested. She liked dinosaurs.

'Before people knew there were real live dinosaurs, back when there were just bones in the Earth and in people's imaginations, there were quite a few Incremental dinosaurs swimming and stomping about in the collective unconscious. Clemmy used to know a Brontosaurus. Now it's no use saying that there's no such thing as a Brontosaurus and there never was any such thing as a Brontosaurus. Just because Professor Challenger went and found a load of live animals and used them to prove that what we'd call a Brontosaurus is just an Apatosaurus put together wrong, that didn't do very much good for Bronwyn did it?'

Iris wasn't sure she was following this, so she took another swig of her drink to help her concentrate.

'Bronwyn?' she asked, slightly afraid of the answer, 'Are you saying you know a Brontosaurus called Bronwyn?'

'Apparently not, apparently she's an Apatosaurus. That's what I mean, you see. She's now stuck being a creature that never existed because the popular imagination insists that it did. It's very confusing for her.'

'Look,' said Iris, keen to make amends, as well as drag Molly out of the slough of despond, 'if you reckon that me singing your song has a bigger effect on you than normal, the same would be true of Clemmy, right? So, why don't we get Panda to put down his brush, and get back on the old Joanna for a quick burst of "My Darling Clementine". We'll use the oldest and muckiest set of words we can think of – and see if it can rustle up Clemmy? The real Clemmy? All bosoms and temper. How about that?'

Molly looked at Iris, excited and engaged for the first time since she'd arrived. 'That would work! You singing about old Clemmy would give her a hell of an incremental kick as it dragged her over from whatever dreary Episcopalian hut she's currently stuck in!'

'That's what I thought,' said Iris beaming at her own cleverness, 'And then, Molly Malone, once we've got your pal back, we three girls can make a night of it. Wadda ya say?'

3: Power

Winterisle

The Laird of Winterisle surveyed the building works at his island's harbour with a proud eye. The splendid new dock, built with government money and at no cost to the Laird or the people of his island, was even in its unfinished embryonic form, hugely impressive.

The harbour was of practical necessity as well as a thing of great beauty. It was how his community was going to survive. Winterisle, the most northerly of four small islets to the west of North Uist, had an environment that, entirely coincidentally, lived up to its name.

When his father had come to the islands more forty years before, purchasing them and, against the wishes of the locals and in line with his own paganism, naming each of the four after one of the seasons of the year, he had already made elaborate plans for his own future. He had always intended to invoke the entirely un-Scots principle of 'feudal dues', and have a wife on each island. He had always intended, if possible, to leave the islands individually to the eldest son of each of these four 'marriages'. He saw it as a way of perpetuating his own practices, ensuring the survival of his line and his way of looking at the world.

But Winterisle's father was not a practical man and it was only his own personal future in which he was interested. That, for example, at least two of the islands could not feasibly be self-sustaining in the long term was of no interest to him at all. He wasn't a farmer or even someone with an abstract or schoolroom knowledge of agriculture. He was a nouveau rich dilettante with pretensions; a boring man with an interest in, but no understanding of, the occult.

Winterisle lacked the rich harvests and loamy soils of the islands named after warmer seasons; the famous corn and barley rigs, the huge, profitable harvests, of the Laird's older brothers' inheritances. The fishing wasn't bad, but it was barely subsistence level within even a small community and exporting to nearby islands with better catches of their own was obviously impractical.

Hence the Laird's willing acceptance of the offer from the Government in London. The new submarine base built deep into the island's only substantial cliff edge was to be served by a splendid, and entirely modern, dock and quay which the people of the island were permitted to use at their own discretion. The London Government had also agreed to pay for the dock's maintenance in perpetuity, regardless of how long or short the Naval base's own tenure of existence was. The Government was also paying the Laird handsomely for the rent of the parts of the island the Naval base occupied.

Once the base and its dock were finished there would be an influx of newcomers to the island. The Laird was determined that the islanders would do their best to make welcome these newcomers, no matter whence they came. None of them would be islanders. That was inevitable. Few of them would even be Scots (although Winterisle had been pleasantly surprised to discover the team leader, due to arrive shortly, was himself a native Scot; born in Ayrshire and trained, as the Laird had been, at the University of Edinburgh.)

However this lack of good breeding was not to be taken as sufficient excuse for poor manners and cold welcomes. He had made this absolutely clear at one of his fortnightly open meetings with the people of his island and they had seemed to accept his view on the subject with surprisingly little resistance. Perhaps they were finally beginning to understand what the base would mean to the island.

While these strangers would bring much that was new and unfamiliar with them, they would also require sustenance and entertainment. Some would even require lodgings. They would, if slowly at first, assuredly mix with the locals over time. After a generation of neglect, there would be new investment in the loneliest of the Seasons Isles.

With new money, new people and new facilities, Winterisle could dream, as ambitiously but less self-centredly than his father, of a future for his island that would provide for all its inhabitants. The Laird was confident that the concrete infrastructure of his quay would prove more long lasting than the wicker foundations of the agricultural prosperity of his brother's island.

4: Rage

Regent's Park Road, London NW1

George Edward Challenger was not noted for being a reasonable man. It would be closer to the truth, in fact, to say that he was noted for being an entirely unreasonable man. However, should one make such a statement within earshot of his wife, or anywhere she might read it in print, the action would invite affronted and determined censure. That tiny, frail, birdlike woman, to whom the Professor was entirely devoted, would stand no criticism of her husband on grounds of insensitivity.

She was, as she explained at length in a letter to *The Times* after its leader criticised the Professor's conduct during, and his publication of his notes concerning, the so-called 'Poison Belt', quite simply not prepared to stand by and let lesser men claim her husband as an insensitive brute. He was, she explained, the most sensitive of all men and it was this sensitivity that made him unable to cope with the crassness and stupidity of so many others.

Few at *The Times* were convinced by the argument but the correspondence pages were lively for several days, and during a parliamentary recess at that, which was reason enough to print it. Had the leader writer of *The Times* seen George Challenger fuming at the breakfast table in late October 1917, he would have thought his initial misgivings about the Professor's character well founded.

Challenger's great bull shoulders were shaking, the vast head with its spade like beard twitching from side to side, the arms (that more properly resembled those of a wrestler than those of a member of the Academy) flailing around madly. There was a real danger that one of those great fists would make contact with the parlour's low ceiling.

'This IDIOT!' bellowed Challenger, once he had recovered the power of speech. 'This mindless simpleton! This oaf!' His ability to speak failed him again and he simply stood there and shook in incoherent rage.

His wife darted around him, slipping into his line of sight, knowing that he found it hard to sustain such a rage when she was in full view. She asked him what it was that had enraged him so and what it was that had been contained in the letter he had opened as she had gone through to the kitchen to give cook instructions for dinner.

Grimacing, her husband told her that the letter was from the Chairman of the House of Commons All Party Committee for the Exploitation of Dinosaur Resources and that his rage was at said chairman, his committee, its conclusions in general and its demands of, and recommendations for, him personally and in particular.

Mrs Challenger nodded in agreement with every criticism her husband made of the Committee. Not because she was afraid of him or because she was unable to tell him he was wrong, but because he wasn't wrong. He was right and she agreed with him with a whole heart. It was, frankly, bad enough that they both had to leave London in order for George to take up a post that he did not desire in a place neither of them even wanted to visit, never mind base themselves in for the duration of the war.

It was, Mrs Challenger agreed, both rude and, yes, inconsiderate of Mr Lloyd George, installed now as Prime Minister, to demand these things of them. It was, she concurred with her husband, outrageous to make veiled hints of detention under wartime emergency powers should his unreasonable demands not be met. It was, absolutely, in no way her dearest's fault that the cover story prepared to justify Malone's trip to South America, that of an exhibition of live specimens from the Lost World to be held at the London Zoo in the Regent's Park, had proved damaging to the government. Her beloved had, she acknowledged, cautioned against such a cover story precisely because it would be seen as a frivolous use of valuable resources in a time of war.

It was, she affirmed by nodding furiously, quite likely that Lloyd George was behaving so abominably because of the threats that George Challenger had made against his person and it was especially unforgivable because, yes, those threats were entirely legitimate. Lloyd George had refused to leave their home at the Professor's politely and calmly phrased request and he was well within his rights to escalate that request to a demand and to back up that demand with a warning of the use of force.

Gently and slowly, Mrs Challenger guided the conversation away from the First Lord of the Treasury and indicated to her husband that there were other items in today's post that might, at the very least, cause him less rage. When pressed for an example, she plucked a smart envelope, the handwriting on which she recognised, out from the pile on the table.

'It's from Edward,' she said brightly.

His rage calmed, his mind keen for distraction, Challenger plucked the letter from her hand with a grateful smile. He somehow slid one of those vast sausage like fingers under the flap of the letter and ungummed it with a flourish. He unfolded the letter within, and several other pieces of paper fell out of it onto the floor. Mrs Challenger picked these up and arranged them in what seemed like a sensible order on the table, while her husband's eyes skimmed the letter itself.

Unfortunately the communication from his old friend began with yet more news that pricked the Professor's ire, and only the calming influence of his wife's hand on his arm prevented him from resuming his stomping about the parlour once more.

'Malone has more complaints about that dreadful man, what's-his-name, the one from the Ministry! Can't say I blame him!' said the Professor, paraphrasing aloud. He paused, as if suddenly captivated, 'Though he does say that the fellow was useful when some...that can't be right, surely...Spanish-speaking bandits dressed in pink carnival masks attacked their camp. What nonsense! There'll be some inadvertently ingested hallucinogen at the back of that story, make my words, my dear! Well, well, he goes onto to say that he's made some sketches of a possibly unknown species of tree! Well, that's more interesting!' Fascinated now, the Professor slipped into his seat at the breakfast table and absentmindedly picked up the slice of, now cold, toast he had throw down in his earlier rage, 'Says he includes them with this letter, but...' The Professor turned the Malone's letter over in his hand, briefly puzzled at the absence of the promised sketches.

Even with the Professor sitting down and his wife standing by his side she was barely taller than he, so unequal were they in height. She slid silently in next to him and placed the drawings that had fallen from the envelope into his line of sight on the table.

The Professor beamed, cleaned his glasses and began to examine the drawings with little clucks of delight.

'The letter also says something about a vase he found in the mud, says he's bringing it back with him,' he said absentmindedly, 'There's meant to be a sketch of that too.'

He shuffled the papers in his hands, turning them over until he found the sketch of the strange, glass object that Malone had found in the mud.

'It's some sort of carboy,' said the Professor, but his wife shook his head.

'It's not a carboy,' she said, 'It's more an ornamental jar or a perfume bottle. It's decorative, not practical.'

George nodded his assent. Had it been a scientific instrument Malone would have had the wherewithal to point it out in his notes.

'It looks like a lovely thing,' said his wife, looking round the Professor's shoulder at the drawing and he nodded in agreement, placing his arm around her waist affectionately.

'It does, my love, it does. Should Malone be inclined to let me have it, I shall give it you as a present,' and he smiled at her, for the moment all anger forgotten.

5: Bargaining

Ypres

At breakfast in the mess that morning, the visiting Colonel, newly arrived from British Intelligence, had made an odd announcement to his recently seconded staff. The junior officers, all of whom had been assigned to the Colonel from the chateau's permanent complement at their own request, had found this rather unusual, but didn't feel themselves in a position to comment or contradict.

The announcement the Colonel had made was this; he wished to be absolute clear that it was his opinion that, upon his arrival later that day, their aristocratic guest would unthinkingly take the chair at the head of the negotiating table.

This had seemed like an odd thing for a visiting Colonel (who was a decorated hero of the Afghan war and a famous author to boot) to insist would happen but, as it turned out, he was entirely correct. Their visitor, whom they had been instructed to refer to only as 'The Count' when not in his presence and as 'Your Highness' when speaking directly to him could not possibly be avoided, had an oddly egoless arrogance. His was the sort of supreme confidence that can come only from centuries of breeding and privilege. The Colonel had wanted his juniors to know that. He had also wanted them to understand how that sort of mind worked. Even more importantly, he had needed them to understand that he had the measure of their visitor. That he understood the Count and that whatever may eventually transpire as a result of this meeting, it was not outwith the Colonel's own plans.

It was incontrovertibly true that His Highness was the kind of man possessed of an arrogance that meant he saw such trifles as the best seat at a table as an innate right, not something open to any kind of question. He was not in his own country. He was a guest. What is more, he was a guest of whom his hosts were deeply suspicious. One in whom they had no measure of trust. Yet the assumptions of status were so deeply buried in His Highness that the Colonel had rightly guessed he would not even consciously select a position in which to seat himself. Like so much to do with power, it had been assumed. The Count sat now, reclining in the chair, feral and catlike, his tall, pale body spread across the wood and upholstery like it was a burnished throne.

The Colonel had never believed the more outlandish tales told about this Wallachian Prince, but now he sat before him he was tempted to push aside all notions of the probable and accept much of the rumour and innuendo that had passed across his desk. Once in his presence, a story about this man that seemed mere penny dreadful frippery when neatly typed on a sheer of foolscap on a Whitehall desk, took on an entirely different tincture; one of total and chilling conviction.

The Colonel selected a chair to the Count's left and sat. To sit at his right hand would be too much, under the circumstances. It would feel too much as though he were offering the Count advice or counsel, rather than opening a negotiation.

The Colonel had dismissed his adjutant and the Army stenographer shortly after the Count's arrival and at his request. For this most private and mysterious of meetings, the Count had suggested, the Colonel could surely take notes himself and then only if absolutely necessary?

This meeting had taken months of careful planning to set up. Even the chair the Count had barely noticed had been transported from Balmoral only a week before and then after a month's difficult negotiation with the private and diary secretaries of Queen Mary herself. Everything had to be both exactly right and seemingly thrown together with indifference and speed. It was vital that they seemed surprised by his overtures.

'Your Highness', began the Colonel, leaving enough of a pause for the Count to suggest an alternative form of address should he so choose, 'His Majesty's Government is both interested in, and gratified by, your desire to seek an audience with his representatives. We respect your integrity in travelling to meet us here, but we are still none the wiser as to your reasons for requesting this audience.'

That was it, the first big lie of the meeting. The Colonel had kept his eyes level, his tone peppered with concern. Had this extraordinary individual been paying enough attention to even notice the performance, or too much attention to be convinced by it? Had he seen through their plan already? It was hard to tell.

The Count's eyes flicked around the conference room, surveying the shell damaged former grandeur, the paintings in ribbons and the windows replaced by wet and rotten slabs of wood. 'This war,' he began, in his unaccented but oddly toned English, 'This folly of the Kaiser's... it drags on.' He smiled sadly, showing his teeth, and leaned across, his breath hot in the Colonel's face, 'My Kingdom... my Principality has the great historical misfortune to be a client state of the Austrian Empire. My people have fought three winters of war for the sake of a worthless paper treaty and a quarrel not our own. It is long enough. Too long.'

The Colonel had not anticipated an answer of quite this tone. Its content was much as expected but he had not expected the old man to express it in such a manner. The Colonel chose his next words carefully, as much for fear of enraging the Count's sense of honour as with regard to his own secret purposes.

'Your Highness, are you saying that your Kingdom would be prepared to negotiate a separate peace with the Allies? Independently of the Emperor? Independently of the Kaiser?'

The Count nodded, 'The Kaiser is a weak fool, henpecked and surrounded by idiots. Franz Joseph is an old, sick man bitter beyond measure at the death of his son.' He laughed but there was no joy in it, 'I make these criticisms with love in my heart, not anger, Colonel. These men are my own distant kinsmen. Family. We are tied by blood.'

His reverie caught him unawares for a moment and there was suddenly terrible sadness on the ancient face. The Colonel almost felt sorry for him. The Count summoned the will to continue and returned to the matter at hand. 'I admire the British, Colonel,' he continued, 'The French I admire… somewhat less so. My admiration lessened when they disposed of the,' he searched for a euphemism, running his tongue across his teeth, 'aristocratic principle. More pertinently I have no need – no desire – to send the young men of my country to die at the hands of either of you,' The Count stroked his moustache and looked askance at the Colonel, 'The longer this conflict extends itself, the clearer it becomes that the Austrian Empire will not survive the war's cessation – and where will my poor Transylvania be then? Broken up. The Romanian nationalists will demand unity with the land of their supposed fathers, with no thought of their loyalty to the House of Tepes that has protected them without fear or favour for centuries. They are an ungrateful rabble.'

The Count pulled down his collar with an index finger that ended in a distractingly sharp nail. 'See?' he asked with sudden hissing insistence, and his eyes were briefly those of another kind of man.

Reluctantly the Colonel admitted that he could not see and the Count pulled his collar down further, indicating a scar that ran across his throat. 'The result of an attempt on my life by my Romanian subjects some twenty years ago. They were assisted by some of your countrymen, I believe….'

The Colonel made to protest but the Count dismissed this with a wave of his hand and the apology died in the Colonel's throat. 'Your countrymen, Colonel, but not acting in the interests or the service of their country. It was a private matter. Indeed a family matter. This is something I understand.'

Something else the Count clearly understood was that the small army of his principality controlled a stretch of trench that had frustrated British forces for months. The British public and His Majesty's Government were as sick of war as His Highness was, and the withdrawal of one of the Kaiser's coalition of willing allies, even a seemingly insignificant one in terms of men and resources, would be an enormous political coup and a propaganda victory of unimaginable proportions.

The principle behind this meeting was out in the open, and subtly but not slowly the Colonel pressed the Count on his terms for a separate ceasefire. Details of the dates and time that his soldiers would lay down their arms emerged slowly. The terms and treatment they could expect as prisoners of war required careful negotiation and very precise description.

As the meeting wound down and the Colonel began to allow himself to anticipate his dinner and the conversation and company of someone other than his counterpart, the Count withdrew a piece of paper from deep within his robe.

He slid the paper across the table and tapped it with a long, gnarled forefinger which, the Colonel suddenly noticed, was the exact same length as the index and third fingers of the same hand.

'It is in the interests of both your country and mine,' said the Count, 'for the exact contents of this piece of paper to go unrecorded by history, I think.'

The Colonel picked up the paper, trying not to make contact with the Count's skin as he did so. He unfolded the paper and read its contents silently. He felt his cheeks redden and then burn at the words before him. There was a small, inhuman snicker from the Count.

'I never thought to see so experienced a man blush for shame at mere diplomacy,' said the Count and his eyes glinted with something unnatural and inexplicably joyous.

The Colonel paused, swallowed and pushed the paper away from him, as if afraid that he would be contaminated by its contents.

'I believe that this can be arranged, although it will require some co-ordination with the Americans, of course.'

'Of course,' said the Count, 'this I expected. I am aware of the practicalities of that which I ask.'

'Is this all you require?' asked the Colonel, experiencing a sudden stab of horror at using such a dismissive turn of phrase to refer to the contents of that paper.

'There is one more thing,' said the Count quietly, 'I require a submarine.' He let the outrageous demand hang in the air for a moment. 'Do you think, my very good friend Colonel Watson, that this is something that can be arranged?'

Part Two: Spring 1917

6: Training Day

Maryland

On a train from Washington to New York, in the late hours of the evening, two old men were having dinner in the first class buffet compartment. The older of the two, the Englishman, had arrived there first and taken up residence at the car's best table.

When his ostensible host, an American, arrived they had greeted each other warmly, as old colleagues often do. For formality's sake the Englishman asked if he should address his old friend as 'Mr Secretary' or 'Mr Ambassador' or even 'Mr Lincoln' and, after a small laugh, was told that 'Robert' would do very well.

Robert Lincoln was then invited to use his guest's Christian name in return, but declined the invitation. It had been sincerely offered but Mycroft Holmes was, especially in old age, a man whom very few felt comfortable addressing with too great an amount of familiarity.

Despite this small distance that still existed between them, the two old men talked openly as the waiter came and took their wine order. Mr Holmes gently mocked the moustache Mr Lincoln had grown since his days as his Country's Ambassador to London and asked the reason for growing such an affront to decency.

Lincoln paused, evidently embarrassed. 'The moustache is because as I got older, every time I looked in the mirror, I saw Father. Which is strange, because I'm older now than he ever was.'

Mycroft nodded and muttered something about his father looming large in his own life and the peculiar indignities forced upon men unlucky enough to resemble a close relative of greater public renown.

Their bonhomie was not artificial. They were old and sincere acquaintances and there comes a time in everyone's life, presuming one is lucky enough to reach it, when one is so old that anyone with whom sufficient experience has been shared, automatically becomes an old and dear friend.

They were both aware, however, that there was business to be done here; unpleasant business at that. That the fine dinner and passable wine, the good conversation and shared reminiscences, were all building up to something that neither man quite wanted to face. Mycroft tried to delay asking the question he knew he had to ask by enquiring further about Mr Lincoln's children and grandchildren, which unfortunately turned the conversation to the death of Mr Lincoln's son in London in '93. Something Mr Holmes had done all in his power to prevent but which could not in the end be avoided.

'Terrible business,' said Mycroft, and felt a very foolish old man for uttering such a banality to the child's father.

A moment of utter silence fell between the two old men. Light from the carriage window flicked across their faces, the rhythmic click-thud of the engine's wheels suddenly unbearably loud. There was nothing to say, and Robert Lincoln seized the moment to say exactly that which needed said.

'The box,' he said, 'is in the furthermost luggage compartment. It contains that which your telegram asked for. The President sends the box with his compliments, but wishes it to be known that he is horrified by your government's need for that which it contains.'

Mycroft was unable to meet his companion's gaze.

'Do you worry, my old friend' continued Mr Lincoln, 'that its contents will be used in some workshop of filthy creation?'

Mycroft flicked his eyes up to meet Robert's and answered with absolute calm; 'I do not worry that they will, Robert. I know that they shall.'

His friend, too aghast to be angry, asked what good could possibly come of such an action. Mycroft held up a hand for silence.

'I cannot tell you,' he said, and continued over Lincoln's attempt to interrupt him, 'but I have told your President. If you wish to know the answer, you must seek if from him'.

'I am not proud of this thing we are doing, Mr Holmes,' said Robert Lincoln with more sadness than passion.

Mycroft nodded his head in agreement, 'Neither am I, Robert, neither am I,' he said and then, with as much enthusiasm as he could muster, he beckoned over the waiter to order coffee, walnuts and cigars and turned the conversation back to Lincoln's grandchildren and watched as the pride slowly returned to his old friend's pinched face.

7: Truth

Bloomsbury, London W1

When she awoke early that morning, Verity Archangel had absolutely no intention whatsoever of going back to being a spy. In fact, she had very few specific intentions of any sort. It was a largely pleasurable consequence of her independent existence that she rarely had to plan her life more than six or seven hours ahead.

As she had brylcreemed her hair and knotted her tie she had pondered the possibility of a walk up to the Regent's Park, before rejecting that in favour of a walk down into Soho. Once there, more tobacco and more cigarette papers could be purchased on Old Compton Street, before an afternoon's entertainment could be found either in the shops on Saville Row or perhaps in the less salubrious environs of Berwick Street and its more specialised establishments for ladies of leisure.

It seemed a good plan for the day, such as it was, and no one could deny that the individual components of cigarettes were something of an urgent requirement, or that she deserved a little relaxation. It was a bright, crisp morning in very early Spring, the sort where the sun sneaks into one's room before one is quite ready for it and somehow before its own warmth has begun to percolate the air. It was quite delightful, in point of fact. But it was not that which had awoken her so early.

No matter how carefree her existence now, or how broadly she painted the smile of her dilettante mask-that-was-only-partially-a-mask, she still had the brutality and terror of trench warfare only six months behind her. She had not suffered, of course, as the men at the front line had suffered. She had not died. Had not seen any of her close friends or comrades die never mind watched as young men died in their thousands. She had killed though. And been close to death herself. Close enough that her Uncle John had demanded that she 'put a stop to all that nonsense' of being 'out there in the field' and return home to an idle life of Dubonnet and gin and seed cake. She lit a cigarette, checked her hair again, and twirled in front of the mirror, making sure the creases in her trousers were exactly right and that the material at the back, beneath her light blue fair isle tank top, hung exactly right. Which it did. Whichever side you dressed on, she was going to set hearts aflutter dressed like this.

Her ablutions all but complete she began to look for her shoes, the patent leather golf shoes with the white leather ersatz 'spats' that she had picked up the week before. She was stretching down to pick them up from under her bed when she heard the telephone ring.

There was a stomp-stomp-stomp as her rather foolish maid Miss Grose travelled in her traditional ungainly fashion up the narrow stairs to the bedroom landing. This was followed by a sharp rap upon the door of Verity's dressing room. During this inelegant kerfuffle Verity busied herself double-knotting her laces and in the process accidentally dropped ash onto her treasured lion skin rug. The maid knocked again, 'Miss Archangel?' she said, 'It was your Uncle John on the telephone.'

Uncle John? That was a surprise, although not an unpleasant one. Though she'd have thought he would have been rather busy at the moment. Certainly too busy to invite her for tea. Verity called out to Miss Grose that she would be down to speak to him in a moment, but found herself being interrupted.

'He's no longer on the line, Miss. He says that you're to go and see him at the Circus at eleven o'clock this morning. He says it's very urgent and you aren't to refuse, Miss.'

Meet him at the Circus? Now that was an odd request, thought Verity, a very odd request indeed. Why would he want her to meet him there? Surely he didn't have something useful for her to do? She realised her heart was pounding at the slightest idea of a return to gainful enterprise; the idea of casting off her idleness and pursuing something worthwhile. She paused and took a long drag on her cigarette. Best not get too excited. Not yet.

She looked herself up and down in the mirror again and waggled her eyebrows at her reflection. She looked, she had to admit, rather spectacular this morning. If Uncle John didn't have something exciting and worthwhile in mind for her, she was sure she could find something exciting and trivial to do before the day was out.

8: A Day At The Circus

Charing Cross Road, London W1

They called it 'The Circus' because that was where it was based; beneath Cambridge Circus at the intersection of Charing Cross Road and Shaftesbury Avenue, on what had once been the old Cambridge Road.

The base had been designed and built as a Tube station, a logical stopping point between the Strand and Tottenham Court Road going north to south, and between Leicester Square and Covent Garden going south west to north east. Military intelligence had put a stop to that when they'd requisitioned it during its construction, a dozen or so years before the old Queen had died.

The place's intended function was visible in the long wooden stairwells and the vast, cream and blue tiled lobby that replicated the shape and size and design of the circular ticket hall of Leicester Square's Station. The entrance to the place was a permanently locked iron box signposted as a public convenience, which had, once upon a time, been earmarked as the Shaftesbury Avenue access to the Underground station that never was.

Because of who her parents were, Verity had been allowed the privilege of visiting the Circus as a little girl, and she had liked visiting the Circus very much indeed. The bustle of it delighted her. The atmosphere of it intrigued her. The noise as the tube trains went through, their little engines huffing and puffing as they clanged through the Circus's sealed platforms, amused her almost endlessly.

As she'd grown older she'd come to appreciate that the Circus's library was amongst the finest in the Western world and that its canteen served some of the best cakes she'd ever tasted. These were two very good reasons to visit the Circus as often as possible even as an adult, which was why Verity's was a face known to almost all of the place's staff despite her having only officially visited it once in her entire life. That was in order to receive her final briefing before heading out to Belgium in the second winter of the war.

On that day she'd been 'Victor'. Dressed up in the green and khaki uniform and thumping brown boots of a Captain in the British Expeditionary Force. Her hair had been chopped and parted and pomaded (although, on reflection, it was longer then than now) and she'd been wearing a stage moustache of the very finest quality on her upper lip. None of this was true today. Although the Verity in carefully chosen men's casual country wear more strongly resembled the 'Victor' of the winter of '15 than she did the younger Verity who'd enthusiastically embraced the opportunity to become him.

After she'd passed through the required security and been escorted through what seemed like a mile of tiled, curved corridors, she found herself in the familiar environs of Uncle John's office. It would seem a strange place, she supposed, were you not used to it. Cramped, with the same ceramic wall decorations as the rest of the Circus, it had an odd mixture of furniture, most of which she recognised from childhood.

Uncle John was standing behind his desk when she entered, facing slightly away from her. His hands were clasped behind his uniformed back and she got the feeling that, had the office not been dozens of feet under the ground, he'd have been squinting out of the window as he gathered his thoughts.

He dismissed her escort and offered her a seat and a cigarette. She sat, lit up and crossed her legs, getting comfortable. She could tell from his manner that the pleasantries would be skipped. This was much as she would prefer it, to be honest. She had long considered the banality of pleasantries unnecessary when dealing with one's own family.

'A few months ago,' began Uncle John, 'when I was in Ypres, I set up an above top secret operation. I arranged for a Wallachian Count of some renown to visit a secret Royal Navy base up in Scotland. He's inspecting one of the new Icthyasubs, with a view to taking it away with him if he happens to like what he sees.'

Verity wanted to ask why someone who, judging by his title alone, was a member of the nobility of an enemy country at a time of war, was being allowed to visit a base so secret that she had never heard of it.

More, she wanted to know why he was being allowed to see, to take away, a piece of experimental technology that she had heard whispered of as a generation ahead of anything anyone had seen in the field. But she knew better than to interrupt without being cued, and she allowed Uncle John to work towards his explanation in his own time. She didn't have to wait long.

'This was part of a deal which could see the Count's country remove itself from the Austro-Hungarian Empire and thus the Central Powers.'

Verity nodded. Now she was intrigued. This was high quality intelligence, and of potentially vast impact on the war effort, but she wasn't sure what it had to do with her.

'Unfortunately,' continued Uncle John, 'the whole operation has since been taken from me.' His eyes showed no wounded pride, not a trace of venality at what lesser men would have perceived as a slight against their competence. He was concerned, not insulted. He was clearly desperately worried that he no longer knew what was going on with something he himself had initiated. He feared for the consequences of this lack of contact with his own project and that was the sum total of his personal feelings on the matter.

'Who took it?' Verity asked, assuming the question was required of her at this juncture.

'EDICT,' said Uncle John and despite herself Verity was surprised.

'And you let them?' she said, louder than she'd intended. She realised that it sounded more like a rebuke than she'd meant it to.

'I didn't have much choice,' he said. 'The docks where the Icthyasubs are based are EDICT's already, you see. Once there was doubt as to the Count's true intentions they were able to slowly wrestle the operation out of my hands.'

'There are doubts as to the Count's true intentions?' she asked, smiling inwardly at the entirely cued nature of her response.

'There were from the start,' he said, evidently trying not to enjoy himself. 'My methods aren't so crude as EDICT's, but the discovery that there was more than one aspect to the problem was all the leverage they needed.'

'They don't trust him?'

'No, but they shouldn't. The other thing they shouldn't be doing is what they've got planned.'

'And that is?'

'I think they're going to try to kill Count Dracula.'

'I see.' She inhaled deeply on her cigarette. 'Why?'

'Because they doubt his motives, because they doubt that he really does want what he says he wants and because they see an opportunity here.'

'You said "try to"?'

He nodded, 'They simply cannot kill him. I am now convinced – and your Uncle Sherlock and I are in complete agreement on this – that Dracula cannot be destroyed by any means available to EDICT. We are not dealing with a creature of ordinary flesh and blood.'

It was a lot for Verity to take in, but the immediate question was obvious.

'Why don't you intervene?'

He looked embarrassed.

'Until this morning I didn't know the location of the EDICT base. I had no idea whatsoever. There are times when one's own side can be particularly efficient in ensuring that you don't get what you need.'

'So what changed?' she asked.

'This arrived,' he said, throwing a piece of paper down onto to the desk with the sort of melodramatic flourish he disdained in others.

Verity picked it up, and as she read it he explained that the Laird of a remote island off the coast of Scotland had been given the letter while touring an EDICT installation on his island. He'd smuggled it out and then simply had it couriered down to him in London.

'This letter gives me the information I need to move against EDICT but, as it also confirms that Dracula is due to arrive in Scotland within the week, I also need someone who can do it efficiently, anonymously and very, very quickly,' said Uncle John.

'And you think I'm the man for the job?' said Verity, smiling.

'I know you are,' replied Uncle John, perhaps more warmly than was appropriate in the circumstances. 'And I know I can trust you entirely, which is not something I can say about some of the other officers at my disposal.'

'What do I need to do?' asked Verity.

9: Easy Speak

Berwick Street, London W1F

'An exceptionally good game,' said Iris, 'is for two people to go together into a darkened room and then each of them necks a bottle of whisky as quickly as possible. The first person to finish leaves the room, then comes back and knocks on the door and asks if they can come in, at which point the second person has to guess who they are!' She knocked back her drink, put her empty glass down on the bar and then spread her arms widely, as if expecting appreciative applause.

Verity waited for a moment, partially to be sure that, now Iris had stopped holding onto the bar rail, she wasn't going to topple face first onto the carpet. When it became absolutely clear that this wasn't going to happen, she told her friend that what she'd said didn't actually make any sense.

'Just because you don't understand something doesn't mean it doesn't make sense,' said Iris curtly. 'And anyway, don't you talk to me about sense, Verity, not after what I heard about what you're up to this week!' She winked and mimed playing the bagpipes using her cocktail glass (which had been miraculously re-filled during its brief excursion out of her hand) and its frankly ludicrous curly straw.

Verity, as was frequently the case, was astonished at Iris' indiscretion. She asked her to be quieter but Iris refused, clucking and cooing and waving her hands around to indicate just how unnecessary quiet and secrecy were.

'You can trust everyone here!' she said, laughing. 'The only reason I come here is because the company is beyond reproach. In fact, I only come here for the company,' she continued, her voice now as dry as her martini, 'in much the same way as I only read The Strand for the articles!' She paused. This time she was unsure if what she'd said made sense, but there was no comeback from her audience, so she ploughed on.

After sitting patiently through a few minutes more of this, and before Iris could demand another drink, Verity quietly and firmly reminded her why she was actually there. She followed that up by mentioning once again that she needed to take custody of the items Iris was keeping for her within the next twenty minutes, because she needed to visit Dege & Skinner on Saville Row this afternoon.

'Dege & Skinner? The military outfitters? Oh Verity, love,' Iris said, 'are you going to be Victor again? I don't like you at all when you're Victor, I'll tell you that for nothing. He doesn't suit you at all.'

'You mean he doesn't suit you,' said Verity with a small smile. 'Victor allowed me to do my duty,' she continued. 'For a time, at least. Uncle John practically admitted as much. I think Victor is going to be rather useful in future.'

'How is your Uncle John?' said Iris, trying and failing to repress the lascivious undertone of her question.

'You stay away from him,' said Verity, trying to balance the tone of the conversation with her horror at the idea of Iris setting her cap at Uncle John. 'He's been married enough times as it is.'

'Oh, I'm not the marrying kind,' said Iris expansively. 'Although, I rather suspected he wasn't either, or at least not on Mondays, Wednesdays and Fridays.' Any faint subtlety in her drunken suggestion was lost when she performed a vast theatrical wink in Verity's direction, which Verity deliberately ignored.

'He is very handsome, isn't he? Even now. Dear me, I could be your Auntie! Wouldn't that be nice? I mean, you don't have an Auntie, do you? You just have two uncles!'

She drained her drink. 'Where was I?'

'Falling off the bar?'

'Quiet!' Iris's face puckered with concentration. Then she broke into a broad grin.

'Look!' she cooed, waving, at the other side of the room, 'That's the divine Lady Molly,' Iris confided. 'The world's first lady policeman, so to speak. The world's first lady police-lady, I suppose. She packed it all in and got married but then she lost her husband in the war and went straight back into CID. Quite right too. She should never have given it up in the first place!' She sniggered slightly. 'Given up police work I mean.'

'All very interesting,' hissed Verity, who would normally have found such frivolities hugely fascinating, but who was preoccupied with other things.

'What did Uncle John send me here for?'

'Oh, I don't know, duck. As I said, I don't know why I come here myself, really, apart from the company.' She sighed. 'Take Sir Charles Berry,' said Iris. 'Outside of his club this is the only place he ever goes, and I can hardly attend a Gentleman's club, given that the only ladies allowed in there are ladies of the night. I *may* be slightly too old for that game.'

'Uncle John sent me here to meet you!' protested Verity, 'To collect something. What I don't know is exactly what that something is. He said you would. It's *important*.'

All the play, if not the kindness, went out of Iris's face. She knew when the game was up.

'Ah, yes, that's it,' Iris replied, suddenly as professional as she'd previously been indiscreet. 'I have to give you a very important box.'

10: Stir

Islington, London

William Wordsworth Fletcher had been named after the late poet laureate, with whose work his mother had been enamoured as a romantic, and indeed revolutionary, young girl. The work of the poet exerted little influence on his life beyond his name and his early childhood. His mother died bringing his younger brother into the world and at that moment any attempt to introduce such lofty concerns into his life had come to an end.

His father, William Wellington Fletcher had been hanged shortly before his son's fifth birthday. It was the only act of note of a short and tedious life of petty crime and drink. For William Wellington Fletcher went into the history books as the last man to be sentenced to death for sheep stealing; an offence which ceased to be a capital crime mere weeks after his internment in the prisoners' graveyard at Holloway Prison. The unfortunate younger William was passed between various distant and semi-distant relatives until eventually entering the parish workhouse in St Pancras at the age of twelve, eventually emerging into the world in adulthood as a fully qualified petty thief and an intermediate trainee housebreaker. He juggled these parallel careers with the inevitable third of being a relapsing/remitting recidivist and by the age of forty had spent roughly twenty of them, including the most recent one, behind bars.

He was currently 24601 Fletcher, W W (Pentonville) serving five to ten years for a spot of injudiciously judged housebreaking. It was, largely, water off a duck's back by now. Or would have been had age not begun to interfere with his ability to keep quiet and go to sleep.

Fletcher was now waiting in some sort of visiting area of Pentonville. He'd been sitting there for some hours. The room was unfamiliar to him. Before this morning he'd never been in it before. Not that there was anything surprising or unusual about it. It had stone walls that were indifferently painted. It had an iron door with a small window covered by iron bars. It had an identically barred window which looked out onto the prison's breakage's yard. It was entirely uninteresting and Fletcher had been in there without so much as a newspaper since shortly after breakfast. The boredom that had descended was so smothering that the banging open of the door and the shrill bark of a warder's demand that he stand in the presence of his betters was blessed relief. The surprise when the warder was followed by a uniformed solider wasn't quite large enough to translate into actual interest, of course, but it was at least something unexpected.

The army officer half walked, half marched in. Fletcher looked the lean form and oddly shiny face up and down. He was barely more than a boy but he clearly meant business.

The officer sat down, dismissed the warder who'd escorted him and closed, locked and bolted the door behind him. He indicated with a maroon gloved hand that Fletcher should sit. So he did.

'I was told,' said the officer as he slid into the chair opposite, 'that you were the best safecracker in London.'

'Not were, sir, am, sir' replied Fletcher with some professional pride, 'the only skill I lacked was the one of never getting caught.'

'Yes,' said the officer with a small smile. He withdrew a thin manila file of papers from under his arms and began flicking through the file. It was obvious after a few seconds that he was merely wasting time, searching for unexceptional conversational gambits which would allow him to delay other, more important matters until he had something of a measure of the man opposite him

'You've never been in the army, have you Fletcher?' he asked, eventually.

'You know I 'aven't,' Fletch replied, 'You're reading my file, ain'tcha?'

The officer nodded.

'Yes, but it's hardly comprehensive. We don't keep files like that. I thought there might be something missing.'

'Well there isn't. Is it important?'

'Perhaps. Do you think you could impersonate an army sergeant or a navy CPO?'

Fletcher, unsure why he'd want to attempt such an impersonation, asked if, as he suspected they were, the 'other ranks' of the services were much like prison officers.

The officer's eyes briefly alighted upon the grizzled prison officer visible through the window of the office and clearly found it rather difficult to restrain a smile.

'I think you know the answer to that.'

'Then it'd be easy,' said Fletcher, 'But I can't see why I'd do it. Or are you expecting me to get all fired up about King and Country and all that cobblers?'

The officer's eyes went very hard.

'You do realise you're likely to die in prison before you complete your sentence?'

'I do,' he said flatly, 'But I've spent most of my life in prisons, I can't say I'd notice the difference until I died. And after that, I'd be dead, wouldn't I?'

'Stone walls do not a prison make,' muttered the officer, in an accidental indication of understanding.

'Nor iron bars a cage,' said Fletcher. The officer's eyebrows flicked up, raised in surprise for the briefest of moments.

'I'm not an ignoramus you know,' Fletcher said, in part because he was genuinely affronted, but mainly because he could never resist the opportunity to make an officer squirm. 'I can read. And I 'ave read and all.'

'And I've done time,' said the officer, 'Prisoner of war, of course, but it's not like the Hun are renowned for fair play.'

Fletcher nodded. Calculated though it was, he appreciated the attempt to create common ground between them.

'What's in it for me?'

'You'll get a full pardon,' the officer began.

'With all due respect, sir, I can't see that seeing me through me few remaining years. I'd be better off inside. At least I'd know where me next meal was coming from.' The officer tapped his teeth with a pencil, thoughtfully.

'Well, lets say you'll get a full army sergeant's pension which treats your years in prison as if they were spent in the army. You said you've spent half your life in prison. How long, exactly, have you spent in stir?'

'Twenty four years, on and off.'

Verity did a quick mental calculation of the cost to the War Office of a Sergeant's pension for twenty-four years service and quickly reconsidered.

'Sergeant might be pushing it,' she said. 'You can be Lance Corporal Fletcher. Does that suit?'

The prisoner's rotund face considered the offer for a moment, then he nodded.

'Can you sew?' asked the officer suddenly. Fletcher tensed very slightly, then nodded again.

'Good,' said Verity, smiling, 'I brought your uniform with me but I need someone to attach your stripe.'

Standing outside Pentonville with the newly uniformed Lance Corporal Fletcher by her side, Verity couldn't help feel pleased. With the third of today's four unexpected errands accomplished, she could concentrate on the last. Now all she had to do was make sure that she and her new batman caught their evening train.

Part Three

11: Tiger, Tiger

When Sebastian Moran came back from India he did it the hard way. He travelled up through Afghanistan and on into Russia, across into Norway and then by sea from Fredrikstad. The papers noted at the time that, in this as in all other aspects of his behaviour, Colonel Moran showed his highly developed sense of honour and his general devotion to duty. On this matter the papers were, as they usually are on matters of importance, entirely wrong.

When, in '93, Moran was suggested to have been the former chief of staff to the late, unlamented Professor Moriarty, the papers were reluctant to turn on him. The man had been Mentioned in Despatches, damn it!

Moran's eventual dishonourable discharge from the reserve list, and subsequent public trial for the murder of the Honourable Ronald Adair, damaged his relations with Fleet Street. Had Ronald Adair not been Honourable, they may have found a way to continue to support a hero of Rourke's Drift, but an attack on the establishment of this sort carried dangerous echoes of the extremist end of Russian politics. Moran's conviction for the murder, with the jury deciding on his guilt in a matter of hours, removed any reservations the papers' may have. They attacked him daily in the strongest terms. They called him a coward, a bully, a dissembler and – for the killing of Adair and his multiple attempts on the life of Mr Sherlock Holmes of Baker Street – some sort of traitor. He was, they declared, the very embodiment of an entirely un-British way of being.

Once again, however, the papers were wrong. Moran was no hero, but he was certainly no coward. His personal courage was immense, his martial skills indisputable. The reasons for his lengthy trip across Russia, once lauded as of National, if secret, importance were now written off as part of some dastardly scheme of Moriarty's, a threat to national security even, but this was by no means true. Moran's devotion, in his own manner, to the ideals of Empire was as perfect and as hard as the diamond he had smuggled across Europe to convince Moriarty of his desire to buy into the most spectacular criminal syndicate the world had ever known.

Moran's main flaw as a human being was simple and ancient; avarice itself. His greed allied itself with his ambition and together they turned a man who had been able to serve his society with something approaching distinction into someone said society was willing, with faint pause, utterly to vilify. Moran was shocked by his terrible fall from grace. Bitter, aging and surviving on an army pension that many felt he should no longer be entitled to, he limped into the twentieth century nursing a terrible rage and an all-encompassing desire to once again be regarded as a hero.

Many long and lonely days were spent staring, rheumy eyed, at the simple type of his Mention in Despatches and wishing that his past had not led to this particular present. Not that Moran regretted his association with James Moriarty. He merely regretted its becoming public. Regretted its impact on a reputation he had once treasured. He did not wish he had not committed his crimes. He wished that he had not been caught.

So it was then that, on the eve of the greatest conflagration the world had ever known, Colonel Sebastian Moran found himself able to do his country service once more and, once his conditions were met, he swore ancient and terrible oaths to the effect that he would not be found wanting. This was a chance for redemption, not necessarily in the eyes of the public, but certainly in the eyes of the establishment, perhaps in the eyes of history itself.

These oaths were foremost in his mind when, dressed in dull and despised mufti, rather than the uniform he had treasured and lost, he sat behind the desk in his office at Winterisle's EDICT Base and watched through the window as a young CPO from his staff greeted, and checked the paperwork of, visitors from London who had come through on army intelligence passes.

He quite understood why army intelligence wanted an observer here today. Denying them the right to one, even making sure that they'd not quite known where today's important event was occurring, had been a petty, personal matter for Moran. His resentment for John Watson had burned for more than twenty years and he saw no reason to forgive his old foe now that they were both on the same side against the Austro-Prussian hordes. That Watson, of all people, now carried the rank of Colonel merely provided Moran with another reason to hate him.

Watson had somehow identified the location of this base and had sent the observers that he, in fact, had every right to send. Moran mentally shrugged. He could hardly stop them coming in, now they'd arrived. Even if his mission here were a total success, he'd have to answer questions afterwards if he did such a thing. It would take the shine off of his triumph. There was no point.

He viewed the visitors coolly through the glass.

They were an odd pair, a steel-eyed army officer and a rotund and oddly uncomfortable looking Lance Corporal who was struggling with his kit and complaining about it far more loudly than was appropriate for other ranks in the presence of an officer. In Moran's younger days, such blatant indiscipline would have result in a flogging. The sight of them, and the certain knowledge of their link to Watson, gave him a vicious stab of envy in his gut, and he gritted his teeth and seethed at what he had lost.

The wave of bitterness that washed over him was almost sufficient to briefly stop him from thinking clearly. But only almost.

'Victor Archangel' he muttered to himself, remembering the name on the papers. Why was that name familiar?

As the errant memory forced its way to the forefront of Moran's mind, he stood up behind his desk and sauntered out to confront his guests.

12: A Nice Chat

The door behind the CPO who had stamped her papers opened and an aging man in grey herringbone suit came through it. He fixed Verity with a very odd look, and then walked over and stood uncomfortably close to her. His face was gaunt, and as he leant forward there was a glint in his eye that reminded her of a guard dog.

'Young... man,' he said with as much irony as he could muster, 'do forgive the intrusion, but I saw you from my office over there and I came to the conclusion that we had met before.'

Verity looked straight into the face of the strange old man and recognition dawned.

'Sebastian Moran,' she said, deliberately lacing her tone with contempt.

The CPO to Moran's right looked up from the paperwork, suddenly concerned at the atmosphere in the room. Moran dismissed him with a curt wave that was clearly familiar to the younger man. Once he had gone Moran turned his stare back to Verity.

'*Colonel* Sebastian Moran, Captain Archangel. I outrank you,' he said with a growling, slimy resentment. 'You should call me Sir.'

'Colonel?' she smirked. 'I don't think so. It's a nice suit, Sabre, but it's not the uniform of any of his Majesty's Armed Forces, is it?'

Moran seethed at her, his face reddening.

'Rank is a piece of personal property gifted to one by the crown,' he said, more upset than he meant to show. 'It cannot truly ever be taken away. If you were really a soldier, you would know that.'

Verity was unimpressed and she told him so, by dint of simply refusing to acknowledge what he'd said.

'Listen to me,' he rasped, spraying spittle at her.

'I don't really see why I should,' she said curtly.

The portly Corporal to her side made a comment about Verity and he outnumbering Moran two to one that made the ex-Colonel jab a finger into Fletcher's chest with fury.

'You're not a solider at all, are you?' he spat, patronisingly, 'I can tell that at a glance. So shut up. There's a gentleman talking.'

He turned back to Verity and this time his tone was, barely, more conciliatory.

'I am Winterisle Base's head of security, Captain, effectively its Commander in Chief. I control all non scientific matters which don't fall within the recognisance of the Laird himself.'

'And your point is?'

'My point, Captain, is that I assume that you believe yourself to be on business that will benefit the war effort. And I can guess what it is.'

She opened her mouth to speak but he held up a wizened hand.

'In deference to your uniform, I shall not interfere in what you do unless it directly affects my duties. If it does, I shall take every pleasure in taking revenge on your Uncles by shooting you dead. Are we clear?'

Verity stood, stiffened almost to attention at Moran's words.

'You are clear, Mister Moran'.

Sabre scowled at her.

'You two may go. Enjoy your stay at Winterisle Base.'

13: What big teeth you have.

The creature in the Aquarium was apparently called an Icthyasaur. Despite it being firmly behind six-inch glass and entirely uninterested in her, something about in unnerved Verity profoundly.

'It looks like an evil dolphin,' she said suddenly to herself. The enormous, tweed clad bulk of her companion rumbled with laughter at this and he shook his huge bearded head in amusement rather than disagreement.

'I can see what you mean,' he said in a deep voice that rolled upwards from his barrel chest, 'But when I asked what you thought of it I meant the base itself, not its oldest resident.'

Verity hadn't actually heard Professor Challenger's question. She'd been too transfixed by the black-green scales and elongated, razor toothed snout of the prehistoric creature in front of her. That she'd said something that could be construed to be an answer to the question she'd inadvertently ignored was nothing more than good fortune. She'd have hated to provoke one of her host's notorious rages with her inattention.

Not that this man seemed to be someone who could live up to that reputation. He was physically imposing, yes. There could be no reasonable dispute of that. His head was enormous. His shoulders the widest she had ever seen on a human being. His face was almost square, with a sort of classical brutishness about it that was not entirely dispelled by the obvious intelligence and candour of his blue-grey eyes. He would probably have looked better, or at least more approachable, without his curious spade-shaped black beard.

She realised he was still waiting for an answer, so she told him how impressed she was with the facilities here. She said the Navy had done an amazing job carving the base out of the cliff face and then shoring it up with local timber and imported steel. She mentioned her astonishment that an aquarium on this scale, utilising artificially heated and pumped seawater was even possible.

To an extent she was playacting, and the conversation annoyed her. Dracula was due to arrive at Winterisle in a matter of hours. There would a small reception and then he would inspect one of the submarines. He would be gone before first light tomorrow. This man, George Challenger, had sent a hurried note to Uncle John a matter of days ago to inform him of this fact and ask for his help in a related matter; yet he was seemingly determined not to talk to her about either matter. He had blustered over her enquiries, even in the quiet of his office, and insisted that he accompany her on a tour of the base. She had assumed that this would give them an opportunity to talk privately, but he'd spent the whole of the tour making small talk.

Challenger's conversational gambit was hardly subtle but it was frustrating; and her frustration was only increased by the fact that she was genuinely staggered by the scope and scale of EDICT's installation. She had never seen anything remotely like it, despite a lifetime visiting government institutions and military installations the world over. She had to hand it to EDICT's puppet masters in HMG; they clearly had a knack for this sort of thing.

She told the Professor this and again thanked him for agreeing, despite the pressures incumbent on him as the base's scientific director, to undertake her tour of the base personally and her repetition only made her wonder, again, why he done it and what on Earth the point of all this circumlocutionary conversation was.

'It's nothing, Captain,' he replied with something resembling a twinkle in his eye and offered to show her ADC around as well, once he'd finished, as she'd put it, 'sorting out the luggage'.

They walked up a sloping ramp that led from the lower aquarium to the vast raised gantry that circled not only the aquarium but also the greater artificial water body into which it fed: the submarine tank. Her first sight of it literally took Verity's breath away. The three magnificent metal beasts in it, obviously modelled in many ways on the vile looking prehistoric creature she had just been spooked by, sat resplendently above the water line on shining steel docks, waiting to be lowered into the inky, frothing water. They were magnificent. She wanted to tell Challenger this but he was too busy asking her about her journey from London and rather than interrupting him she found herself muttering a reply. Telling him about how odd she'd found the Scots she'd encountered on Winterisle itself.

'That would have nothing to do with their being Scots, Captain Archangel, it's entirely down to them being islanders.' He pursed his lips slightly before continuing, but the look in his eye told her that he was not offended and what followed was for her information only and not a rebuke, 'I myself am Scots, and I could hardly be said to resemble those people in any way.'

'You don't sound Scots,' said Verity doubtfully.

'Largs,' said Challenger suddenly, and for a moment Verity thought he was merely clearing his throat. Then she realised he was naming a place. She thought it best to refrain from mentioning her initial confusion.

Continuing their conversational niceties, Challenger led her to the edge of the walkway and waved an arm towards a large circular hole in the wall above the water tank.

'This is how the aquarium is refilled!' he announced. 'I'm very proud of the system, which I designed myself. It brings in saltwater from the sea, pumps it through circular heated pipes and, when it's reached an appropriate temperature, drops it into the aquarium. It does it rather nosily though.'

As if on cue, water began to pour out of the gap, lashing down into the aquarium with a thunderous roar and a loud, whistling hiss of steam.

Suddenly, Challenger grabbed Verity, almost knocking her off balance, and spoke insistently into her ear in a hoarse whisper that proximity caused to resemble a shout.

'This base uses a variation on the system of naval whistles to communicate between decks. Pipes and things! It's quite effective! It also means that every inch of the place is easily eavesdropped on by EDICT's own security! They have a team of girls, shorthand typists and stenographers, in a room downstairs whose sole job is too report what people in the base say to one another!"

Verity nodded her understanding at him. Of course. They were being listened to at all times. The astonishing noise of the water would prevent any sound from being accurately heard and taken down and this was why he'd brought her here.

As quickly as he could the Professor told her about how he'd been briefed only this week on the planned visit by Count Dracula and how he'd persuaded the Laird to smuggle information about this to London in a diplomatic bag. Recent discoveries on the base had taught him that EDICT's staff could not be trusted and he knew from past experience that John Watson was a man within Intelligence with sufficient integrity to be trusted.

Verity started to ask Challenger a question but he held his huge right paw up in a gesture that unmistakably indicated a need for silence, momentarily resembling some glowering Pentecostal preacher. The epic noise of the sluice ebbed away surprisingly quickly and the gushing water stopped with a final gulp. Something near silence broke out. Or would have done had the Professor not thundered in mid sentence, near shouting –

'.. and so he thought at first it was an Archaeopteryx! That turkey like beast identified by the great Christian Erich Hermann von Meyer when I was just a boy, but it was something rather more extraordinary!'

'Excuse me?' asked Verity, unsure how what Challenger had just said fitted into anything.

'Didn't you hear any of that?' asked the Professor, feigning surprise. 'The Archaeopteryx. Fascinating creature. Rather like the Komodo dragon in a lot of respects.'

Verity shook her head.

'Well, never mind, it's a shame that you didn't catch it, as it would be rather interesting to you, I think. But, as you heard, the water is rather loud, isn't it?'

'Yes!' she said back, nearly matching his volume despite the lack of any pressing need.

He laughed with his mouth and face but not his eyes. 'I really must find a way to improve the water gate, don't you think?' he said. 'It's fortunate,' he said, his eyes indicating he thought the exact opposite, 'that the tank is only refilled every quarter hour or so, so we won't have to put up with that noise again for quite a while!'

Seeing the deadly serious expression on his face Verity reluctantly conceded that any useful, unoverheard conversation on this topic, or any other, would simply have to wait for rather longer than was practical or convenient. She went to leave down the ramp but the Professor caught her arm. The expression on his face was grave.

'If you could wait here, Captain, we have very much more to discuss,' he said, indicating the water hole with his free hand, 'It should only take about twenty minutes.'

14: Key Notes

It was, if he was honest, the easiest job that Fletch had ever done. The safe wasn't quite the easiest he'd ever cracked, but the time and space allowed to him to do the job meant he'd never been more relaxed in his working life. The knowledge that being interrupted here meant merely a pause in proceedings rather than an encounter with the Old Bill added a marvellous ease to the whole business. So much so that he unselfconsciously started humming sections from Gilbert and Sullivan.

He span the wheel at the front of the safe in his right hand again and leaned into the door, resting his ear against the cool metal panel. He listened to the insistent 'click-click-click' of the lock and a grin spread across his chubby face as the tell-tale 'clunk' arrived. Highly satisfactory bit of work, that, he thought to himself with the pride of a skilled man. It was a great thing to enjoy your work, wasn't it? And it was all in a good cause this time too.

'King and Country and all that cobblers,' he muttered under his breath as he heaved the door of the safe open and peered into its gloom at a large and battered packing case. He withdrew it and began working on its own lock, which gave easily under his skilled ministrations.

He knew what would be in it but the sight was still repellent. Human bones. Not chalk white but sandstone yellow, like Pentonville Prison's walls, and pitted and scarred. He gagged slightly but he did as he'd been instructed, lifting the small, dark cylindrical container he'd been carrying since they left for Euston from his pocket and dropping it in amongst the unsettling remains of his fellow man. He then shut up the case, placed it in the safe, relocked both and made his way out of the office of the base's security chief with the practiced wariness of the professional housebreaker. The whole job had taken him just under twenty minutes and couldn't, it seemed to him, have possibly gone any more smoothly. But then he had no idea that he'd been closely observed throughout.

15: Food and Thought

Against the noise of crashing water, Verity and Challenger compared notes. Verity told George of her meeting with Sebastian Moran and how she was certain he was, on EDICT's behalf, going to try to kill Dracula. Challenger concurred that Moran, whom he knew well and despised, was more than capable of such a thing. What he didn't understand was why it would be a problem to dispose of the Transylvanian monster. He had assumed that that was what Verity herself was here for.

She quickly disabused him of the notion.

Instead, Verity explained why Dracula could not be killed and both the secret part of Dracula's price for attending this meeting and how she, at Watson's instigation, was planning to frustrate that design. At all three, Challenger's eyes widened with shock and he shook his head in both wonder and anger at what war would make men do. Then he told her why he needed her help – and the horror of it took her breath away.

Fletcher was impressed by the haggis roll served in the NCO's mess. A steaming pile of meat shoved into a crusty lump of bread, it was one of the best things he'd ever eaten in his life. He'd been having rather a good time swapping stories with the embarrassed CPO from earlier who had, it turned out, done time in the smoke for receiving stolen goods just before the turn of the century. They were about to move back to the mess's counter to fetch a fourth roll and third cup of tea when his new found friend suddenly stood up and snapped to attention. Fletch wondered why, raised his eyes and saw that Captain Archangel had just entered the mess. The Captain indicated with a hand that the CPO should leave, shot Fletcher a look that indicated that he should have stood to begin with, and then sat down opposite him.

Archangel pushed a piece of paper filled with information and instructions across the table at Fletcher.

'That is what we're going to do,' said the Captain, tapping the note.

16: Bone Idol

The gathering of figures seemed insignificantly small in the huge, echoing chamber of the submarine dock. Even Dracula, resplendent in scarlet, seemed somehow tiny as he walked into that great space to little fanfare. The Count noted the lack of significant ceremony with just a hint of resentment and distaste, but nodded the patronising approval of those born to power to the naval ratings, recently seconded to EDICT, standing to attention with unloaded rifles. He shook hands, his cold, wet hands, with Challenger, Moran and Verity, each of whom was nervously watching the others as well as the Count and made quiet comment to the base's security chief about the parcel he required. With obsequious formality Moran stepped back and summoned a fourth rating, who brought a large wooden box to him, which the former Colonel then handed to Dracula. The effect on the saturnine figure was immediate. He almost snarled at the innocent seeming case, and then hurled it to the floor in a fury, spilling its contents across the concrete floor of the dock. The Count dropped to his knees, nearly howling, all formality and superiority forgotten as he pulled at the ruined box and ran his hand through its contents, his nose twitching like an animal scenting its prey.

'Yes!' he cried, exultantly, 'They are here!' His eyes were hideous, the pupils sunken and red, blood pulsing in somehow horribly visible veins. 'The bones of Quincey Morris! My murderer!'

The Count used a long, sharp fingernail to open up a vein in his right wrist and dripped blood onto the pile of ashes and bones on the floor. The pile of carrion began to fizz and pop obscenely, thick red ooze pouring out of cracks in the bones while muscles and sinew began to knot around their ends. The noise it made was awesome, a terrible unnatural wind howled as impossible magics pulled a man dead for a quarter of a century from the ether and forced his soul into the smashed pieces of his own body. Eyeballs began to grow in the fragmented remnants of the skull and even before they were half complete Verity could see the consciousness behind them, desperate with pain and despair. A dead man was coming to life on the floor and his suffering was unimaginable.

'Why would you want to resurrect this man who you say did so much harm to you?' she screamed at Dracula above the noise. Dracula's expression would stay with Verity for the rest of her very long life.

'Why, child, to kill him again, of course.'

Verity saw Moran move suddenly to attack Dracula, something flashing and sharp-seeming in his hand, but his attempt was over as soon as it had begun. Dracula didn't even stop him, he simply forbade Moran to move and the old soldier froze in his tracks, panic on his face, his thin arm shaking with the muscular effort of enforced stillness.

The Count shook his head, a patronising leer crossing his face. 'You really do not understand do you? Did either of you think you could kill me? Do you even know what I am?'

'Actually,' said Verity suddenly, 'I do'.

At that moment, there was a sudden, distinct explosion in the mess of flesh that was the once and future Quincey Morris. Dracula stepped back, suddenly confused, as something else exploded outwards, expanding with a tearing noise and a terrible resounding scream into something that was almost instantaneously too big to properly see. It was a plesiosaurus. Its vast head smashing against the ceiling of the submarine base as a creature dead for a hundred and forty million years suddenly roared back into existence.

'If you're going to use blood magic to resurrect some bones, Count Dracula, I suggest you take care to make sure which bones you're dripping your precious fluids onto!'

That was my moment and I seized it, throwing myself into the fray and attacking the Count with all my strength. As I did so I heard Professor Challenger screaming at the top of his considerable voice for someone to open up the sluice gate. Oh, I'm sorry, didn't you realise that I was a party to this story? I am no mere narrator, I assure you. Will you allow me to explain overleaf?

You will? Very kind. Very kind.

17: A Matter of Death & Life

Whitby, 1893

I knew that my neck was broken. I hadn't felt it happen but I had heard an obscene snap as He closed his fingers around my throat. The noise was profound, grotesque but I didn't immediately realise what it was. I only knew what He'd done because He told me and even in that knowing I didn't understand. Madmen often fail to grasp the simplest of things and at that moment I was quite, quite mad.

He dropped me to the cold stone floor of my cell and, standing above me, cursed my name for my treachery against him. I did nothing. I could do nothing. I had nothing before me but the imminent moment of my death and He knew it. He told me that He would have stayed with me, and waited for that moment to come purely for hate's sake, but that I was simply not important enough for it to be enough of a pleasure. I had been a bad servant and now I had been disposed of. His ending of me was no more than that. He left the way He had come, transubstantiating into mist and slipping through the cracks in the stone walls as easily as the air that I breathed did.

I lay there. I do not know how long for. I remember those moments now, and I remember them as being endless, as a purgatorial nightmare. But I am not sure I experienced them at all at the time. I have read, in the years since, that the brain stores memories by electrical impulses. I think that these moments were stored in my dying brain by such impulses, leaving me able to recall them without having truly lived them.

Time passed. Then they arrived, entering my poor cell as He had done. The three of them, the unholiest trinity, His creatures: the Master's 'brides'. Carnal, monstrous, unimaginable things, two of them dark and one of them, the senior of the three, fair. The dark ones, with their reddened eyes and long, roman noses, looked as though they should be the master's kin, not His consorts. I had longed for them, these voluptuous monsters, as I had cringed at the Master's side, and even though I lay dying, I feared them, feared them more than the imminent slipping away of my mortal existence, more even than the hell that I knew my God would commit me to the moment my life was over.

Their leader knelt over me, spilling out of her dress as she did so and even as I lay dying I felt my heart fill with lust. She leaned forward and licked my face, the inquisitive, rough lick of a cat tasting food. She laughed her whispered, a wicked laugh of silver and smoke.

'Dear Renfield,' she said in a soft voice that caused me terrible pain, 'My poor, dear mad, Renfield. We have come to save you.' The rest was silence.

I was cold when I awoke. I was cold and naked and tormented by the beginning of a sensation then new to me; a feeling which would, though I didn't know it then, grow into an unimaginable, unslakable hunger. I lay in the dark, alone and afraid and discovered something that must surely have been clear to you, you who have been reading my words, for some time now: my mind was clear. My madness had gone. The brides had given me back my sanity.

Why?

As I scrambled to my feet in the dark I fell from the bench on which I'd been lying, crashing into the hard, cobbled floor of whatever room I had been imprisoned in. I was alive. I stood and looked at my arms, inspecting them for damage caused by my ungainly fall. There was none. I turned my hands over and saw the faintest outline of curled, white hair on my palms. I was engulfed by fear. A terrible, terrible dread overwhelmed me and as I reached up to my neck with my hands I knew what I would find. Two puncture marks. In denial, I scrambled to the window of the mortuary (for that was what it was) into which I had been placed. The night was dark outside and the glass reflected the room I was in back at me as well as any mirror. The cobbles. The benches. The bloodied sink and locked door. I searched in vain for my reflection in the glass. The Brides had restored my mind, yes, but at a terrible price: they had taken my soul.

18: Redemption

Hampstead, 1894

Mist and pollution rolled together onto the Heath, coating the hill with a dank and foul smelling fog that tasted of the imminent twentieth century. She was waiting for me there, as I knew she would be. The fair one, with eyes like vast sapphires, the one who had made me feed on her as I lay dying. Their leader, and my leader now: the beautiful beast that had condemned me to live.

She was dressed more demurely than I had ever known her to be and she greeted me with a warmth I had not thought she possessed. She could have passed for a human being but for the brilliant white teeth that shone like pearls against the ruby of her voluptuous lips; her feral, catlike teeth that matched my own. I wept at her feet and she held me, tenderly. I asked why she had done this to me and then left me alone for a year. I had spent a whole year of scavenging and fighting and living as a beast. A year in which I'd never seen the sun and daily choked on the filthy, red effluent that was my only sustenance. Why had they done this?

'We mended you,' she told me, 'So that you could serve us. We have watched you carefully these months, hoping that you would not destroy yourself. Knowing that every day that you survived made you stronger, made you better fitted to our purpose.'

I asked her what this purpose was but she shushed my interruption as though I were a child and continued with her story instead.

'Marya has gone, now. Destroyed. We are two now, only, and we need you more than ever.'

I begged her to tell me what they needed me for and she wrapped her arms around me and spoke gently into my ear.

'You are ours,' she said, 'as we are His. We have our freedom now because He is not here. Not dead. Not alive. Not Undead. Not here in this world. But He will return. He always returns. When He does, you will be able to fight Him in ways we cannot.'

'Fight the Master?' I gasped, sobbing.

'Fight Dracula,' she said, cringing at my subservience, 'Fight him because you can and because you hate him as we do, with the fury of the betrayed.'

She took my face in her hands and raised it so I was looking at her. 'When He returns we will no longer be able to resist Him, just as you cannot resist us now. You must destroy Him for us. Free us. Free yourself.'

I nodded, choking on my despair, and told her that I did not think I could possibly destroy the Master. This was not reluctance. I simply did not have the power.

'With time and training,' she said kindly, 'you will,' and with that she took my hand and together we dissolved into the fog.

19: One Way To Find Out

Dracula hissed as I crashed into him. He turned to me and bared his teeth, his eyes feral and all pretence of humanity gone. Even in the terrible, chaotic circumstances they found themselves in the people in that dock were shocked.

Shocked at what Dracula became at that moment, at the pure beast within him. Of those there, I alone had the advantage of knowing what to expect and I took advantage, recovering from my long fall down into the dock. I stood my ground and, as he lunged at me, parried him, turned away and briefly insubstantiated to avoid his blows.

The great prehistoric beast above was still growing as Dracula and I fought. He changed shape as I did, both of us struggling to defeat the other. The dock was filling with water now, the Professor's command to flood the base having been obeyed as we fought. Dracula roared at me, telling me how pathetic I was, in thrall to his creations like I had once been in thrall to him. He told me how I could never destroy him because I would never know how. I screamed at him. I told him that he was wrong. That I knew what he had actually come to Scotland for and that I had made sure that others knew.

And I told him that I knew what he really was. That I had bent the mind of Iris Wildthyme to my will and used her to quiz his fellow Incremental, Molly Malone.

I saw in his terrible face that he understood me. I did not mean his pretence at humanity. I meant his pretence at vampirism. For the first time in the decades of our sickeningly intimate acquaintance, I saw shock on his face – and seeing it was, even in this moment, impossibly sweet. In his moment of confusion, Dracula was weakened. I reformed, became solid again, and pushed back into him with all my strength.

The Count was thrown against the nearest Icthyasub, his face crunching against its metal hide. Above us the plesiosaur, confused, enraged and out of its environment, screamed and then thrashed its neck down into floor beside us. The concrete began to crack. The people around us stopped staring, their will to live reasserting itself over them – and they ran, Verity and Challenger carrying a nearly resurrected Quincey Morris, Moran scrambling for his own safety, able once again to move due to Dracula's lapsed attention. Above us the plesiosaur tore at the walls and ceiling of the base in a frenzy. If I had not been so preoccupied with my revenge I would have taken the time to appreciate what was surely the most awesome sight I would ever see. If only I could have seen such magnificent things while still alive.

Struggling now against the waist deep water I tried to force Dracula into moving to his right by charging at him in as ungainly a fashion as I could fake. It worked. He stood, unknowingly, in the doorway of the Icthyasub and I threw myself at him and we tumbled together into the submarine. As he struggled to get to his feet I turned and shut the door behind me, spinning the great green wheel on the door with all my strength. I had timed it exactly right, for as I did so the water level rose above the portholes in the door. Dracula stood and stared at me and I saw him realise that the skin of the metal beast would not yield to his attempts to pass through it.

'We are surrounded on all sides by running water!' I told him and I was surprised to hear laughter in my voice. We were drifting out to sea and he knew it. The submarine tilted in the water around the island and I felt it sink. So did Dracula and he moved towards the little ship's controls, only to realise that they'd been smashed to pieces before our arrival. I had seen to that. We were trapped together, unable to escape, in a metal bubble sinking to the bottom of the sea. He raged at me, incoherent at his entrapment and it was only when he had finished his ranting that I told him of the other thing in the submarine with us; the only finalised samples of the obscene weapon that he had really come to Scotland for.

He lunged at me, as though to prevent me breaking the canister of poison. The poison that he himself had requested be loaded onto this submarine. The poison he had discovered had been brought back from Challenger's Lost World. As he did so I saw him realise that it was too late. I had broken the seal as he lay on the ground. I told him that I doubted it could destroy him, not an abstraction such as he. I didn't think he would ever have desired its use if there was the slightest chance that it could. I did not know if it could destroy me either, but I was willing to embrace the end of my barely tolerable existence to dispose of it, and for the slightest chance of watching the agony that I thought using it in this sealed compartment would cause him.

As I finished speaking, he turned to me and I saw the poison had started to do its work. 'This is what you would have done to world,' I told him as he retched. His face was a mass of sores and suddenly growing pus-filled buboes. He lifted his hands, screaming in misery and anguish and pain.

20: Coda

From: J H Watson ("C")
To: Control ("M")

Quincey Morris came to see me today at the Circus for full debriefing in relation to recent operations in Scotland. He has now fully recovered from his long period of incapacity and was proudly wearing his 2nd Stryker Cavalry Regiment uniform. He's bound for France with next month's shipment of US troops to France where he'll take command of a regiment of horse in time for the movement to [CENSORED] on the [DATE CENSORED] next month. Colonel Morris was concerned that the whole operation had been undertaken for his benefit and that lives had been risked for him. I was able to assure him that this was not the case and brief him on the following.

The Circus's initial interest had been in eliminating Dracula, with the possibility of agreeing peace with him if he were sincere. Once it became clear that peace with Wallachia was not practicable the US State Department expressed an interest in utilising Dracula as a resource to resurrect Colonel Morris, as this would be advantageous to the war effort. This was something that, having read his books on tactics, I was quick to agree to for military and humanitarian reasons.

My initial plan was to kill Dracula after Morris's resurrection but I then became aware that this objective was unlikely to be achieved. My circle of contacts included some of the more abstract figures in the London netherworld and through Miss Iris Wildthyme I had come to understand that Dracula was not a vampire at all.

The historical Count Dracula had perished centuries before. The creature I had met in Ypres was the creature Morris had killed back in '93. He was an incremental. An idea. The notion of Dracula that existed because we let it exist.

This was not uncovered until arrangements were made by my contacts to move Morris' remains from the family vault in Texas and it was only after this had been done that the operation was moved out of my hands by EDICT (with whom I had been reluctantly co-operating do to their control of the Icthyasub base and their refusal to release full details of its location) forcing this department to extemporise in response to changed circumstances. EDICT, it seems, continued to work on a variation of the Circus's initial design, using Colonel JS Moran as Dracula's assassin. Moran, it seems, was already in place on the Malone/Roxton expedition, having been sent there to acquire venom glands from the plateau's many living Sinorithosauruses for use in research into poison gas weapons of a kind of which Dracula had expressed an interest once EDICT had taken over my negotiations.

My department's response to this threat included the acquisition of freshly cremated dinosaur bones from Edward Malone, the utilisation of George Challenger's fresh intelligence about EDICT's location and intentions, the unfortunate abuse of diplomatic privileges, the involvement of Captain Archangel and the pardon of a petty London crook. I wish it put on record that I did not intend or design the destruction of EDICT's base in Scotland, nor the closing down of much of their funding, however...

'Panda!' shouted Iris from the bar, interrupting the little bear's reading. 'What are you doing? You're on in three minutes. Molly and Clemmy have nearly finished their turn!' The little bear looked up from his papers, secreted out of the British Library using the old security dodging disappearing bus trick, and nodded. He jumped down off the bunk in the back room of *The Tradesman's Entrance* and checked his bow tie in the mirror. It was time for a song.

The Irredeemable Love
by Nick Wallace

The Changing Location of Manleigh Halt

The cover illustration depicts (amongst others) members of the Manleigh Halt constabulary. For reasons never fully explained, the Manleigh Halt Police Station blinked out of existence in 1920 to reappear in 1930, complete with the two Policemen who made up its full complement. Now accompanied by the mysterious Isiah Dogberry and spirited widow Clarissa Miller, the occupants find themselves moving back and forth in time and space, determined to both uphold the law and embrace each adventure in which they find themselves.

i. Wilson

It wasn't meant to be like this.

Wilson could barely breathe. The woman was naked beneath him, her body hot, open, wet. He barely dared move. It wasn't meant to be like this. It wasn't right.

Together with Sergeant Whitney and Miss Miller, he'd spent the previous day on the hillside, looking down over the estate grounds. Occasionally changing their vantage point, all the time aware of the strange force that still pushed at their minds. They'd watched the staff going about their business; neither Wilson nor Whitney had any real experience of a house like this, but Miss Miller had assured them such bustle was not uncommon. Except, once again, they all felt it. There was something wrong below, but not one of them could say precisely what it was.

When they'd returned to the inn, there had been an envelope waiting. Scuffed at the edges, the paper grimy at one corner, it had been addressed to Miss Miller. Inside was an invitation, for Miss Miller and guest, to attend dinner at the estate the following evening.

Whitney had said nothing, while Wilson had been dispatched to the bar to uncover how their presence had been discovered. While Whitney had been greasing the locals the previous day, Wilson had spent most of his time leant against the bar, talking with the barmaid. Dark-haired and hazel eyed, she'd had a wide smile and brilliant teeth. She had laughed at his jokes and been unafraid to tell her own. It was the barmaid he turned to when he wanted to know about the invitation.

But all she could tell him was that the envelope had been delivered by a bearded man, dressed in a starched jacket.

The invitation made Wilson uneasy, but only seemed to invigorate Miss Miller. It was clearly a trap, she said. But that itself only confirmed their suspicions: her relative had been murdered, and (in identifying their presence, if nothing else) something strange was underway on the estate.

Miss Miller had then announced her intention to accept the invite.

Wilson would accompany her as her guest and immediate protection in case of any danger. Shortly after they arrived, Whitney would follow – in his official capacity – and begin enquiries with the staff. When Wilson had begun to protest, believing they should wait for Dogberry to arrive, Whitney had just coughed in response. It was a cough Wilson had come to know well over the years; Whitney's gentle reminder of who they were and what they represented. They were members of the police force and right was on their side, they would prevail. It said they would make the world a better place.

Wilson was trying hard to remember that, to keep it clear in his mind now.

The woman was naked beneath him, her body hot, open, wet. Slit open from the chest to the pelvis, her blood soaking through his dress shirt.

Wilson should have got to his feet, or tried to help her somehow, restore some dignity. But he couldn't. The first thing he'd seen when he'd found the body, when he'd fallen on the body, had been her eyes. Hazel eyes surrounded by dark hair. It had taken him more than a flustered moment to realise just what had happened. That she was dead.

A wide smile that would never be seen again.

He stayed there, unmoving, listening for any movement in the house around him. Finally, he whispered a quiet apology – to the heavens, to the girl – then reached up and drew her eyes closed.

It wasn't meant to be like this.

Wilson finally pulled free, scrambling back, away from the body, from her body, until he bumped up against a cabinet and could go no further. One hand sunk into his hair, pulling it tight, he just sat there, staring at the girl.

It wasn't Elsbeth. He knew that. But that didn't change a thing.

It wasn't meant to be like this.

When they'd arrived, they'd been met by a manservant. A mono-syllabic Scotsman who ill fit the clothing, dark hair and beard barely kept in check; likely the same manservant who'd delivered the invitation. He'd guided them up the stairs to their rooms, deposited their bags, and told them drinks would be served at eight. Wilson had been given instruction from Miss Miller as to what might be expected from him; the laid back lifestyle of the party guest. He unpacked his bag, had a wash, laid out his clothing for the evening, but it was still unsettling to find himself with nothing to do for the remaining four hours.

Books lined the shelves of the room, and Wilson picked one at random, flicking through the pages before returning it to the shelf. He tried again, several times, over the next couple of hours, but was never able to settle with a title for more than a few minutes. The print was too small, the story-telling impenetrable, there was no action or conversation to grab him, and so his attention wandered to other things.

He looked out of the window, studying the grounds to see if there were any clues he might decipher. But there was nothing of consequence and after a few minutes he stepped back.

It was then, returning to the bookshelf one more time, that he realised it was more than just a shelf. A double joint at a partition led him to search for a catch and, finding it, he swung the hidden door open.

It was a disappointment to discover there was no secret passage behind. Rather, it was a connecting door to the next room; the bookshelf frontage a matter of style, not secrecy.

With his own surroundings exhausted, Wilson hesitantly rapped on the door. When there was no answer, he tried the handle and pushed. The new room was empty. It appeared to Wilson to be more akin to some kind of trophy room. Various animals – from bodies to busts – were stuffed and mounted on the walls or in the glass cases that lined them. In addition to the animals, there were also numerous weapons, ceremonial swords and modern firearms pinned alongside them. Wilson had glanced over the cases, tried the door out onto the corridor – locked – and then returned to his own room.

He had dressed for dinner. After struggling with the cufflinks, when he finally gave up on the bow tie he had checked the clock and found there were still another ninety minutes to go. Wilson had drawn the curtains, blocking out the woodland and the grounds, and laid down to sleep.

He woke suddenly, flailing, convinced there was someone there with him. It was properly dark outside, and – with the thick velvet curtains – darker still in the room. Wilson laid still on the bed, studying the shadows as best he could. Then he heard a sound from next door. Climbing down, Wilson worked his way over to the bookshelf and found the catch once more.

Thinking of Whitney, he straightened his back and marched forwards. Wilson got two steps into the pitch black room before his foot caught on her leg and he was thrown on top of the woman.

The door swung shut behind him, followed by the click of a lock being turned.

Wilson had watched as his sister died. He'd been stuck in a cupboard in the dark, looking through a crack in the door as the butcher took his knives to her body. The man was a doctor, according to his father. A surgeon. And a surgeon was what was needed.

It seemed like he'd spent his whole life at her side till that day. It was Elsbeth who taught him to walk and talk. It was Elsbeth who played with him and comforted him at night when he woke. She was the one who'd taken him to school and helped him with his letters when he returned home.

Then their mother had passed and the house had changed. Elsbeth had to stay longer at the oven, and no matter how hard she or Wilson tried, they were never the same. Wilson saw it long before their father, probably before Elsbeth. She was not well, could not keep up with the pace of their life anymore. Thinner, paler, the colour slowly seeping from her lips.

When he'd tried to talk to her about it, Elsbeth had smiled and told him to look into her eyes. Had they changed? And when Wilson answered that they hadn't, Elsbeth had smiled again and told him that everything was all right, then.

Except her eyes had never changed. Not even when she died.

Until two days ago, Wilson had thought he'd never see those eyes again. Then he'd spent the evening talking to the maid behind the bar, not even knowing why at the time. That night, when he fell asleep, that he dreamed of Elsbeth. It was then that he realised that, despite being possessed of different features, the maid had the same eyes as his sister.

Hazel eyes that would never see a smile again.

When Elsbeth had finally been diagnosed, the doctor had agreed there was little chance. Wilson had tried asking her what was wrong, but she just waved him away. When he asked his father what was happening, why it was happening, the man had just shook his head.

The world, he told his son, was too big. It should have been a better place. But it wasn't.

When the doctors had come that afternoon, Wilson was told to find somewhere else to be. His father had taken him to a neighbour, but Wilson had gone out the back door before the front had even closed. He'd made it back into their house, creeping up the stairs and into Elsbeth's room. His sister had been asleep, her skin white and glassy. Wilson had kissed her once and promised he would stay with her like always. And then he had heard the footsteps on the stairs, and tucked himself away in the cupboard.

As the doctor had examined her, Elsbeth's back had arched and she'd cried out in her sleep. They couldn't wait for the ambulance, the doctor had said. He would have to operate immediately if she was to stand any chance.

And so Wilson had stayed and kept his sister company as always, as the final minutes of her life were cut away, soaking the sheets and slowly pooling on the floor.

Wilson didn't know how long he sat there, unable to move.

He'd heard feet on the floorboards out in the hall. A light, delicate step. Then some time later, others, heavier, more hurried. Not once did anyone try the door handle. He knew he could not wait there forever. The door may have been locked, but it was an old house, and a good kick might have been enough to clear the hinges. Failing that, his earlier inspection had revealed ammunition in the drawers of the cases, enough that he could find a functioning firearm to shoot the lock if it was required.

He knew all this, but could not summon up the strength to open the door.

The world outside was too big.

ii. Whitney

As instructed, Sergeant Whitney took the path around to the rear of the house. He'd kept his distance from its walls, just in case any of the guests should happen to look out, but most of the windows were dark and, for the handful that weren't, all the curtains were shut. Past the dining room and the glasshouse, on round the corner with the water pump, navigating a tight passage between outhouses, and he reached the back door of the kitchens.

There were no curtains here, but little real light either. The windows cut dull squares on the cobbles beneath Whitney's feet, but there was no brightness or warmth to their light.

Whitney paused and took a step to one side, peering in through one of the panes, the glass cracked down the middle. Inside, the staff moved back and forth, pans bubbling on the ranges, china and silver clattering on its journey from the cupboards through the kitchen and on to the servers. Whitney had had cause enough times in his thirty-year career – barring time given to military service, of course – to visit houses such as this before. Like tonight, he had invariably been directed round to the rear of the property; sometimes for fear of scandal if a policeman was seen at the front door, sometimes because it was a member of staff he was there to apprehend.

Whitney paused to brush off his uniform jacket, then straightened his back and gave a firm rap on the door. Before anyone could answer, he pushed it open and strode into the room.

As the servants turned towards him, he gave a thin smile and removed his helmet, tucking it under one arm. This done, he pulled a notebook and pencil from his pocket.

He began his questioning in what had become his well-practised manner. The briefest of introductions, followed by a stern look; said look being comprised of a slow turn of the head that encompassed all the parties present, thus enabling him to assert his authority over them as well as identify the likeliest candidate for his questioning.

While not one for strategy as such, Whitney had been in the job long enough to have a natural sense of how to approach most situations. In a case such as this the victim had been a young man. In the event anyone in the house had known him, the most obvious suspect would either be a girl of a similar age who had formed a romantic attachment to the boy, or an older woman with some maternal instinct.

The difficulty he had that night, slowly surveying the room, was that none of the candidates wanted to meet his eye. The handful that didn't continue in their own business kept their heads down or glanced towards the dark at the rear of the kitchen.

Whitney cleared his throat loudly, attempting to draw their attention once more, but nothing happened.

He stepped further into the room. One of the kitchen staff looked up. A young girl, carrying a row of cooking knives on a tray; barely in her teens, the skin on her fingers was cracked raw, her eyes sunk deep in a hollow face. Like the rest of the staff, she wore austere below stairs uniform; but the fabric was worn in places, dirt held in the creases at the elbows and waist. The lace holding the girl's hair in place was fraying.

The staff, like the exterior of the house, had seen better days, and Whitney had seen enough of the future to know this was a life which would pass into history within the girl's lifetime.

He started to smile, but the girl broke away from his gaze; like the others she glanced back into the kitchen. This time Whitney followed her look.

A massive figure detached itself from the darkness. A woman, both high and broad, her frame pushing at the seams of her starched black dress, her hair drawn up in a vicious bun, her eyes hooded and invisible. The housekeeper, Whitney presumed.

Only she too made no attempt to meet his gaze, did not acknowledge him at all. Instead, she was looking past Whitney.

The sergeant snatched around to see what had her attention. He heard the action before he saw it. The harsh double rap of something solid on the window, sharp enough that any more weight would have broken the glass. The light was such that Whitney caught only a glimpse of the figure who had made the noise – tall and thin, receding black hair and beard – and then he was gone.

As he turned back to the room, he realised the housekeeper had already crossed the kitchen to meet him.

Thirty years earlier, Whitney had been fresh in his uniform. Baby-faced, pink skinned, and carrying little of the weight he now had. He had been mentored by an older officer – Sergeant Lester – who had taken it upon himself to teach the young Whitney everything he knew about policing. He'd taught him the importance of walking the streets every day, of knowing which youngster to encourage and which to cuff around the ear, who to give a smile and who a scowl. And he had taught Whitney about the most important weapon in a policeman's arsenal: his whistle.

The whistle, Lester had explained, was the most important item he would ever carry. More than the uniform or truncheon or buttons or badges, it reminded an officer that he was just one part of something bigger. Everything he told Whitney about the people he would deal with was important, but the bobby's strength lay in the body of men he stood with and what they represented: the weight of the law, the importance of order. They were mighty forces, and if Whitney was ever in trouble, he had to remember that he was part of something more powerful than any foe he may be faced with.

All he ever needed to do was blow his whistle, and his fellow officers would hear and they would respond.

It was a lesson Whitney had always remembered, and it was the first thing he had told young Wilson when it had come his time to play the teacher.

The whistle was at Whitney's lips now. There was a sweat on his face, his eyes wide open in the dark, chest heaving with exertion. No fingers held the whistle – it hung loosely between his teeth – his hands against the wall, pressing back against it.

When he had turned back from the mad face flitting past the window, he'd found the housekeeper already crossing the room towards him. There had been a moment where that had felt like progress; the onset of co-operation, the natural order of the world asserting itself once more. Then the woman had collected a blade – a hatchet – from the tray the maid was carrying. Whitney had blinked, uncertain. The housekeeper hadn't even paused, had taken another step and swung the steel towards him.

Whitney had stumbled backwards, his heel catching on a flagstone. A moment which had saved his life. As he fell, the hatchet had cleaved the air in front of his face. Helmet still tucked under one arm, he'd landed heavily. There was a sound – high pitched and full of rage – and then the housekeeper had stomped one foot down, catching his ankle under her immense bulk.

If she had taken the opportunity to bring the blade down once more then, he would have had no chance. But the woman's head had snatched around, surveying the maids' response as she once more opened her mouth and screamed. The staff had stepped back from the ovens, put down their burdens and turned en masse towards them. Towards Whitney.

His leg still trapped beneath the housekeeper's foot, he'd seen the maids picking up knives of their own. As the housekeeper refocused, Whitney's composure had left him. He'd thrown his helmet at the woman, catching her full on the nose as she turned. There was a crack of bone and a burst of red, but the pressure holding his ankle did not relent. Whitney had pulled back his other leg and kicked out, furiously, his heel connecting full with the woman's kneecap. And there had been a moment's respite, just enough for him to pull clear.

He'd rolled away, underneath the heavy kitchen table to his right. The hatchet came down behind him, striking sparks on the stone floor. The staff were closing around the table, some already dropping down to flick at him with their knives. That was the first moment where he'd put the whistle to his lips. But then one of the faces had looked at him, and the breath deserted him and the whistle fell away.

Something primal had taken over. Whitney had rolled onto all fours, then up into a crouch, braced his back against the underside of the table, and ignoring the pain from his ankle, he had pushed upwards.

The table had toppled backwards, and as it did so, Whitney had run, pushing his way through the crowd of bodies, striking blindly at anyone in his way. Through the pantry, out into the corridors. There was brief silence behind him, confusion he'd left in his wake, then the scream again – the housekeeper's scream – and he heard the sound of footsteps, of bodies pushing after him. Hearing the footsteps behind but not once looking round.

He didn't need to see, did not want to see.

At the earliest opportunity – rounding a corner, out of sight for just a few moments – he'd ducked into another doorway, stone steps leading to a cellar of some kind.

He'd waited as his pursuers passed by, then slowly and carefully begun to make his way down, careful not to make a sound. There was a cable pinned to the wall; power for haphazardly strung light bulbs. Reaching the bottom of the steps, he'd paused, taking in the damp, chill air. Even with the electric lighting, he couldn't see far enough to be sure, but guessed it was a wine cellar or some such. He'd followed the wiring further in, stopping when he reached the switch.

His truncheon had been in his hand. He couldn't remember drawing it, but the wood had been slick with blood, telling him it had seen use in his flight. There were scratches on his face, the buttons ripped from his jacket.
He'd tested the cable and found enough slack to slip the truncheon in behind it, then levered back and forth 'til the wiring was wrenched from the switch.

The only possible light now was that from the corridor upstairs – be it candle or the light of the moon through a window – and with his eyes adjusted to the gloom, Whitney was certain he would see anyone approaching long before they saw him. But try as he might, he couldn't shake the sight of that face, looking under the table at him.

And Whitney had shrunk back against the wall, holding his truncheon in one hand, and put his whistle to his lips once more. That long-held certainty that all he had to do was blow the whistle and help would arrive was still strong. But he remembered the face, and knew there was nothing a whistle could do to save him in a hell such as this.

It took him a while to realise it, but there was still light.

Whitney thought at first it was a trick of his mind. That his eyes had failed to adjust to the darkness or were seeing patterns not there. He'd kept his vision fixed on the stairs, watching shapes move across the top of the stairs. First, in large groups, tearing up and down the corridor, the housekeeper's scream barrelling them along. But eventually, the screams had begun to fade and the bodies had grown less and less frequent.

And then one shape had paused at the top, feeling around for a handrail as it peered into the dark below.

Whitney had tightened his grip on his truncheon then. They couldn't see him in the blackness. His teeth had born down on the whistle. They couldn't. They couldn't.

And then another shape had appeared next to the first. There were no words – there could be no words – but a message was passed. And the first body stepped back, drawn away from the stairs. At first, he had thought the search was over. But then there was a creak from above and the cellar door had begun to swing shut.

Whitney had had to stifle a scream, fight the impulse to charge back up the stairs. He would not panic. He was member of the police force, he was not alone. And that strength would secure his release.

Thus he had stood silently as the door closed and bolts were drawn.

It was then that he saw the light, the faintest of glows from deeper in the cellar. Whitney blinked, then turned towards it. So dim, impossible to tell how far away it was. But as his eyes adjusted once more, the more he became convinced this was no imaginary figment.

He had a book of matches in his breast pocket but was reluctant to use them. Whoever else was down here had given away their position, there was little to be gained from him doing the same. Instead, Whitney began to edge forwards, keeping one hand on the wall, moving as slowly as possible in an effort to avoid walking into some object in the dark. Except, in the end, that was exactly what he did.

His toecap tapped against something, and there was a whisper of wind at his trouser leg and a crash of metal that echoed off the vaulted ceiling. Again, he fought panic, keeping perfectly still as the sound rolled away.

Ready for the fight, he waited in the dark for them to come, but the cellar door never opened, the distant light never moved.

Eventually, Whitney sank to his haunches and carefully felt the ground before him. A horrible suspicion grew as he touched the object. He gave the far off light another glance, then drew the book of matches from his pocket. His fingers struggled with the task – too fat, too sweaty, too awkward – but eventually he struck a flame.

He found himself in a forest of death.

The object on the floor before him was a trap. Intended for animals, yes, but if he had set if off with the weight of his foot rather than jarring the mechanism, Whitney had little doubt that would have signalled the end of his escape. But worse, as he lifted the flame and looked around, he saw the trap was just one mechanism among dozens; different sizes and shapes, most hung on the walls, but some – like this one – lay primed on the cellar floor. He remembered a picture book he had caught Wilson reading one time: a mouse negotiating a room full of traps to reach a sliver of cheese.

Whitney let the flame die, then studied the distant light once more. Still no movement, still no sound. He lit another match, searching the floor around him. There was a pile of rubbish nearby – old newspapers and offcuts of wood, almost too good to be true. Whitney took a deep breath and reached out, prodding the pile with his truncheon. Sure enough, it exploded with a snap, kicking the truncheon from his hand as the match burnt out.

He took another deep breath, considered. Then Whitney slipped his jacket from his shoulders, pulling at the seams until the fabric started to come apart. Working blind, he found the likeliest strip, winding and tying it around the head of his truncheon. This done he lit another match, leaving just one more in the book. Whitney set about clearing the papers and kindling from the sprung trap, racing the flame as it flickered against his fingertips. He bundled the papers in amongst the fabric, putting the flame to it just as the match guttered. There was horrible moment of stillness, then the fire caught.

He raised the improvised torch above his head and moved forward, negotiating the open traps, avoiding the other detritus scattered across the floor. He had to move quickly – the torch would not last long – and he needed to be clear of the traps before it was extinguished.

Whitney was not a thinking man. He did not cogitate on the rules and laws he upheld, did not think hard on the principles he enforced, simply trusting to the importance of order. But he was smart enough to know that traps were laid for a purpose. Outside, they would be used to catch game, but the fear of them would also deter the unwary. And it was that second cause, he was sure, for which they were being used here.

As he made his way through the varied metal jaws, Wilson thought about the house he was in and the people he had seen. He had not been expecting to hear from Miss Miller or young Wilson before his arrival – indeed, their plan had been to meet the following day to exchange notes and plot their next move – but, now his own pursuit had come to an end, he wondered what fate had befallen them. For while they had chased him with vicious abandon, Whitney felt sure the staff were as much victims as he.

The traps, he surmised, were being used to guard something. As he moved through the vaults, he gauged the light was getting brighter. His watch had been broken in the initial pursuit and he wondered how long he had been down here, whether it was the sun penetrating some distant exit. Something that had to be guarded, to keep the poor souls here prisoner.

But as he cleared the traps, Whitney realised that the geography of the cellar had misled him, and this was not the case. The light was not getting any clearer, but remained diffuse. It was being reflected from somewhere deeper inside the house.

Whitney sunk to his knees at the knowledge this was not his way out, that his journey could only take him further into the madhouse.

Then he heard it. So distant, and impossible to tell from where. It was just the faintest echo and soon cut short, but there was a scream. Not the housekeeper's cry of rage, but one of terror and pain. It was, Whitney was certain, Miss Miller.

Whitney hurried on. He'd not heard the scream again, and could not truthfully say whether it had come from in front or behind. All he knew was he could not navigate back through the field of traps without the torch, and that was now burning low. If he was going to be of help, he needed to find a way out of the cellar.

The torch smoked, then dimmed. But free of the traps, Whitney no longer needed it. There was enough ambient light ahead to light his way forward.

He checked each vaulted arch as best he could as he passed; ensuring he wasn't missing an exit, but expecting none. The way out lay with wherever the light was coming from.

In the end, it proved to be something as mundane as worn stone stairs; set back in an alcove, curving up in a tight spiral; like the ones in castle ruins Whitney had visited on holiday. The curve explained why the light was so diffuse. Unfortunately, it also offered him little insight into what lay ahead.

Whitney straightened his back one last time and advanced.

As he climbed the stairs, the light remained a constant presence, never getting clearer or brighter, showing him just enough. Drawing him on, Whitney realised.

Only there was no-one waiting for him.

He emerged into a small room. There was no visible exit, save the one through which he had entered. The walls were plain and devoid of illumination. The centre of the room was occupied by a large wooden chair; fashioned out of rough oak beams. Big enough that Whitney would have struggled to fill its frame, but then, as he circled, he saw much of the frame was already occupied. A wrought-iron grid had been beaten into shape around it; cogs and springs grown from the sides; ratcheted rails lined the chair back, holding long, curving metal teeth.

Fascinated, appalled, Whitney leaned closer. The teeth were hinged, could fold back once a catch had been released, allowing access to anyone who should want to sit in the chair. The device was crude, and he was still unsure how it worked, but just looking at it, he knew that work it did.

The wood of the back and seat was stained thick with dark, dried blood.

He backed away from it, bumping up against the wall.

Only then did he see the box. An alcove of sorts had been carved into the head of the chair, and positioned within it was a small metal box, pictures and writing etched on its side. The metal was dark and heavy looking and yet…

It was the source of the light. Indeed, as Whitney looked around, he realised that there were no candles or light fittings, that there was nothing else in the room that could have been the source.

He was still considering this when he heard the sound of bolts being drawn and the wall behind him began to move.

iii. Dogberry

The boy had been murdered. That much was obvious, or so Miss Miller had insisted.

It was a statement which had caused disagreement in their own ranks, yes, but perhaps more pertinently, the conclusion was disputed by the surgeon who'd examined the body. The injuries, he'd indicated, were entirely consistent with an animal attack; the boy had got on the wrong side of a stag or aggravated a bull or some such. The boy's coat pockets had revealed line, hooks, and fly, plus the remnants of a bottle of chloroform. There were also traces of gelignite on his hands. Items that told their own story: the accoutrements of a poacher.

From that deduction, the circumstance unfolded thus: a night time expedition gone awry, the boy trampled underfoot and his abdomen ripped asunder. When the beast responsible had let him free, he had crawled off in search of help. The trouble was, that far from a town or main road, he had stood no chance. With earth and blood under his fingernails, his ribcage shattered, trailing viscera, the boy's strength had finally given out on the boundary of the old Austin estate to be found, possibly days later, by a passing farm labourer.

There had been no papers on the body, and none of the local villagers had recognised him, nor the local constabulary. He had remained anonymous until Miss Miller spied the notice in the paperwork at the Manleigh Halt station. The circular mentioned a distinctive birthmark on the boy's cheek, and on reading the description, Miss Miller had been insistent: she knew the child. Except, she had said (after calculating the years in consultation with Dogberry), he would hardly be a child any longer.

He was a distant cousin of her late husband, a relation she had met just the once on a visit to the country. With her husband occupied on family business, Miss Miller had (she'd explained) been entrusted to the boy's care, and – in the way of small boys – he had delighted in showing her his playground. A long summer's afternoon was spent navigating hedgerows and undergrowth, being inducted into a secret child's world of animal tracks and broken branches, disturbed mosses, slow flowing streams and slippery stepping stones. The boy – George – had been an insistent and commanding guide. When they returned, Clarissa was flushed with exertion, her elbows dusty and her hair astray.

Once they had been in touch with the investigating forces, it had been simple to confirm his identity.

And when that was done, Miss Miller had insisted: the child who had guided her through the wilds that afternoon could never have been taken by surprise by some animal. To her mind, that left just one conclusion: if it was not an accident (which it could not have been), then it was murder. And that, she had said, made it their business.

Dogberry had described her reasoning as fragile and refused to become involved, even as the others drew their plans.

The trouble was, now he was stood there, looking at the scene around him, he was certain Clarissa had been right.

Isiah Dogberry was concerned. Firstly, there was the worry that he had made a mistake, and secondly, corresponding to said mistake, there was the concern that his error had only begat another. Namely, that his comrades-in-arms had rushed headlong into a situation that was worse than they might have expected, and while that error was theirs, it was born in his own misjudgement that there was nothing to be concerned about.

The depth of his own concern about all of their poor choices, Dogberry thought last (or was it fourthly?), was indicated by the manner in which he was relapsing into circular exposition and inaction. Old habits, he mused, died hard and such thinking was, for him, an old habit indeed.

He shook his head and returned his attention to the matter in hand.

The device he held had been a present; a parting gift from a red-headed man in a city of sea and sunlight. Since their discovery of the unique properties of the Manleigh Halt police station, Dogberry had always been wary of removing advanced scientific material from its walls. Their own peregrinations seemed to be tolerated by the laws of the universe (such as they were perceivable), but he was careful not to test them too much. Future knowledge was to be protected, he told the others, meaning they should never speak of it outside of the walls of the station nor carry anything that could not be easily accepted by those they met.

It was only the particular nature of their current problem which had prompted Dogberry to break his own rule.

He had brought the torch in an attempt to finally prove his point and dissuade his fellows from their activities. As it was, he had arrived too late and then, in the hour of his arrival, only succeeded in finding the truth in Miss Miller's theories and the depth of his own misjudgement.

Reaching the inn, Dogberry had discovered his companions had already departed for the house; an unexpected dinner invitation so exquisitely timed that he should have immediately been concerned. Instead, their absence had only exacerbated his bad temper. He had made his way to the local constabulary and, verbally bludgeoning both the desk sergeant and police surgeon into submission, surveyed their reports on the incident. From there, he had proceeded to the estate itself and begun his inspection. He was, he gauged, only a few hours behind his colleagues. With luck, he would find the proof he needed quickly enough. Then down to the house to reveal his findings and accept their apologies, and they might all be on their way before supper.

As had been explained to him, the apparatus emitted a light which could reveal traces of blood long since passed from plain sight. His intent had been to locate the blood trail of Miss Miller's long-forgot relation, follow it to its source, marry the details up with the existing police reports, and establish the truth once and for all.

Except, as soon as he had located the scene in question – the line of trees marking the estate boundary – it became apparent that no such marriage was possible.

Dogberry worked the light back and forth, carefully studying the glistening trails it revealed on the earth and surrounding foliage. Long before he got to the relative age of the blood stains, the patterns themselves told him this was no accident.

He doubted that the local police had even bothered to visit the scene themselves – and why would they for an easily explained accident befalling a perceived vagrant? – but even if they had, they would have found enough to support their existing theory. It was only the instrument in his hand that revealed the extent to which this stage had been set.

Blood at the scene, yes. And blood tracing from the scene away from the estate, back towards the moorland, to where the deer and stags roamed. The story fit the supposition: the boy had been attacked by an animal and dragged himself this far before dying.

But there was not enough blood and it was in the wrong pattern. The body had lain where it was found, yes indeed, but the boy had not died there. Dogberry leaned closer, working back along the trail until he found what he was looking for: another path. A thin line of spots, running away from the main trail, leading back towards the woods and into the estate. As he followed its path, Dogberry kept casting glanced left and right, up and down, murmuring an occasional sigh as he moved deeper into the woods.

And then the trail had blossomed into a bright flower on the ground before him.

Dogberry had finally switched off the device. Tucking it back into his coat pocket, he had allowed a few moments for his eyes to shake off the remnants of its purple glow. Then he had drawn another, more conventional flashlight and begun an inspection of the earth. There was a scrap of wool on a branch close to head height. Dogberry suspected this new clearing was where the boy had died, that his body had been wrapped in a blanket or a rug (more to staunch the blood trail than anything) and then transported off the estate to where its 'discovery' had been carefully crafted. All that remained was one final piece to tip the scales in his mind from supposition to belief. It did not take long.

Angling the flashlight, Dogberry worked his way around the clearing.

The boy had supposedly been gored. It still wasn't beyond the realm of possibility that some stag had achieved this in the woods and that the boy's body had simply been moved. Except, as he examined the ground, it became clear that no animal had come close in weeks. Indeed, he thought, there was no sign any wild creature had ever visited this place.

It was enough to give him pause, and Dogberry stood and pocketed the flashlight. He braced his hands on his hips and arched his back, trying to clear some of the stiffness the evening's exertions had brought on.

As he did so, he examined the trees around him. They were all commonplace for the English countryside, but there was something strange about them. Almost like they had travelled through a magnifying glass and become twisted, engorged versions of themselves. A woodland as seen in a travelling hall of mirrors.

Except, Dogberry realised, that was not quite right. This was not a circus. He remembered a book from his youth. Such a long time ago now, and the finer details of its narrative were lost to him. But he could recall the thick volume and the intricate frontispiece; a fine ink drawing of a girl making her way through a dark grove that loomed and curled around her.

Stories of wolves and princess and evil witches.

Looking at the trees around him, Dogberry saw those same dark surroundings. The oppressive world of a fairy tale.

There was a long stretch of open ground, cutting through the trees and leading down towards the terrace of the house below. It was here that Dogberry sat, looking at his ultimate destination, yes, most certainly. But also to study the grass around him.

Tracking back from the scene of the crime, he'd headed in the general direction of the house. However, in doing so he had also had occasion to cross back over the more circuitous route – guided by the trail of blood – which had led him there in the first place. He suspected he had noticed the issue the first time, but solely on the level of the subconscious. It was only when it registered at that second crossing that he recalled the first. In isolated spots – amidst the bracken and on the leaves – autumn had come like a disease. Dogberry had paused, and made a more careful study. The patches of brown and withered foliage drew their own line in broadly regular spaces.

Dogberry had dropped to his knee to study closer, picking up a leaf only to find it turn to dust in his fingers,

After some consideration, he estimated firstly that the regular spacing was akin to his very own stride, and that lastly the patches in question were of similar size and shape to his own foot. And while he was now concerned as to the fate of his colleagues in the house below, it was a matter which required further thought and study on his part.

Thus it was that he, Isiah Dogberry, was found watching the grass around him.

Except he was not only watching the grass, but also cogitating and attempting to further the previous conclusions he had already drawn.

A fairy tale was what he had thought, and fairy tale fit the woods behind him still. But what was the nature of the wood in such stories? The lair of the beast or the supernatural, a place into which the unwitting traveller would be drawn to meet their fate. And yet, the woods behind him were, to all intents and purpose, devoid of life. No birds or beasts to be found. And, as the blood trail had proven, the one killing they knew had occurred there had likely been at the hands of one of the household. Therefore, while the trees may have looked threatening, there was no threat to be found within them.

Yet, Dogberry knew, there was purpose to their appearance. He had seen enough to recognise familiar plant species in his surroundings, indeed, enough to imagine how the woods would have looked five or ten years previously, but all were now twisted from their natural form. And he could not believe there was no intent to such a change.

The answer, he came to surmise, laid with his original thought. While they were not in themselves dangerous, the tree lines around him represented well-signposted, primal threat. The kind of threat that even a child would be able to recognise. It was a deterrent, to keep idle trespassers – from the playful to the poachers – at bay.

Such a wall of protection made Dogberry then think about what lay behind it. What secret did the house beneath him hold?

He climbed to his feet, surveying the circle of grass around him. Here the effect was not autumnal, but the height of summer. The green had vanished, replaced by worn and tired looking blades. Browner than a well-worn wicket, he concluded. And while the appearance was of a different season, the conclusion was the same. As far as the matter of this woodland was concerned, his touch was death.

The curious thing, Dogberry thought as he surveyed the landscape, was the sense the geography provided.

His first impression, of defence, was, he still believed, an accurate one. But coming to the matter again and again, as his mind was wont to do, another possibility was slowly raising itself to his attention. It was only as he progressed down the slope towards the house that it occurred to him to look back for another perspective. The glance had revealed nothing that he had not expected; the surrounding woodland raising tall and faerie thick, curling up to form its own horizon. And yet, time and again, he would pause on his journey to look back.

A most assured signifier that his subconscious was trying to communicate with him.

Yes, Dogberry thought, the trees were impressive. From the outside edge of the estate, they had looked overgrown and impenetrable. A false impression – he had navigated them, after all – but, as he had deduced, one with clear intent.

However, stood there, looking back up the slope, he wondered what it was he had missed. He studied the woods for a minute more, then sighed and gave up – he had delayed long enough, and mischief was likely underway below – intending to return his attention to the house. As it was, he never fully completed this latest about face; making a three-quarter turn before slowly swinging back.

Flat on, there was no perceivable difference to the woodland. But at one point, the tree line curved back around the slope to his right. And as he turned, it might be glimpsed in profile.

The trees had grown upwards and massive, yes. But they were also reaching, too, curling inwards; a profile only betrayed in that sideways glance. The effect, Dogberry mused, was also like a fairy tale. Massive wooden fingers, clawing their way up out of the earth. Slowly he rotated on the spot, and now that he had noticed the pattern of growth, he could see it repeated all along the tree line; as far as his eyes could see, forming a near complete circle around the house. The only exit was the gravel drive. And while it was straight and true, Dogberry wagered that the woods were such that it looked like a road that led only to darkness.

The growth of the trees followed no natural rhyme or reason; neither wind nor sun would stimulate such uniform growth.

For as much as they appeared from one side to be a barrier intent on keeping intruders out, from the other – curling inwards, looming over the bowl in which the house was situated – they would serve a similar purpose. To deter anything from escaping.

To hold it here.

Dogberry stood, turning the flower over in his hand. A daisy, gently plucked from the lawn. It was the third such flower he had pulled, consulting his pocket watch on each occasion, timing how long it took the plant to curl up.

His premise was now thus: the growth being experienced by the local vegetation was not natural. Therefore, it was being influenced by something. What that something was, was the matter currently pre-occupying him. The closer he had got to the house below, the more he saw the more questions arose in his mind, the slower his progress had become. On another day, it would have disturbed him to realise how much he relied on his companions to keep him for such pre-occupations; today, shorn of their influence, his thoughts turned only to this present challenge.

His initial, and admittedly obvious, premise was that it was a disease of some kind. But thinking such begged other questions. Why was it that his touch posed such a material threat to the plant life? And what was its precise nature?

Because it was this precision which had led to the current experiment.

As he had walked, Dogberry had been retracing his journey in his mind. His faculties could, he granted, be somewhat slipshod. Yes, a train of thought might be lost in a moment's distraction or consume him to the detriment of all else. When focused, however, he had learned his recall could be quite extensive. And thinking over it, he had come to realise that the extent of the faerie woodland marked precisely the borders of the Austin estate. Given that the phenomenon was man-made, Dogberry's initial thought had been that it was a substance which had been sprayed to so mark the territory. A biological deterrent for stray animals which had mutated beyond the grasp of its inventor, maybe.

It was, he thought, a respectable reading of the facts at his disposal. Even given the act of murderous deceit which had drawn them all here, he would struggle to refute the logic, but that did not shake off the simple conviction that, as an answer, it did not feel true to him.

Thus he had begun his examinations over again, seeking out new information to lead him to a more honest conclusion.

Considering what it was prompting him to this belief, Dogberry decided it was the shape of the trees themselves. They did not feel like an accident. They felt alive and formed. Controlled, was the word he was searching for.

Something had control of this place.

There were considerations here that Dogberry could not immediately resolve. Such control would have to be powered somehow; material change such as that in evidence around him would require energy – literal or metaphysical – which would have to be provided. This force would need to be fed.

But it was the nature of the control that Dogberry was now seeking to test. The first flower he had plucked he had sung to; the second he had spoken at. And while both had wilted, it had taken the second considerably longer to do so than the first. While there would be different harmonics between his speech and song, Dogberry considered the major difference was intent. The song was but mere noise; the speech was composed of intended words. They had weight and they had meaning. They expressed thought.

And so now, he was concentrating – imagining verdant fields and bright grasses and colourful blooms – on the daisy in his hand. The vegetation was once again browning, but at a noticeably slower rate. Perhaps with time and effort, he would be able to counter whatever deadly effect his presence was having entirely.

It was then that the various elements came into focus for him.

If the substance that had infected this place, whatever it was, responded to thought, then someone's thoughts were governing it. The effect bordered the lands of the estate, because that was the extent of that person's dominion. The house's owner would have been the natural suspect, of course. Except he was dead, and – according to the local constabulary – had been dead for a year or more. His remaining family had departed the estate not long after. Which begged the question, who else would be so bound to this place? The answer was the staff.

But not just any random scullion, Dogberry thought. Their territory would be the house itself, lucky if they saw beyond the kitchen or the pantry. No, it would be someone who knew the lands.

And as he thought it, the flower in his hand turned to dust.

It would be the gillie.

iv. Miss Miller

Clarissa Miller stood at the top of the staircase, waiting, and on occasion, glancing behind to where a grandfather clock stood, marking the time it was taking Constable Wilson to join her. The pendulum was producing a satisfying constant tick, indicating that the timepiece was oiled, freshly wound, and well-maintained. But by Clarissa's best guess, the hands themselves were awry by more than three and a quarter hours. The type of contrast that was becoming more and more commonplace the longer they stayed in the house.

She wondered how George had come to die in a place like this.

The circular had been four months old when she'd found it in the Station, idly leafing through paperwork abandoned on the front desk as years ticked by outside the window. It had taken her a minute or two to work out why the notice had held her attention, why she had felt immediately that she knew the victim. It was only when she had looked up from the paper, had seen the flickering of light at the edge of the Station door, that she remembered. The summer sun, caught behind the leaves of a poplar tree, waiting with George, still as a statue, for a pheasant to emerge from the undergrowth on the opposite side of the clearing.

That feeling of stillness, that you were the fulcrum the world turned on, was one she experienced every time she visited the police station at Manleigh Halt. But prior to that, she had only felt it a couple of times in her life – on her wedding day, and that afternoon with George.

She had made discrete enquiries with Rodger's relatives. They hadn't heard from the boy for years; the last they knew he had travelled south, moving with the seasons around the big estates.

It was only when they reached the village where his death had been reported that Clarissa's suspicions had begun to grow into certainties. Dogberry had dismissed her initial conclusions and refused to indulge them, staying behind when Sergeant Whitney and Constable Wilson had offered to accompany her. Their conversations with the officers who had dealt with the boy's death and the surgeon who had examined his body had not impacted on her one way or the other; she believed George could not have been taken by surprise and so badly gored by any animal, but could prove nothing.

As they'd left the village, they had taken the ridge way that passed the edge of the woods where George had been found. In the distance, they could make out a break in the trees; the angle and thickness of the woods was such that they could not see the space itself, but there was a hard line of stone that cleared the treetops. A large house, the centre of the kind of estate George had been working in.

In retrospect, that alone would have been enough to pique Clarissa's curiosity. It fit what they knew about George's movements and his death.

That alone would have been enough. But there was more. They'd stood there – Clarissa and Whitney and Wilson – and had been unable to move. Eyes drawn to the distant line of the house, the landscape pushing them away, the wind driving their attentions on. An unnatural push-pull that had continued for minutes on end. It had been Clarissa who had broken first, snapping her head away, shaking it clear. And when she had moved, the spell had broken and Whitney and Wilson had followed suit.

Without a word, they'd returned to the village and taken rooms at its sole inn. Clarissa had made her way to the post office and sent a telegram to summon Dogberry. Because, while they didn't know exactly what it was, they had all felt it, something drawing at their minds as they'd stood there watching. Something unnatural.

When she'd returned, Whitney and Wilson had changed out of their uniforms and were seated in the snug. Three pints of ale on the table; two barely touched, one drained almost to the bottom. Clarissa had understood and moved straight past without a word. Only when she'd reached the stairs did she glance behind, to see – as expected – a well-worn local weaving uncertainly back towards their table, drinks in hand.

Intelligence gathering, she'd thought, was fully underway.

A half-hour later, Whitney and Wilson had convened in her room. The building they had seen was indeed the centrepiece of an estate. The place had belonged to some minor noble or new money, no-one was quite sure. He'd had a bad reputation among the villagers; too loud, too carefree. When the man had died – a year or so back – there had been little mourning, not for him or his estate.

The few members of staff who were a regular sight in the village shops had drifted away, no orders for meat were placed with the butchers, no fruit or veg taken from the grocers. The gates at the head of the drive remained closed, paint beginning to peel, iron turning to rust.

There were occasional rumours of staff being employed, but no-one from the village ever filled any of the positions. No-one would try. They were just rumours. The estate was dead, everyone could see that just by passing it by. There was no future for anyone there.

In the end, Clarissa had tired of waiting. She'd crossed the hall to where Wilson was roomed and knocked on his door, but there was no answer. She'd tried the handle, but the door was locked and there was no response to any call. Lacking a suitable alternative, she'd descended the stairs alone, following the sounds of the party.

They'd enquired about the house's owners at the local police station and had received hushed, reserved answers. The owner – one James Austin – had fallen to his death. Though nothing had ever been conclusively proven, suspicions about his character had been raised by visiting members of the Metropolitan Police. Items had been removed from the home, and monies and papers seized. The police would say no more, so Clarissa had again dispatched Wilson to the bar to enquire further.

The locals were, however, unable to expand on Austin's criminal status. But – Wilson admitted – rather more widely spoken of was the nature of the parties Austin had been known to hold. More than one serving girl had returned home to the village with tales of debauchery. Clarissa had wrinkled her nose, opting to treat the tale with naked scepticism.

However, since entering the house, she had spotted a number of items tucked in alcoves and on shelves which piqued her curiosity. All were coated in dust and cobwebs, but she had been able to get close enough to ascertain that they were not heirlooms of the usual country provenance. She'd not been able to say anything to Wilson – and doubted he'd noticed – but the longer she spent in the house, the more of an idea she gained as to the owner's troubles with the law.

As she crossed the hall, her heel caught on an imperfection in the marble floor; a deep grove that her been worn into the tile. Never a man around, thought Clarissa, to hold you upright when you wanted one.

It was only when she heard the laughter and music at the entrance to the parlour that she thought of the other stories. She hesitated for a moment, wondering if she should go in search of Wilson once more. Then, shaking her head at her foolishness, she pushed the door open.

Clarissa felt a little disappointed when that first glance revealed a scene no different to any other party. The people were grouped in little clusters with drinks and cigarettes in hand – the men stiff-jacketed and square backed, the women looking demure and slight in long dresses – while a gramophone played in one corner and a pair of servants slowly made their way around the room.

Their heads swung towards her as she stepped into the room. Clarissa had assumed that their host would be there to greet her, or – failing that – the manservant who had ushered them into the house would announce her presence. But there was nobody at the door, and as passively as the heads had turned to her, they turned away again. Clarissa stood there, uncertain as to what to do next. No-one took an interest, and – thinking about it – she was not sure the conversation had paused at all even when they had glanced in her direction.

Her brow creased in irritation, and Clarissa stepped into the room proper, closing the door behind. Still nothing. And so, with a brief sigh, she picked out a couple of young women close to her and crossed to introduce herself to them with a smile. Only while they turned at the sound of her voice, no reply came. Their mouths remained firmly closed, their eyes lowered, and then they turned away altogether.

Clarissa tried again, this time with a couple of the men, but the response was the same. All the time, the gramophone continued to play, despite being drowned by the ongoing murmur of conversation. By this time, Clarissa was standing in the middle of the parlour, midway between a sofa and a chaise longue. Her initial irritation at being snubbed was slowly changing to curiosity, because that snubbing was only the most obvious sign that something was amiss.

Taking a glass of wine from a passing servant, Clarissa paused as she raised it to her lips. There was a chink in the rim of the crystal. More than that, she could feel old grime on its surface. She raised the glass to the light to examine it more closely, then sniffed the wine itself. Corked and almost turned to vinegar.

It looked no different to any other party she had attended, yes. But, like the house they stood in, that look only passed the most cursory inspection. The tables were carelessly dusted; gleaming in places, grimy and inlaid with scratches in others. The clothes that the guests wore were in a similar state: the edges were fraying on the hems of dresses; once crisp and proud, gentlemen's cuffs flapped loose without links. And then there were the people themselves. They were grouped like respectable dinner guests, but their eyes did not lift and their shoulders were heavy. And while their heads bobbed in conversation, half the mouths never seemed to open in speech.

She turned slowly around the room, trying to come to terms with the incongruity, certain she must be mistaken. But it only got worse. No-one spoke, yet the hushed dialogue continued unabated. It was only then that Clarissa tried to pin down who exactly it was speaking, and only then that she realised something was horribly wrong with the voices themselves.

She had seen one gramophone in the corner, playing the music, when she entered. Except despite the revolution of the wax disc, she couldn't make out a tune and, as she surveyed the room, it became apparent that there were two more such devices that she could easily see. As she crossed to the nearest, the sound of one set of voices became louder and she could, finally, make out the words.

A Midsummer Night's Dream.

Scarcely able to comprehend what she was doing, Clarissa leaned over the gramophone, lifting the needle from the spinning disc. And sure enough, one set of voices vanished. Glancing back into the room, she saw one group of guests had stopped their movement with the sudden silence. Almost immediately, the maid who had passed her the glass of wine, laid down her platter and pushed past Clarissa to replace the needle.

And as the needle touched down, the guests began to move again.

Clarissa studied the room some more, then crossed to the second gramophone and removed its needle. Once again, the same thing happened. Silence – but from a different group of guests this time – with activity only resuming once the needle was replaced.

Another glass of wine was presented, drinkable this time. And Clarissa watched from the edge of the room for a few minutes more, sipping the wine and slowly drawing her own conclusions. The truth was none of the guests was speaking; not even the ones whose mouths flapped open and shut. The only conversation came from the overlapping soundtracks of the gramophones; an unintelligible babble of theatrical recordings.

Trying to rationalise this, Clarissa wondered if the elaborate charade was part of some sort of joke, the stories about the parties returning to her thoughts once more.

But that answer did not feel right. Not with the chipped glass and soured wine, the general decay in evidence all around the house. This, she resolved, was exactly what it felt like: a masquerade of life.

Clarissa's patience finally gave in.

When the maid ignored her call as she passed by, Clarissa grabbed her wrist and spun her about. And when her head shied away, she took hold of the chin, tilting her face back and up to meet her eye. Except Clarissa never asked any of her questions. The maid's eyes sat in dark hollows, the skin tight on her face. And just visible – only now so because it had caught the nearby light precisely – was a gossamer line, criss-crossing her pale lips, the skin pinched and taught in places around it, thick in the manner of an old wound. Torn and healed, over and over again.

Clarissa stifled a cry, but could not help but take a step back. In doing so, she caught a vase, perched on the edge of a table, which balanced for an eternal moment, then crashed to the ground.

While the conversation did not stop at the sound – it could not stop – all of the heads swung towards her. The mouth of every woman was drawn in a thin, tight line. Just like the maid's, Clarissa thought, and, she guessed, with the same cause, too. The men, though, the men were different. As one advanced towards her, she could see the mouth open. The lips curled back around yellowing gravestone teeth. He gave voice to a sound, but no words, just a deep, guttural breath that seemed to have no end. There was no tongue visible in his mouth, just a thick ridge of calloused flesh.

Clarissa was so transfixed by the sight of him that she did not realise the danger he posed until it was too late.

His hands grasped her shoulders. His jacket was cloaked in dust and the scent of aged moth balls, but beneath that, escaping from it, was old dirt and perspiration. Hot, stifling odours. When she resisted, he released his hold, swung his elbow, catching her on the temple. The blow gave him enough time to take control, pushing her head sideways, exposing her neck for his mouth to close around.

Clarissa scrabbled behind her for a weapon, finding none.

The man's hold vanished and she stumbled away, grasping the wall for support. All the time, the overlapping Shakespearian voices continued their charade in the background. The man who had attacked her was bent over, clutching his head, blood trickling between his fingers.

One of his fellows stood behind him, a candlestick in hand. When her attacker looked up, the man with the candlestick simply shook his head with a schoolteacher's disappointment. Clarissa thought for a moment that she had been forgotten entirely.

But then, as her attacker straightened, all of the other guests slowly turned towards her.

Clarissa realised that the entire time since she had entered the room, the party had been under some kind of spell. A fantasy of ordered behaviour which served no purpose other than to mimic real life. But that spell had now been broken, and it was the real creatures who occupied the maid's uniforms and the worn dresses and stained suits who were looking at her now.

The house held secrets.

When the lights had flickered and died, Clarissa had run. She had fled the parlour, and locked, then barricaded the door – courtesy of a bell rope around the handles – as best she could. But she had little illusion that the door would stay shut for long. Which left her with choices to make.

She crossed to the front door, but paused with her hand on it. Through a window to the left, moonlight lay the grounds open for her. The drive led directly away from the house, up through the surrounding woodland. But it was a straight line, and there was little hope of escaping unseen. The alternative was to flee through the woods, but she thought of George and of what might await her in the trees.

The handles on the parlour door were rattling, hands thumping on wood, the rope she had tied already straining.

And then there was the issue of her friends, both of whom had vanished. Both of whom had almost certainly met with foul play of some kind. Could she abandon them? And as importantly, inside, she knew what motivated her to stay. The need to know, to understand what had happened. To George, to her, to everyone within these walls. With every breath she felt it: the house held secrets.

And she had to know.

Her hand dropped away from the door. She turned and surveyed the hall. The door to the parlour would not hold much longer and she needed to be quick. While not a welcoming sight, she had seen the upstairs rooms and suspected there was little more to be learnt there. Her attackers had been conducting a masquerade, play-acting at host and guest. It followed that they genuinely filled neither role; thus the guest and family rooms would reveal nothing.

She had learnt long ago that one's concern should be the puppet master, not his puppets.

With no sign of the electric lighting being restored, Clarissa grabbed a candelabrum from a shelf and advanced into the darkness at the back of the hall. She went swiftly, but attentively.

The deep grooves scored into the marble floor, the ones she had tripped on earlier, were immediately clear, beginning some ten feet from the back wall and leading back towards it. Clarissa followed the path they presented, but was momentarily baffled when they disappeared into the skirting board, with no sign of whatever had made them.

She knelt down, looking closer. There were dark brown traces in the grooves, and – yes – they did not stop at the wall, but disappeared behind it.

Clarissa rapped her knuckles against the surface. The sound was hollow. A secret passageway, she smiled. She set the candelabra down and pressed her hands against the walls, feeling for the switch which she knew would grant her access.

A wave of nausea flooded through her, and Clarissa stumbled away.

She blinked, then pressed back against the wall.

Something was screaming inside her head, liquid and glass and gold.

Clarissa's fingers were burning against the wall. She was supposed to be searching for a way in, a secret escape, but the actions never came. Her hands remained pressed against the false panel as the light glittered in her mind, brighter with every breath she took.

Her heart began to race. The light was seduction. It was the heat of her husband's skin against hers, the press of his body, and the touch of his fingers. Casual and private abandon. The most basic of human comforts, yes, and the most simple escape from the world. Almost like he was still there with her, part of her still.

But, she remembered, he was not.

She snatched her hands away again, and as she did so, realised the sound from the parlour was growing more intense. The door would be open in moments and they would have her.

Picking up the candelabrum, she ran for the nearest doorway.

It was apparent almost straight away that she had found the way below stairs. The wood panelling had vanished, replaced by decaying plaster; the floorboards were bare beneath her feet; the electric lighting – still extinguished – hung bare here. The noise from the hall grew more intense and Clarissa knew that her pursuers were free. At the sound, she also realised she had left the door ajar behind her.

After a moment's consideration, she went to pinch out the candles. Licking her fingertips, she found them coated with a thick layer of ash or sawdust. Something she could only have picked up from the wall she'd touched.

Liquid and glass and gold.

Clarissa shook her head, then extinguished the candlelight. That done, she looked back the way she had come. Shapes moved across the entrance, darting back and forth, searching. They had no idea as yet where she had run to, but that was, Clarissa knew, just a matter of time. She had to press on.

Gently setting the candelabrum down, Clarissa slipped off her shoes, then, keeping her back to the wall, began to finger her way deeper into the dark passage. The air grew heavier as she progressed, condensation slick on the plaster behind her. In the distance, there was a dim glow falling across the corridor.

She glanced back, but there was no indication the voiceless hunters had caught her scent.

And yet here was a voice.

She was unable to make out the words, but she could hear it in the distance, whispering down the corridor. Clarissa edged closer to the light; the glow of candles showing through thick, textured glass. Guessing that shadow would hide her presence, she moved on – pressed against the opposite wall – intending to get past the partitioning as quickly as possible. Instead, she stopped.

The partition was made up of multiple glass panels in a lead surround; almost all of them undulating or distorted in some shape or another. But in one corner, there was a single pane of clear glass. At a guess, the original had broken at some point and been replaced with a cheaper substitute. Nonetheless, the effect was to provide a window through to the other side. The square of light from it did not reach her, lay on the flagstones a foot or more away, and she was confident she could see but not herself be observed.

It was a kitchen. Clarissa had been below stairs in houses like this before, had seen the energy and fury which normally occupied rooms such as these. And there was evidence – pans still steaming on the stove, soapy water in the massive sinks, chopping boards and half-cut vegetables – that this was a kitchen like any other. Except it was almost devoid of life. There was only one person present, a massive woman, hair just edged with grey, sat at the big wooden table.

The woman was leaning forwards, head resting on her colossal hands, and the hands clasped together . There was something odd about the angle of her nose and her face was streaked dark brown. Her back rose and fell steadily as she spoke. Still Clarissa could not make out the words, but she didn't need to. The woman's manner made it clear this was prayer.

Watching, Clarissa stood, fascinated by this moment of calm in the bedlam of the past half-hour.

And then she realised the woman was not alone. There was a movement in the darkness and a man slowly stepped into the light, closing in on the woman. There was something in his manner; the soundless intent, a hunter's movement. Sure enough, a knife hung at his side, and judging from the rest of his attire, Clarissa gauged he worked the lands of the estate.

This, she knew with absolute certainty, was who had killed George.
It was the answer she had suspected. George had come here, looking for work, and stumbled into a nightmare much as she had. Only, she thought, he might have seen it sooner. He was the same breed as the man in the window, she could see the resemblance in the way he moved, the way he watched the world around him. And George had seen the danger the man represented soon enough to run. An escape, she believed, he had almost made.

A life now unlived.

She studied the man a moment longer, suddenly realising it was the butler who had met them at the door and escorted them to their rooms. Dressed differently now, of course, with his hair ragged and eyes raised. The only person in the house she had found who switched between upstairs and down, the only person she had heard speak with their own tongue.

The puppet master they were looking for. And yet…

One hand reached out for the woman's hair. She was praying still, and so silent was his movement, she had no idea he was behind her. Only Clarissa saw that while that single hand reached, the other rested on the hilt of his knife. But her immediate reaction was that this was not a hunter's movement. There was hesitation and nervousness in that hand, and it was why the other one held the knife. It gave him confidence he did not feel.

There was tenderness there, desire.

Seduction.

Something glittered in her head, liquid and glass and gold.

And the man's head snatched up, looking through the window pane, into the darkness. Looking at Clarissa.

She turned to run, only to find her path blocked. The darkness was filled with soundless bodies. Dressed in servants' uniform – scullery maids and cooks – they stood across the passageway, a line three or four deep. They all looked tired, some were nursing bruises and blood, the remnants of a desperate fight that they surely never had a chance of winning. For like the guests at the party upstairs, each had pinched and taught skin, what Clarissa had come to recognise as the hallmark of the thin line of wire thread. Only here, rather than their mouths, each had their eyes sewn shut.

Clarissa finally broke. And as she screamed, the crowd of bodies surged towards her.

Clarissa had fought, and as she fought, she felt it once more. Liquid and gold and glass. With every scratch, every kick, every blow she landed, she felt it more. Every inch of her body, the muscles, the tendons, skin and bones. She fought and she ran.

It was the gillie who landed the blow that took her. Stepping out of the dark to connect with a fist, straight to her face. Clarissa's head had snapped back, and before she'd had a moment to recover they were on her. As hands pinned her arms, she was aware of blood running from her nose, down over her chin, onto her dress.

Her chest heaving, skin damp with perspiration, hair coming loose, she had not felt so alive in years.

She attempted to straighten, to look her captor in the eye, but he showed little interest in responding. He studied her like meat, looking her up and down, pinching the flesh on her cheeks and her torso, but not once regarding her as a human being.

Then he inclined his head, and the others – the servants – began dragging her back up the corridor, back into the house proper. When Clarissa screamed and struggled once more, he hit her again, catching her on the temple. Dazed, Clarissa could feel her legs give out, her bare feet dragging along the flagstones as they pulled her on.

By the time she had gathered her wits once more, they were back in the main hall.

The gillie was joined by the cook. Both of them stood in front of the false wall

Clarissa had identified earlier. Then the woman pitched her head back and screamed. Clarissa winced as the noise dragged on at a frightening volume. Then her mouth closed and there was silence. Again, Clarissa tried and failed to catch the gillie's eye.

And then she understood the significance of the cook's cry. Slowly the doors around the hall began to open, footsteps were heard on the stairs, the house's other occupants – mouths sewn shut, tongues burnt out – returning from where they had been searching for her. Summoned.

She could see the gillie scanning the crowd, totting numbers and faces. After a few minutes he was satisfied, and turned to the wall behind him, levering free a panel to reveal sturdy bolts holding the rest of it in place.

As he swung the wall back, the hall slowly lit with a glow that was, Clarissa immediately knew, the same light which had been glittering in her mind.
She wondered if the others could see it, see the way it drifted around the casket that the gillie was picking up from the alcove.

Then he stepped back, bearing the box aloft and two of the servants stepped in, taking hold of the chair that it had been resting on. As they began to pull it forwards, Clarissa remembered the grooves worn into the marble that had brought the false wall to her attention.

Finally talking note of the device being dragged across the floor towards her, she did not scream, merely shook her head in disbelief.

The gillie stepped up in front of her and raised the casket to her face. He smiled and then released the lid, unveiling the object within. Liquid and glass and gold.

Clarissa took a sharp breath, breathing its light, and then they pulled her into the chair's embrace. Her breathing began to slow, and she offered little resistance as the straps were tightened around her wrists and ankles. There was no fight left in her. As the gillie placed the casket atop the chair behind her and she took its light into her lungs once more, the feel of the device was all there was left in the world.

Not just the leather pulling at her skin, but the metal arms being pushed into position around her, under her arms, reaching around her torso, finding the midline between her breasts. Except they weren't arms, but teeth, pushing against her, pushing her back against the chair, slowly, one by one being wound down, digging into the fabric of her dress, then on into her skin, into her flesh.

She gasped, tears came and she closed her eyes. There was no pain. Just the light from the casket, in and out with each breath.

The light was seduction.

There was a ratcheting noise, and she could feel the tension against her back, building in the chair, ready to be unleashed.

Casual and private abandon.

And then they waited. With utter calm, Clarissa wondered what they were waiting for. She could feel the gillie's hand on the lever that would release the device, that would snap the jaws apart, tear her body asunder.

The most simple escape from the world.

Then thunder sounded and something sprayed across her face.

Clarissa opened her eyes.

Wilson was there, coming down the stairs into the hall, trailing smoke from an old revolver. His hair was loose across his face, and there was a look of anger, of rage and pain, on his face that Clarissa had never seen before, would never have thought possible. A child raging against the world.

He raised the gun as the crowd swarmed towards him, thunder sounded again, the bullet catching one of the servants in the head, an explosion of blood and brain, a gossamer line across his mouth, unable to make a sound as he fell.

There was another sound behind her. She did not hear the words, but she knew the tone, A commanding voice telling everyone to stop. Whitney's voice. He was emerging from a stone doorway behind them, his uniform ragged, truncheon in one hand, the other raising a whistle to his mouth. Order attempting to impose itself on chaos.

By the time Wilson had cocked the trigger again, they were on him, and the next shot went into the ceiling as they pulled and clawed. By the time Whitney had raised his arm to strike, there were half a dozen man and women pinning him back against the wall, till all he could do was blow the whistle

They were all breathing it in, liquid and gold and glass.

She knew now what the gillie had been waiting for. He had been waiting for this.

The child had to grow up. Order had to be broken on chaos.

And seduction would become death.

v. Gillie

Gillie stood on the roof of the house. His hand drawing the hunting knife back and forth across the edge of the parapet; a slow, practised movement he could do without concentration. A movement that left his eyes free to watch.

On a night like this, this quiet corner of the roof was the only place he could see the moon, a silver coin low on the horizon.

Just over a year ago, he had been searching the house. Not quite knowing why, but he'd finally come to the library.

It had been near-empty, most of the books had been taken away after the master's death. The few that remained leant against each other like drunken soldiers; still on duty, but in a post that counted for nothing, where no-one cared. As he'd moved around the room, Gillie's foot had caught on another soldier, passed out on the floor; this one fat with pages of small words, left open on a picture of the moon. Gillie had picked the book up and blown the dust away, tracing his fingers over the drawing. After a few moments, he'd drawn his blade down the edge of the page, lifting it from the book. He'd folded it neatly, slipped it into his bag and carried on his search.

At the time, he was still unsure what he was looking for, or why. Only later had he realised he was only seeking and, in the end, finding because the Ghillie Dhu was already a part of him, had always been a part of him.

That evening, he'd handed it to cook and made her tell him what it said. The page had spoken of old gods and goddesses, of the moon as Diana, and of what she was said to represent. After a few minutes, Gillie had waved cook into silence. The words made no connection with him. The moon was not the thing that glittered in the back of his mind.

He'd never liked the moon, did not trust the way it bled colour away. It made silhouettes out of everyone. Travellers in the dark.

And that was what Gillie fancied he could feel tonight. Something hiding away in the moonlight where he could not see.

There was nothing wrong with the house. Yes, the strangers were there, but only because he had brought them. The party was underway in the rooms below, overlapping voices making themselves heard. More than that, if he concentrated he could feel the creak of the ropes on the dumb waiters, the ring of the pans in the kitchens. From the outbuildings, he could smell the residue of smoke, still seeping from the pork side hung there, and iron from the blood that had dried between the flagstones.

The Ghillie Dhu let him know all of these things.

No, the trouble wasn't the house or the strangers. These would all look after themselves, because that was how Gillie had made them. Instead, it was out there in, in the dark shadows cast by the moon. Out in the wood, purple light was flashing back and forth, breaking through the cover of the trees.

Something was moving that Gillie could not properly see. An old fear.

After drawing the knife back one final time, Gillie tested the edge of the blade against his thumb, and satisfied, looked up once more. The light was gone now. He watched for a minute, but it did not reappear.

Whatever it was would wait. He would trust in his defences, he would not be swayed when there was work to be done.

Others had come before. Never the travellers in the dark that Gillie feared, but desperate men, calculating men. They came for the Ghillie Dhu, but the imp itself always let him know.

The first had been just weeks after Gillie had found his prize. He had been standing on the roof, just like he was this night, still getting used to his new role in the house. Only something had made him look up. Their relationship was still in its infancy those days, and he had not yet come to understand what the Ghillie Dhu wanted from him or properly hear its cries. But, he knew later, a cry it was.

There, standing at the gate, a mile or more distant was a man, just looking down into the estate. The oaks and the conifers still stood straight back then, and – in the end – he had moved off. There had been nothing for him to see.

Later that same day Gillie had passed the gates and there, pinned to a gate-post, was a thin rectangle of pasteboard, a visiting card ornately inscribed 'Mr D Davies esq.'.

He knew the imp had a siren song of its own. It was what had drawn him to Austin's hiding place; secure enough that the police and the travellers had never found it. He'd found it in the half light of dawn; dust caught in the first rays of morning through the hall windows, drifting out from the edges of the box. Releasing the catches, Gillie had pushed back the lid, far heavier than it should have been, and breathed deep. And while his eyes had been closed, he'd seen the imp nonetheless.

It had been waiting for him all his life, ready to take him in its embrace.

That morning, looking at the man in the distance, was the first time Gillie understood that others felt like he did. Others coveted the imp and, inevitably, more would come for it.

In the months that followed Gillie had studiously charted the Ghillie Dhu's new domain. Every time he opened the box and breathed deep, he saw the imp. Every time he opened the box, the imp's hold grew stronger and Gillie's hold grew stronger.

Outside of the domain, he learned what tales to tell and to whom. What stories would spread, and how to keep people away. After a few months, he knew that anyone who entered their lands was most likely a stranger, ignorant of the stories, and could be taken into the household. But there were others, like the man, who knew what they were doing. More careful, more cunning, unsuited to a role on staff.

And they needed to be drawn in, to be broken against the Ghillie Dhu.

The Boy he had already taken care of. He'd not seen Gillie at the inn, but Gillie had seen him with the girl, seen the Boy's weakness straight away. The Woman was inquisitive, would occupy herself until everything was ready. All of which, he thought, left only the older man, the Giant.

Back then, Gillie had gone by a different name; the one given to him by his mother on a chill autumn night. It was the name he'd worn as a child and on into his teenage years. He couldn't even remember the different name now, but he knew he had been a different man.

A dark and impenetrable world loomed over the village, one that only the grown men had access to. The woods were dangerous, all the children were told. And like all the other mothers, Gillie's had told him about Lame Jackie. As a boy Jackie had been lost in the woods, and the men had spent days searching for him. When they found him, one foot was torn almost clean off. A bear or a wolf, the parents told their children. And so, they were never to go into the forest alone.

An old man now, Lame Jackie could still be seen, shuffling around the village, so there was no reason to doubt the story. But one thing had puzzled the young Gillie, if the woods were so dark and dangerous and vast, how had the men ever found Jackie? His mother had waved the question away, but Gillie had persisted, day after day until, one evening, she had given him an answer.

Leaning close to his bed, she had explained about the Ghillie Dhu; the spirit who watched over the highlands. An imp, a faerie, and like all his kin, sometimes capricious, sometimes kind. The men, his mother explained, knew how to speak to the Ghillie Dhu, and it was he who had eventually led them to Jackie.

His mother – a widow – had regular visitors across the week, afternoons when Gillie would have no choice but to go and play, regardless of weather. There was one who would smile and make a present of an apple or pinch his cheek; another, heavier set, would catch him with the back of his hand at any delay on leaving the house; most never saw him at all.

The children outside had been no better, commenting with mouth and fist. Gillie had been too small to fight back, and so he had learned to run and hide. But the boys were persistent and any hiding place in the village, any respite, lasted for no more than an hour or two.

On a morning like any other, Gillie had turned a corner to find the village children massed and waiting for him. Except this time there was something different in the set of their faces, arms and fists. Gillie never found out what had provoked the change that day, but he'd known if they'd caught him it would have been a beating like no other.

He ran, putting speed over cunning, pushing for distance between him and his pursuers. And while he made a little ground, he knew it would not be enough for him to find any safe place to hide.

Nowhere, the thought had suddenly come, in the village.

He'd turned left, back into the narrows, losing speed as he fled uphill. The houses thinned out, and he was past cobbles onto grass, then into bracken, and he could feel the determination of the pursuing children waning. The forest rose up before him, but he did not break stride. He slowed as he broke the tree line only because he dared not risk tripping on a stray branch or root.

The gang were slowing also, but still following behind. There would come a point, Gillie knew, when their fear of the wood overcame their desire for him. He just had to push on until that point came. It was the same instinct that was drawing the other children on: the belief that eventually Gillie would prefer the beating over being lost in the trees.

And as his pace slowed, Gillie became more and more aware of the depth of the forest around him. Its scents and textures, the uneven ground beneath his feet, the height of the evergreens above, the darkness that thickened with every step he took. And then he saw it, a distant glimmer of light in a deep shadow catching his eye.

Sometimes capricious, Gillie had remembered, sometimes kind. And he'd turned and headed into the darkness, fixing on that sole point of light as his guide.

He just kept moving, secure in a child's knowledge that if he reached the light, he would find the Ghillie Dhu and she would keep him safe.

He broke through a final curtain of heather, but caught his foot on a rock and fell. It was only then, the magic spell broken, expecting to be found at any moment, that he realised his tormentors were no longer behind him.

Slowly he got to his feet. The forest was silent, with no other creature in sight. Gillie stood there, panting, the rich damp scent of the wood filling his nose and his lungs, his body steaming in its chill air.

He turned, looking once more to the glimmer of light from the Ghillie Dhu.

As he grew older, so Gillie abandoned the village. Now when her visitors came to call, he would kiss his mother good-bye as he had always done and vanish without complaint. Then, out of sight, he would head for the woodland, collecting his things from wherever he had hidden them the night before.

The other children had been cowed into silence that first day. They'd waited for him at the edge of the forest, but when he had emerged from the trees at dusk, he had stood tall before them. While there would be the occasional whispered comment as he passed in the street, they never bothered him again.

After that, he'd slowly spent more and more time in the forest. Now the fear had gone, it was a place he was free to explore. Picking up scents, following tracks, charting streams and gullies.

Gillie had known of a couple of men who went hunting; the heads of families whose clothes were threadbare, but who never went hungry. He knew better than to ask either outright, because an adult would never, could never keep his secret. Instead, over a period of weeks, he had shadowed the pair; watching what they did, listening to what they said. Eventually, when he felt he could do so without giving himself away, he followed them into the woods and from his hiding place, watched them lay traps and lure fish from the streams. He watched and made their skills his own.

Then one day, he was returning home when he caught a strange scent. Smoke, growing thicker as he neared the border of the trees.

He did not hurry, but walked slowly into the village. He knew. Before he could see the flames, before the people parted at his approach, watching him but unable to meet his eye, before all this, he knew. His home was gone and his mother with it. He had looked at the smoking skeleton of their home for a minute, then turned, intending to head for the woods and never once look back. Only then did he see the man staring at him. The one who'd always smiled, now standing tall and unbowed. Like Gillie had been the day he'd returned from that first venture into the forest.

Confident and untouchable.

Gillie passed him close by and while he was cloaked in the same smouldering odour as all the others, there was a trace of something else. A sharper smell of paraffin. Gillie had paused for a moment, taking a long look at the man's face, then silently walked on and out of the village.

The months that followed saw him make a home in the wordless forest. His body grew stronger and leaner as he worked the hills, travelling for days just following deer across the highlands. From time to time, he would return to where the forest bordered the old village, never emerging from the trees, just staying in their shadow, watching. His new home had taught him the value of patience.

Indeed, it was years before the day finally came. The man who had smelled of paraffin emerged from the inn one night, intent on relieving himself. Gillie — taller and thicker, growing into a man's frame — had not made a sound as he crept up behind him.

He hadn't killed the man there and then. Although years away from his old life, Gillie still knew a murder would be investigated and he did not want anyone disturbing his new existence. As far as the village was concerned, the man simply had to disappear. To Gillie, this meant making sure the body was well hidden in a place far enough away that, even if its bones were one day discovered, no connection could ever be made.

He bound the man's hands and made him walk. For days on end, Gillie ignored every plea made, just forcing him on at knifepoint. Every time he tried to run, Gillie chased him to ground; every time he sat down, refusing to move and begging for death, Gillie waited him out.

Gillie had no specific destination in mind. He just wanted distance, thinking that when they reached a suitable spot he would know it.

In the end, that was exactly how it worked. Coming over a hill, Gillie looked ahead and could see they were running out of thick countryside. Another day's walk and they would be closing on road and rail, houses and people. So when they next came to a clearing, Gillie told the man to stop and, without pause, sunk the knife into his heart.

He cleared leaf and bracken away, revealing a square of dirt, then began to dig. He had just thrown the first handfuls of earth back on top of the body when he heard a branch snap behind him. Gillie turned to find an old man, dressed in warm – but not rich – clothing watching him, a rifle in his hands. The man said nothing at first, and Gillie looked between the man and the grave. After a while the man had stepped closer, waving Gillie back. He'd given the body a cursory inspection then asked if Gillie had killed him. Except, Gillie knew, it hadn't really been a question.

Gillie just answered that the dead man had killed his mother.

The newcomer had nodded, considering this, then gestured with the gun again, prompting Gillie to sit down. When he did so, the man also sat, across the clearing, the grave between them. He produced a bottle of water, which he threw across to Gillie. Had Gillie ever killed anything else, he asked.

And Gillie told him of the rabbits and hares he had caught, the streams he had fished and the chickens he had stolen. The man had smiled at the last one, then asked about larger animals, like deer. Gillie shook his head; he'd stalked them, but never had the means or the need for the kill. The man smiled at that too, then told Gillie to get to his feet.

The grave wasn't going to fill itself.

Gillie never knew the man's name, only ever his trade. The one that he was to be taught: a woodsman, a gamekeeper, and hunter. A gillie. Gillie himself never asked how the old man had found him, because as he had watched him work, the question had been answered.

The old gillie would have picked up their trail in the woods and, thinking he was running down poachers, tracked them. Gillie guessed the old man saw in him what Gillie saw in the old man; a kindred spirit.

The estate that the old gillie worked was a prosperous one. His position there was well established and there was no argument when he presented Gillie as an extra mouth to feed. The laird was aware of his employee's advancing years and keen to see a successor put in place. But every candidate put forward, from within the household and without, had been rebuffed by the old gillie himself. Consequently, when the old gillie announced he had found his protégé, Gillie was gratefully welcomed.

Gillie rarely set foot inside the house those first few years. It was a world beyond his understanding; of massive wooden beams and gleaming silver, deep carpets and looming dark paintings, of rich clothes and strange accents. Old gillie could see how uneasy this made his charge and so they spent most of their time on the hillsides. He watched to see what Gillie knew, how he tracked and fished, how he cooked and kept warm; satisfaction was silence, disapproval a sigh or quiet shake of a head.

He taught Gillie how to work a knife properly, how to bleed and skin, how to read the deer and stags, and check the number of fish in the streams. He taught Gillie all of these things, waiting patiently for the young man to master each skill before moving on to the next one.

He never asked Gillie about his mother or where he came from, wanted to know nothing other than what he could do in the wild.

Eventually, the old man had placed a rifle in young Gillie's hands. Gillie was surprised how heavy and awkward it felt. His mentor showed him the importance of respecting the weapon, of cleaning and caring for it, how to load and shoot, and Gillie learnt all the skills as had all the others. But his whole adult life had been spent working with his own hands and reading the shift in the world around him. The gun felt solid and inflexible, and did not belong in the world he occupied.

There would be days when the old gillie would be summoned to the house to organise a hunting party. Again, Gillie was kept at a remove; as with his visits to the house itself, it was felt he would struggle with the mass of people, their hustle and bustle, accompanying customs, and required deference.

In the beginning, he would follow the parties at a distance, shadowing and observing. Eventually, he was allowed to join the beaters. And while he learned to disguise it, he always felt unhappy with such events. The crack of the rifles and the quiet cheers that accompanied each shot felt wrong.

As with the gun in his hands, there was the sense that this was not how it should be.

Old gillie could see the discomfort in his charge. After one such shoot, Gillie had asked his mentor what the event was for. Old gillie had explained that it was tradition; the day marked the turn of the year and the hunt was to celebrate the occasion. Gillie had pointed out the members of the party: reluctant, fat, red-faced and bad-tempered. There was no shame in hunting, Gillie said, but this was no celebration, either. Old gillie considered this and, in the end, agreed.

When the shooting party was over and done with, old gillie had taken him out once more. The light was fading and it was bitter cold, but they had no concern, both knew this countryside well enough. He told Gillie to hunt, to bring back any animal of his choosing. Within a few minutes, Gillie had returned with hare, struggling inside a sack slung over his shoulder. Old gillie had smiled, and asked what they should celebrate.

Gillie thought about it, hugging his coat against the cold, then said the coming change of seasons and everything it would bring.

Old gillie had nodded, then drawn the hare from the sack. He repeated Gillie's words – a toast or a prayer now – then slit the animal's throat, and as it bled out, sliced its body wide open. They left its carcass on the hillside, there for the other animals to eat. An offering to prosperity.

Gillie paid little attention to the lives of household staff. He spent more time in the house as old gillie slowed, but still preferred to spend his time out in the glen. The mechanics of the house held little of interest to him.

The servants' entrance led him through the kitchens on his way to any meeting with the laird, and he found the space oppressive, assaulted by the steam and smells and the heat and the sweat. For their part, the kitchen staff ignored him in return, working round him as he passed.

The exception was a young girl, only a couple of years out of childhood. Her name was Margaret, she told him. She would catch his eye and smile, calling him "Gillie". He would tell her he was not gillie yet, but she continued to call him that anyway. Whenever food was brought to the croft Gillie and his mentor shared, it was Margaret who brought it. Old gillie would make her sit down and eat with them, quizzing her on the household's activities. He was, he said, trying to explain to Gillie that he needed to pay attention to all things, that he was just part of a greater organism. It was during one of these meals that he saw his master smile as she called him "Gillie", and only then did he finally hear the humour in her voice when she said the name.

It was then, when he finally stopped correcting her, that the name itself began to stick.

It had been expected that old gillie would die before the laird. In the end, this was not the case. While their master would still issue orders and tear a strip off his menservants, there was an unspoken knowledge that change was coming. Gillie could see it in the kitchens when he visited below stairs. The smile slowly, day by day, draining from Margaret's voice. The staff saw the change coming, but never dared speak of it. None of the household knew of money and finance, but food orders were being trimmed and repairs to crofts delayed.

The laird's son, old gillie had commented one night, was away in London, and only ever returned to bleed his father for money. It was the only time Gillie heard the old man speak of their master with any kind of disdain. Gillie should settle down, he advised. It was fine to work the land, but only a fool made it his entire life and lived at the whim of the rich.

Gillie had nodded at the old man's words, just as he always did, but was unable to escape the feeling they had no meaning for him.

Then came the day the laird passed. The house fell into darkness, everyone in black, as visitors came to pay their respects and the heir made his way home. Bagpipes played, mourners lined the drive, heads bowed as the funeral cortege passed by, heading out to the family mausoleum that stood on the edge of the loch.

Gillie and his mentor had a brief interview with the new laird, but the man's disinterest was readily apparent. He would nod, mutter a little in response to whatever they told him, but all the while his fingers played with a deck of cards. Shortly afterwards, new sets of visitors began coming to the house. At first it was young women and jovial men and dinner parties that went on until the early hours. Some of the staff embraced the change. It was, Margaret said, just like the tales her cousin wrote to her, of the rich folk at the house she worked for in the England.

But the parties became more and more infrequent, and other visitors – fat, suited men – more prevalent.

All the time, old gillie's health continued to deteriorate; rarely leaving his croft, giving over the running of the estate to his protégé. In the end, the death of the estate and the old gillie coincided.

Old gillie's croft was near the gatehouse, and Gillie had been there, tending the old man, when he heard them approach. Boots crunched on gravel, but not the blundering footstep of the laird and too regular to be a poacher's error. Moonlight cast everything in black and white through the window and Gillie's eyes struggled to make out their form. Misshapen heads and long cloaks, moving with purpose through the long shadows of the drive.

Travellers in the dark.

He'd left the old man's side and, keeping his distance, followed them all the way up to the house. There the heads were revealed as helmets, tucked under arm as they were shown into the house. Shortly after, the figures emerged once more, the laird at their side, not once looking back. There were no handcuffs, but he left with them nonetheless.

When Gillie returned to the croft, he found the old man had died. Slumped in his bed, facing the window that looked out onto the drive,

Gillie intended to bury him himself the next morning, but was thwarted by a summons from the house. Gillie and the other heads of household were met in the study by the laird, dishevelled and grey, and another man who introduced himself as the family's solicitor. The estate had run out of money, he explained. The laird had already secured a buyer for the house – a banker from London looking to retire – but there was no such agreement for the surrounding lands. These would be sold off at auction and were unlikely to be bought whole.

When the meeting was over Gillie had returned to the croft, hefted old gillie's shrouded body onto his shoulders, and returned to his original task. He climbed high up into the woods, burying the body on a promontory, where he stood watch till the day began to ebb.

Returning to the house, he informed the other's of old gillie's death. Only when that was done, stood in the kitchen, did he notice her absence. Enquiring after Margaret, he was told she had already left the house, heading south for work with her cousin.

Gillie spent the following years moving from estate to estate. His old master's financial troubles had been of his own making – too many years bleeding his father dry with gambling debts and an inability to take a hard decision when one came – but they were not unique. After a couple of years, Gillie slowly became aware that he was developing a reputation. When shooting parties came, the richest and the fattest would jostle to have him at their side, believing it guaranteed success in the hunt.

By the time the century turned, the routine was set. Gillie would secure a new position and spend a couple of years making it and the land it came with his own. And then, he would watch and listen as the nobles and businessmen filtered in and out, learning who did what and where, and wait for a likely prospect to attach themselves to him. Because such migration was rare in his position, Gillie was careful always to make sure he left his employers in good grace; the lands and stock in prime condition, staff well versed, a successor (who would be good, but not quite as good as he) on hand.

Slowly but surely, this haphazard pattern led him down across the border. As he did so, his employers grew louder and fatter and the lands he tended became smaller and smaller.

Although he was largely untouched by it, the war, when it came, seemed to change the world around him.

A broken man, his then master had stumbled through the following years, more dead than alive. Eventually, peer pressure (and the man's wife) prevailed, and they began to hold parties once more. But even Gillie could see the change. There was an emptiness at the heart of all their jollity.

Amongst the regular guests was one man who seemed to exemplify this more than the others.

In his mid-thirties, he was full of charm and grace, talking to everyone as an equal and drinking in the detail of the world around him during the day. But Gillie heard stories of his behaviour when the sun went down; the humour ever present in the man's eye being given full vent. He was only minor nobility, and the other guests simply saw a lack of dignity. For Gillie, it was a sign of something more fundamental.

A few weeks later, and his master had been invited by the man – whose name, Gillie learned then, was Austin – to visit his home and enjoy the shooting. Austin had insisted Gillie be brought; ostensibly to show Austin's own beaters the ropes, but Gillie knew the type well enough by now, suspecting he was being asked to provide amusing colour. Except the weekend did not turn out that way. The man was even more incorrigible in his own household, taking great delight in making his guests uneasy and performing ever more outrageous acts.

From overheard conversation, Gillie knew that there was some mystery surrounding the man. He came from a wealthy family, yes, but there was no income to suggest how he was able to afford the house and grounds. After their first evening in the house, his master (at the behest of his wife Gillie was in no doubt) instructed him to converse with the servants and see if he could unearth any more detail. It was a task Gillie had undertaken with great reluctance – even now conversation and social grace did not come easy to him – and was unsure how to proceed. In the end, it was been simplicity itself. A brief rap on the kitchen door, and he had walked in.

The morning after, Gillie had resigned his post and asked Austin for a job.

Something inside him had to change.

Except the change never really came. All Gillie found was an echo of decades past. When the kitchens wound down for the day, he would spend a half-hour in the company of cook and her staff. It had not changed since the time of old gillie. While those upstairs chattered on about nothing, too in love with the sound of their own voices to take note of the world around them, downstairs they saw it all. They knew who was drinking too much, who was losing at cards, who was sleeping with who and how. All the secrets and lies and betrayals were theirs to see and never speak of. All save one.

Their master remained a mystery to them all. They all knew of James Austin's behaviour and strange habits, yes, but none of them – not even Gillie – understood him. They talked when they hunted, Austin pressing Gillie for stories of his past. So Gillie had told him about old gillie, and his first estate, and how it had all come to an end. Austin had laughed at the mention of the family mausoleum, immediately determining to have his own built.

Then, after he had been in the man's employ for just over a year, Gillie saw the change. It took him a while to pin down exactly when it had happened – after Austin had disappeared to London on another one of his social tours – but the man who returned was different.

The behaviour grew more and more reckless, the humour became casual abandon, the casual abandon increasingly dangerous. The late night parties would be punctuated with gunshots and screams as Austin demonstrated trick shots with a revolver. A guest who lost a wager would pay by acting as a stationary target as Austin dotted the wall around them with thrown knives. The general impression was of a drunkard in full swing, but Gillie had seen enough of his master to know he rarely touched a drop. It was merely that everything the man was had been brought to the surface, unashamed, unabashed.

Incredibly none of the guests seemed to mind. When they crossed the threshold into the house, it seemed to be accepted that the rules they all abided by had changed. If he hadn't known better, Gillie would have suspected Austin of doping his guests.

For a year or more, the house seemed to careen along like a carriage drawn by wild horses, furious, exhilarating, barely able to hold the road.

The mystery of the man only deepened with his death.

It happened away from the house, in London. Austin had fallen, the impact awkward enough to break his neck and end his life. The assumption was it had been another joke gone awry. Gillie had remained quiet, suspecting something different entirely.

He may have thought it, but it was the strange woman at the funeral who voiced the idea for him.

Gillie had stood at the back of the mourners, watching as Austin's coffin was taken into the mausoleum. Before him, amongst the long black coats and veils, was a woman in a large velvet hat and a fur coat. The coffin had not even passed the door when she turned to leave. As she did so, Gillie saw the creature at her side. At first glance, it looked like a child's toy, but Gillie caught its eye. Living eyes, he realised. As they passed, the creature turned its head and told him it was rude to stare. Before Gillie could react or the creature could say anything else, the old woman had clamped a hand over its mouth and smiled an apology.

Gillie had felt uneasy for the rest of the day. Even the bustle of the kitchens, in full steam to accommodate the wake underway upstairs, couldn't relax him. He could not stop thinking about the woman and her pet, like they had offered a glimpse into another world.

That of a young boy, alone in the trees, looking for the faerie light that had drawn him on.

That light had never existed, not in the way Gillie had thought when following it. Eventually he'd found a corner of glass, the remnants of an old bottle, half-buried in mulch. Looking up, he spotted a gap in the canopy of leaves where sunlight had penetrated, catching the glass, catching his eye. The Ghillie Dhu he had chased, who had saved him that day, had not been real.

But he had seen the woman and heard the stuffed creature talk.

Shrugging off cook's offer of a hot drink, he had left the house and gone off to stalk the grounds. He had not walked with purpose, but a light and the sound of metal on stone drew him to the mausoleum. Hunting knife in hand, he'd stepped forward, only to find the old woman sat on a blanket, eating the crust of a sandwich. She waved a hello, then turned to the mausoleum, where the small creature was waiting with a miniature pickaxe. The woman snapped at the animal – he'd lost the game of rummy fair and square, so it was his turn to do the digging – and then gave Gillie a welcoming smile.

She explained that she would have frisked the body at the service, but she'd been busy searching the house and, running late, had not made it there before the casket was sealed.

Gillie remembered when his own mentor had found him, digging the grave for the man who'd killed his mother. He'd often wondered how it was the man could have taken such action in his stride, never questioning or passing judgement. Like his mentor that day, in the end, Gillie could not rage, but simply asked what they were looking for.

A trinket, the old woman had smiled. Something had gone missing from the British Museum some fourteen months earlier. It had taken her a while to track the likely culprit. The police didn't have it, which meant it hadn't been on Austin's body when he'd fallen; a rooftop chase with pursuing detectives, she said, not some face-saving slip rescuing a cat. There was no guarantee Austin had the object, she continued, but he'd been the most likely suspect.

His master being called a thief should have spurred outrage. Instead, it merely chimed with what he'd always felt about the man. It seemed appropriate for the woman before him, gaily voicing truths known but never spoken.

There was a cry of triumph from the small creature – a panda, she had called him – and the door to the mausoleum was open. The woman picked up her torch and ventured inside with the animal. More noises sounded, then a billow of dust escaped the entrance along with a fusillade of curses. A few minutes after that, the pair of them had emerged. The woman dusting down her coat, then wedging the door shut.

The item she was looking for, she explained, was not on the body. There were other avenues of investigation to pursue, she said handing him a small card. It was possible the object she was searching for was still in the house. Unlikely it was that well-hidden, but still a possibility. She would, therefore, be most grateful if Gillie ever came across a genie – or anyone else looking for a genie – could he please send notice to her.

Gillie had watched the pair pack up their things into a large carpet bag, then they had trudged off without a backward glance. As they left, Gillie had the impression they were squabbling once more.

He returned to the house, seeking out cook. He didn't make mention of the two strangers, but asked her if she knew about any genies that might have been kept in the household. Cook had laughed at him, but it was not a cruel laugh and had made Gillie smile. Awake before dawn, he had wondered if he'd dreamed the whole episode. But then, out in the grounds as the night breathed its last, he'd seen them come through the gates. The police and the lawyers and the men with dour faces. The same parade of travellers in the dark that Gillie had seen years ago, and he immediately knew where it would end.

Cook knew too. She never said it, but he could see the pain in her eyes. The look of an animal, caught in a trap, knowing its fate, powerless to prevent its world ending.

That night he did not sleep well, and when he woke in the morning something was calling to him. There was a glimmer of light in his mind that would not let go.

Liquid and gold and glass.

vi. The Irredeemable Love

Isiah Dogberry was still a hundred yards from the house when the gunshots cracked and the whistle sounded. On an ordinary night in an ordinary place, he would not have heard the second noise, but the air was still and there were no other sounds to mask this one. It would be Whitney, no doubt, and it meant the trouble he had feared was real.

He picked up his stride, but did not break into a run. If he was right, this place preyed on emotion. The key to survival was, therefore, control.

Control, he thought, and picking your weapon and knowing when and where to strike.

He did not pause at the entrance. No knock or moment of consideration, just grasped the handles and pushed with all his strength. The doors swung backwards, leaving him with a clear view of the interior. At the same time, the whistle sounded again.

In the centre of the hall, positioned directly opposite the front door, was Miss Miller, sat in a rudimentary oak chair. Her hair was bedraggled, and blood soaked her clothing in several points. There was some device framing the chair, obscuring his view of her, but there was no doubt this was the cause of her injuries. And the look and weight of the machine left no doubt those injuries were just a precursor to what would be a greater, almost certainly fatal blow.

Whitney was held on one side, Wilson to the other. Dogberry did not turn his head to look at either; the few details his peripheral vision allowed him – outnumbered, surrounded – suggested there was nothing he could do to aid either of them directly.

Control was the weapon that would break this spell. Control was what he needed.

Because the undoubted target for his theory was standing behind Miss Miller, hand on the device that would end her life.

Gillie stared at the newcomer, at his long thin face and the cloak wrapped around him. A traveller in the dark. And he knew his time had come.

Dogberry stepped forwards. Indeed, he barely broke stride between opening the door and continuing to move. He fixed his eye on the bearded man behind the device, locking on his face, never glancing towards the hand on the lever. Because he was in control and if he did not acknowledge the lever then it would not exist.

He strode onwards, certain of what he had to do in the immediate future to forestall Miss Miller's fate, but not yet sure what would free her from the mantrap in which she was entombed. And as he thought it, he nearly stuttered in his movement, nearly broke the spell. Instead, he pressed on, one controlled step after the other; all the time the crowd around them looking to the bearded man, all the time the bearded man looking to him. What did he see in Dogberry? And what, Dogberry wondered, might he see in the man in return?

Massive wooden fingers, clawing their way up out of the earth. To deter anything from escaping. To hold it here.

There was fear in the bearded man's face. Fear he had fought long and hard to control.

To deter anything from escaping. To hold it here.

He could not, would not, lose this place. He would not allow it, would do – and had done – anything to prevent it.

Dogberry paused a couple of feet in front of him, still looking at their nemesis. And then his shoulders dropped, and he let the breath slowly ease out of his body.

There were tears in the bearded man's eyes.

Dogberry stepped forwards, slowly raised his hands, gently cupping the man's face, and said:

'No. No more violence.'

He tilted the man's face upwards as he leaned in and tenderly kissed him on the mouth. As he pulled back, Dogberry could see the tears had started to flow on the man's face.

'No more violence,' he repeated. 'Only love.'

And Dogberry stepped backwards.

They were still for a few moments, just staring at each other, and then the man's hand dropped away from the lever. He stumbled back, finally bracing himself against the oak chair. The mass of people assembled about them, so still until now, were suddenly fidgeting against one another, uncertain. Still Dogberry did not dare look away from the man, not until he was sure.

Then the man turned, looking around him, searching. He began to push past the gathered men and women, and as he did so, in the fleeting glimpses as he passed behind faces, Dogberry could see him beginning to change.
Like the flickering of the years outside the Station windows.

The hair on his head and beard was lengthening, turning to grey and white; the skin dropping and creasing and tightening around his face; the movements, once smooth and assured, becoming more and more laboured.

All eyes were on the man as he moved now, and Dogberry motioned to

Whitney and Wilson to release Miss Miller. In moments, he could hear them working the straps and her gasps – of pain, of relief – as the device was slowly pulled away, its chunky metal fingers withdrawn from her skin.

The bearded man was moving with purpose, and the crowd started to shift out of his way. Not cowed respect or fear, but losing cohesion, stumbling away having woken from the deepest slumber.

And then, before him, was one who did not move. Who had woken and whose eyes were solely on the man as he closed, step by step, year by advancing year, on her. His eyes were fixed on her and his tears, Dogberry realised, had been for her. He allowed himself a moment of satisfaction in how right he had been with his choice of words.

The man stopped in front of her. His skin continued to leather, his hairline receding further, his hands folding in on themselves with age. He looked at the women before him, dressed in a tired cook's uniform, her face caked in dry blood, and his mouth began to break into a smile too long in coming. He raised his arms, looking to grasp her face as Dogberry had held his.

'Margaret,' he said. 'I –'

But she could not look at him. Her head flicked away, and Dogberry knew what she was staring at. The device behind him, heavy and oiled, its weighty barbs crusted with blood.

To deter anything from escaping. To hold it here.

And she looked back at the man and, as his hands closed in on her face, she shut her eyes and gave a definitive shake of the head.

She had never asked for this, had never wanted it, and could not want a man who had.

Before his fingers could touch her skin, they began to evaporate, skin and flesh turning to dust, bone lingering only a moment longer before vanishing the same way. It could have been a trick of the light, but Dogberry believed that the man's eyes had stayed on her throughout, unmoving, unflinching as his body wasted away to nothing. A final pleading look that would have satisfied a Cheshire cat. And then he was gone, nothing more than a cloud settling around the woman's skirts.

There was a long pause, then the woman sank to her knees, her chest heaving as one hand reached out for the pile of dust. She was whispering something, just one word, over and over. A name, Dogberry guessed.

He turned. Miss Miller was leaning on Wilson as Whitney dragged the heavy machine back into the shadows. Clarissa caught Dogberry's eye, and in doing so, seemed to gain strength. Her back straightened, and one hand came up to brush the hair back from her face. The other clasped the remnants of her dress together, trying to recover some modesty or hide her injuries, Dogberry was unsure.

And having caught his eye, she turned, drawing his attention to a recess build into the head of the chair.

Where it sat, shining. Liquid and glass and gold. So innocuous, and for those with the right perspective, so utterly alien.

Clarissa reached out for it on the shelf – to clutch it to herself or dash it to the floor – but Dogberry caught her wrist just in time.

Whatever this thing was, whatever it had released into the atmosphere of this house and its grounds, it had demonstrated an unfortunate reaction to Dogberry. And yet, the only thing which could distinguish Dogberry's biology from that of other human beings was the same thing which applied to Miss Miller and Wilson and Whitney. Something about their own temporal peregrinations had rendered his touch – and, he'd wager, theirs too – death here.

He did not want to risk what would happen if any of them touched the object directly.

Dogberry reached up, and flipped the lid of the metal casket which the object sat in. It closed with a satisfyingly heavy lead thump.

He made sure the clasp on the casket was firmly in place, then hefted it himself. He smiled and inclined his head towards the front door, which had remained open since his own entrance.

Wilson slipped his arm around Miss Miller once more, and she accepted his support, letting him guide her form – suddenly unsteady once more – out of the building. Whitney looked at Dogberry and gave a simple nod of his head as he tucked his whistle into the back pocket of his trousers. Giving all of the bystanders a hard look to ensure they stayed out of his way, he followed after Wilson and Miss Miller.

The object, Dogberry thought, would have to be properly investigated. Unfortunately, he knew there was no way – given its reaction to him – that he could perform the task himself. Someone else, some scientist or guardian would have to be found.

As he stepped across the threshold, a breath of wind crept in through the door, swirling around the hall, before exhaling once more. As it did so, it deposited a thin sheen of dust on the cuff of Dogberry's trousers. He looked down at it with a sad smile, and whispered:

'Only love.'

Elementary, My Dear Sheila
by Cody Schell

Sheila felt like she'd been turned inside out. She'd almost died, but Señor 105 had rescued her just in time. "Who did this to you? Who attacked you?" Her senses were muddy with pain... his voice sounded distorted. She could hear him asking about the body, but she felt too woozy and light to answer, as if she might just float away. She wanted to warn him so badly, but couldn't. It was up to Señor 105 to deduce things for himself, as Sheila drifted backwards into semi-consciousness and the memories of earlier that morning.

Part 1: Day of the Dead - All Saint's Day

Señor 105 thundered down the stairs of his old house, effortlessly hefting a sizable crate packed with dusty books. "I found some more in the third attic, Sheila!" He concentrated on not stumbling as he hurried through the myriad hallways. Fortunately he was wearing his good mid-calf boots, blue with the reliable tread. He was ready for any terrain, not just the unpredictable flooring of the house. Despite this, he almost slipped on an unsecured Arabian rug lain across a stretch of highly polished marble corridor.

This house had been a home to 105 for a large part of his life, but he had been the sole owner for only a fraction of that time. Generations of Mexican wrestlers, luchadors like himself, had lived here before him. The halls and rooms were full of heirlooms, mementos, exotic trunks, rugs and furniture from all around the globe. 105 was well travelled but no more so than his mentors before him. There were photos, paintings or tapestries on almost every wall, in every room and hallway. Scattered through the house were odd mementos of adventures passed; mounted animal heads, Chinese marbles, collections of miniature spoons, antique bird cages, cigar boxes. Other surfaces were taken up with modern electronic bric-a-brac in varying states of repair. There were bookcases, spiral staircases, dumb waiters, laundry chutes, fireplaces, priest holes and recessed shelves made for phones that had long since become defunct. Pneumatic tubes snaked invisibly through the walls. Touring the house, one could enter a room that looked like a snapshot frozen in history, and the next room would be decorated with minimalist furniture, mirrors, lava lamps and groovy sixties op-art designs.

The house contained a laboratory, a darkroom, kitchens, attics, bedrooms, bathrooms, and an observatory. There were rooms named after elements; The Neon Room, The Silicon Room, The Chlorine Room (which held a pool). But there was a special room where 105 kept his masks, his piano, his jukebox and his cactus. He called it the Map Room, perhaps unsurprisingly, because one wall was dominated by a large map of Mexico. This was the room to which he was headed.

105 had made it his goal to organize and clean the house before the 1970s rolled in, but he was always getting distracted by other issues. He now only had a little less than two months until that self-imposed deadline. Maybe after the weekend he would start. In the meantime however, he had guests and a special project.

The late Saturday afternoon sun seeped into the Map Room and filled the shallow sockets of a skull. When 105 finally set down the heavy crate, particles of dust flew up into the beams of sunlight. He'd thrown a drop cloth over his old upright piano and used that as the foundation on which to create his altar. He'd been working on it since just after lunch and it was almost complete.

Stalks of sugarcane intertwined with marigold flowers, forming an arch over the cloth-covered upright piano. The flat surfaces were covered in assorted items; books, *jimica*, a jar of cubed cactus, a paper kite, a can of *pozole*, a compass, various pieces of jewellery, a collection of faded business cards and several freshly painted sugar skulls. These were the possessions, photographs and favourite delicacies of one of his mentors, the luchadora Viento. She was being honoured on this day, the Day of the Dead.

In the centre of the altar was a framed monochrome photo of Viento in her younger years. She was beautiful, with dark eyes and long eye lashes. Her leather mask was the colour of grey ceramic, stitched with subtle swirls, suggestive of gusts of wind. Even from behind the mask she exuded an air of grace and wisdom. Next to this photo, Señor 105 gingerly placed a battered leather-bound book, *El ingenioso hidalgo don Quijote de la Mancha*.

This was Viento's favourite book, one she had never stopped enjoying. There was still a red cloth bookmark in the book, indicating the place she had last paused reading. 105 wanted to open to that point and read a passage, but stopped himself. That bookmark had been in that spot for many years and he wasn't going to disturb it now. This was her copy. She had given him his own copy, one Mexico City Christmas many years previously.

He picked up another old photo, this one showing the two of them. Young and tattooless, he was wearing what was his first new wrestling mask. Number 93, Neptunium. They were both smiling in this photo, but he remembered they had fought over this mask. Years before, Mexico's Caretakers of the Unusual, the three magnificent wrestlers, *Tierra, Viento y Fuego*, had taken him under their wings. Named after the elements of earth, wind and fire, they had trained him, grooming him to become Río, named after the element of water. However, he had his own ideas of how to do things, and picked a more contemporary definition of the elements. How appropriate that the then newly discovered element Neptunium was named after the Roman god of the seas. In a way, he had honoured his mentor's wishes and served his own purposes at the same time.

As a youth, he had been interested in science, not myths and legends. He wanted to be independent. As he got older, he came to appreciate the way the three of his mentors did things. He had gotten the first of his tattoos at this time. A triangle pointing down, the alchemical symbol for water.

Lost in thought, 105 realised he had his hand on this tattoo, over his heart. He brought himself back out of memories. There were still many things to prepare for tonight. He had invited some special guests to visit him this evening, the night of All Saint's Day, the first day of *El Día de los Muertos*.

He heard a voice behind him. "Is it finished, Monsieur 105?" Sheila was the newest resident of 105's sprawling home. She was still adjusting to various Mexican customs after moving from Europe. Her lovely Parisian accent matched an accompanying flair as she floated gracefully across the room to join him in front of the altar.

He nodded. "Almost."

Placing a few more books on the altar, he looked in the battered wooden boxes for something that might add a finishing touch. A dusty old top hat caught his eye and he perched it on top of his head to see Sheila's reaction. She giggled and said he looked "Tres chic". As he replaced the hat in the crate, a glint of light caught his eye. It was an ornate perfume bottle. Even though it was unfamiliar to him, it must have been important to his mentor if she had kept it with these other treasures. What a shame such a marvel had been tucked away, forgotten in the attic all those years. It pleased him to find a place on the altar where everyone could see it. Looking over the spread one last time, he hoped his guests would admire his handiwork. "What do you think, Sheila?"

She moved back to take in the entire altar. "There is so much to look at! And that perfume bottle is lovely! I'm not sure I've ever seen one quite like it." Sheila lingered on the bottle, there was something about it. It had a sort of timeless beauty, not unlike the photograph of Viento. "You don't talk a lot about her... or the other two." In fact, reflected Sheila, it was hard to get him to talk about his past at all. "Except when you are in a moment of stress and you remember something they taught you."

"That is something I mean to rectify, and that is the purpose of this day. It can be so easy to get involved with my work and forget about...other things." He surveyed his progress and crossed his muscular arms, turning his head to look at the map of Mexico. "It's frustrating when nobody takes my claims seriously. The American government laughs when I contact them in regards to an alien invasion. The British aren't any better." He picked up the centremost book again and gestured expressively. "They think I am like Don Quixote here, mistaking windmills for giants!" He set down the book next to a copy of *The War of the Worlds*. "...or water towers for Martian tripods. Martians don't even *have* tripods! I can understand these government officials not believing in certain supernatural creatures that I have encountered, but it seems the only aliens that concern them are the people crossing their borders illegally."

Sheila hated to see 105 upset. "Perhaps it is their arrogance that they don't think aliens would pick this country to invade over their own? Monsieur, there are many people who recognize and appreciate the things you do. The French government was appreciative of your help when we first met. And I'm sure if we ever find my family, they will express their thanks as well. When they find out I am alive, they will have you to thank."

105 thought about Sheila's gypsy-like family who had disappeared soon after he had freed them from the clutches of an evil filmmaker. "I will find them for you, I promise." He sighed. That was another neglected objective that made it difficult for him to relax.

Stepping over to stand in front of his jukebox, a glowing rectangular block lurking in the corner, 105 pressed a button on the glassy horizontal surface. The time displayed on the vertical panel. "We had better get ready, Sheila. I haven't yet ironed my grey suit and our guests are due to arrive momentarily."

Each of these guests had been involved in at least one of 105's previous adventures. Each had, of their own volition, been so thankful for his help that they swore to him that they would repay him. He even tried to talk them out of making such promises, but from pride or obligation each of them insisted. It had been his intention never to require them to fulfil their obligations, but he was calling in those favours now by requesting their participation in his current plans. He wondered if they regretted making their promises once they found out he was asking them to become involved in the affairs of the dead. He only wished he could have seen their faces when they had received their invitations and instructions.

Interlude 1 - Mr. Tea

Tadaaki Tea was running barefoot through the Antarctic. As he ran, he periodically leapt over the tall yellow flowers that emerged through the snow. The flurries were falling fast, and he had to catch the mastodons before the blizzard became more severe. There! In the distance was the herd! Munching on the luscious marigolds and lilies that got stuck in their teeth, the foolish mastodons were shuffling slowly through the snow. Tea had caught up with them quite easily. He was suddenly glad that he was a white tiger, it was really quite conducive to sneaking. Choosing his victim from the crowd, he stealthily crept up behind the animals.

The mastodons were white now too, and hard to see in the snow, but Tadaaki was almost on top of them. Their camouflage wouldn't help them. Certainly not the young, delicious one in back. He felt a momentary twinge of guilt about killing the baby mastodon. After all, they'd be extinct soon. But that was the way of nature.

He threw an orange frisbee to distract the mother. All the mastodons hurried after the toy, wanting to join in the fun, leaving the youth isolated and alone. In slow motion, Tadaaki the Tiger leapt into the air, ripping into the little mastodon's throat with his fangs. Red red blood splattered on the white white snow and the yellow yellow flowers. The little white elephant's heart lay in the snow, beating irregularly, but somehow more loudly. The red snow was so wet and cold in Tadaaki's fur. The pounding heart was demanding attention, but he felt too sick to eat it.

Someone was pounding on his door. Mr. Tea woke up from his dream in a cold sweat. His brain did an instant repositioning, like a compass that has suddenly had a magnet taken away from it. He was in his small Tokyo apartment, not the Antarctic research station where he'd woken up for the past several months. It was Wednesday, 1st of October, 1969. Someone was still pounding on his door. He leapt out of bed immediately.

In the hallway, the postman counted down before pounding one more time. *San... ni... ichi...* He lifted his fist just as the door flew open. A young Japanese man in an immaculate black suit & tie lifted his bowler hat and bowed politely. "I say old chap, I'm terribly sorry!"

In a series of fluid motions, he flipped his umbrella under his arm, slipped a pen out of his jacket pocket, tipped the clipboard at the optimal angle to sign the receipt, and gripped the package, easing it out of the postman's hand. "Flipped, slipped, tipped, script, gripped!" he quipped. Then with a grin he doffed his hat. "That should take care of it, I'm dashedly grateful! Good day to you, my good man!"

The door slammed in the postman's face. Not understanding a word of English, he looked confused for a moment then checked the signature, "Mr. Tea". He shrugged and moved on. Eccentrics were not uncommon on his route.

Inside, Mr. Tea was immaculate, not showing a sign of having been woken abruptly, nor seeming winded by his speedy exchange with the postman. He took pride in keeping his composure, whether it was waking up from a vivid, savage dream, or whilst escaping from a government raid on an Antarctic research station.

Truth be told, he was getting used to waking up to this type of dream. He threw his new bowler hat across the room with a flourish and it landed on a shelf next to a toy Routemaster bus. His last hat was unfortunately shredded in...an incident. He rubbed his thumb along the bottoms of his upper teeth. Best not to think about that.
He surveyed the room, making sure everything was in its place. It was good to be back home in his native Tokyo. The small flat was crammed with memorabilia from the United Kingdom. England herself! His brother said he was obsessed. His brother didn't have room to talk, being just as obsessed with yo-yo's and American rock 'n' roll.
He straightened his cuffs and smoothed his white gloves. He may have just woken up from a strange dream and would need a hot shower, but the postman didn't detect any uneasiness at all. Mr. Tea had made sure of it.

Satisfied that he looked every bit the English gentleman, he now turned his attention to the package. It was sloppily wrapped in brown paper full of distasteful folds and creases and covered in scuffs and smudges. Not displaying his disapproval of this object on his spotless table, he wondered what it could be. As he lifted a cup of tea to his lips, pinkie out, he turned the package around to read the return address, hoping it would give him an answer.

He spat out his tea and swore in Japanese. Señor 105! Calling in his favour so soon? Tea undoubtedly owed 105 his life, after the events at the research station. Not only did 105 save his life, but also gave Tea an idea of how to save years of research. If only he could find a way to retrieve the genetic information from where they had hidden it from their adversaries. His own genetic code.

Trembling, he again forced composure on himself and steeled himself to accept whatever 105 asked of him. He held a letter opener, poised, ready to cut through the paper and reveal what trial he would face.

Interlude 2 - Diana Gulbronson

Diana swore. The yellow parakeets in her Brooklyn apartment squawked in alarm. She'd already spent an hour going through the contents of the package from Mexico. She was too old for this, but it was only thanks to Señor 97 that she had made it to this age. Señor 105 now, she corrected herself. If it weren't for him, she'd have been buried under the rubble of the United Nations headquarters building.

She remembered back almost 20 years, the two of them running around the foundations of the building. He was Señor 97 then, just getting involved with the New York School art scene. She remembered being amazed how easily people just accepted this strange masked man, his frightening tattoos and thick Mexican accent, without missing a beat, as it were. Many of them were beat poets, after all. Others, like her, were artists and painters or dancers or musicians. What a wonderful time. Then the problems started with Raymond Merritt, the ridiculous fool. He fancied himself an abstract impressionist architect. It shouldn't have been a surprise that the scene would produce such a madman, but it was still shocking in execution. Usually architects were so straight laced, no one had expected it of him. Still, they stopped him in the end.

Diana searched through her paintings and reams of papers until she finally found what she was looking for behind an overstuffed sofa. She apologised to her orange striped tabby, Rugby, for interrupting his beauty sleep. She moved the sofa slightly until she could pull out the portrait she'd done of Señor 97. It was rather abstract of course, but as she looked at it, she remembered looking into his eyes, behind his purple and white mask, and thanking him for his help and promising to repay the favour. The promise had been at the back of her mind for the past two decades. She'd never thought that he'd ever ask something like this of her.

She propped the painting up and crossed back over to the small kitchen area. Rugby rubbed his furry cheeks on the edge of the frame. The phone was ringing and it was probably one of the substitutes from the teaching pool offering to take over her art classes while she was in Mexico.

Interlude 3 - Chago Serpiente

His family, the Terrible Kings, had left him to rot in prison. Being a part of the Snake branch of the family, Santiago "Chago" Serpiente shouldn't have been so surprised to discover they'd be so cold. The public called them *rudos*, after all. The bad guys. It was a fun reputation to possess, but somehow the family didn't seem so savage until you were on the outside looking in. This was not unlike the fearsome snake masks worn by himself and his brothers; scary from the outside. The mask he was still allowed to wear in jail.

Chago serving time served a purpose, namely keeping a more important member of the family out of jail. And it was also his punishment for failing. The only reason he wasn't dead was because of some trickery on behalf of Señor 104 that deflected blame away from him. The Terrible Kings already hated 104 enough, it was not a new burden for him to shoulder. However, it was a horrible burden for Chago to be secretly indebted to 104. It was almost worse than being locked away. It was like having your identity eaten away.

At first, he thought his family had finally broken their silence and sent him something. The package had been the first mail he'd received in the past three years. Before now, the only thing he had to pass the time was exercising in his tiny dirty cell and thinking about how to redeem himself in the eyes of the family. That, and thinking about how he would love to smash in 104's big yellow face. Now he would be released early thanks to 104's intervention. No, not 104, now it was 105. Chago paused to solidify it in his mind that Señor 104 was now Señor 105, due to the discovery of some new space-age element. It would be a big blue face that needed smashing now. Now the thing looming on his mind was why Señor 105 was asking him to take part in this foolish venture. He had a month to prepare, and the time would pass quickly. However, if his well-informed family found out he was taking part, there would be hell to pay.

Interlude 4 - Jorge Zumbido

Rodrigo weaved his way in and out of street vendors. It was easy for a young boy to move quickly through the bustling streets of Mexico City, cutting down alleys, jumping or crawling under fences, squeezing through gaps. The package didn't slow him down, either. He was so excited to be running an errand for his favourite luchador, his hero, the famous Señor 105! The man of over 100 masks! This was no mere errand, this was a *mission*; delivering a *mysterious* package to a *mysterious* location.

Rodrigo finally arrived at the red door 105 had described to him. He looked around secretively, pretending to see menace in every shadow, and knocked loudly and quickly. Waiting, his heart beat quickly.

This was nearly as exciting as the time he and 105 were accidentally transported to Paris. That incident had taught him not to touch the jukebox, but at the time he had only wanted to hear "Mucho Miel" by Jorge Zumbido. It was one of his mother's favourite songs and they were too poor to buy records very often. When he pressed those buttons, he didn't expect to suddenly be clinging to the metal girders of the Eiffel Tower and getting involved in an adventure with his hero and meeting Señorita Sheila.

The red door opened slowly. "Rodrigo? I've been expecting you." Standing there was a man of medium height in the most amazing rhinestone covered suit, wearing chunky jewellery on all his fingers and a massive pair of sparkle-rimmed glasses. It couldn't be. Rodrigo could see through the doorway stairs leading up to a well-lit stage and a heavy red curtain. This was the White Arcade! This was Jorge Zumbido's nightclub! And this man with the giant glasses was Zumbido himself!

"Zzzzzz..." was all Rodrigo could muster, holding out the package in front of him.

"Buzz buzz, aren't you just a busy little bee! Come on in here, *mijo*! I'm Jorge, it's nice to meet you." He took the package from Rodrigo's outstretched arms. "And thanks for delivering this to me, 105 called to let me know you were on your way." He shook the package, but that gave no clue about the potential contents. "I hope it's not another one of those giant brandy glasses, I have enough of those laying around, it just makes me want to throw up into one of them." He laughed obnoxiously and gestured to the baby grand piano which did indeed have a giant brandy glass resting upon it. "I know it's my trademark, but I'm just sick of it. Nobody drinks out of those things anyway, they're just a place for people to put tips. One time I broke one on purpose just to scare a waitress, it got a good laugh from the audience."

"My... my mother loves the song 'Mucho Miel'."

"Oh does she? Bless her heart! She should come visit me sometime, I'll play it for her."

"She has to work most nights. She...cleans."

"Oh well" said Zumbido, waving his hand dismissively and walked over to his desk and pulled out a marker. "I'll just have to give her a copy of one of my 45s. A signed copy! Do you think she'd like that?"

"Oh yes!! Yes, she would, Señor Zumbido!" When asked his mothers name, Rodrigo answered "Andrea Villar".

He signed the record sleeve with a dramatic flourish and held out the record to Rodrigo with a finely manicured hand. "Well here you go, you little scamp. Why don't you run home with that for her, I have to see what old leatherface sent me, then get ready for tonight's show."

"Gracias, Señor! Gracias!" Rodrigo disappeared out the back stage door and was gone. Zumbido's jovial expression disappeared as soon as Rodrigo was out of sight. 105 hadn't been forthcoming with information in regards to the contents of the package. He only told him to expect Rodrigo's delivery.

Zumbido opened the box and peered inside. "Oh god no!" he cried. "Not that...don't ask THAT of me!" He threw back his martini, finishing it off in one gulp. He bit the olive off his toothpick and started to make another drink. He looked at the contents of the box again. The enclosed note read:

"Estimado Sr. Zumbido,

You no doubt recall the occasion on which you promised me a favour in exchange for saving your nightclub from the Tiny Tuningforks. You may also recall I assured you that you owed me nothing in return for my assistance, but you insisted. I relented and allowed you this. Now it is time for me to call in my favour. Please review the contents of this package. You will find a selection of new books published this year. You are one of several individuals I have selected from different backgrounds and possessing diverse viewpoints to participate in my book discussion group. Please arrive at my house in Mexico City at 5pm on November 1, 1969. This Day of the Dead event will be in honour of Viento, my mentor, and founder of the Caretakers of the Unusual. I take this matter very seriously and expect you to act accordingly. This will fulfil your obligation to me. Dinner will begin at 5:30 and discussion forthwith. I look forward to lively discussion!
Cordialmente,
Señor 105"

Zumbido downed his second drink. "Anything but this! I hate reading! I even hate reading music!" In disgust, he knocked an oversized brandy glass off his desk, which shattered noisily on the ground. The tiny shards of broken glass sparkled in sympathy with the sequins on his jacket.

"...and so Vic Mizzy turns to Esquivel and says 'I was wondering how your xylophone got all wet!'". Finishing his joke, Zumbido chortled loudly in his trademark style. He feigned being weak at the knees, his wrist went limp, the back of his hand resting on his forehead. For the next fifteen seconds he was wracked with paroxysms of imaginary uncontrollable laughter that echoed around 105's wood panelled drawing room.

The masked Chago sighed and started on his third beer, a bottle of Tecate with a wedge of lime rammed into the neck. He had missed beer in prison.

Diana smiled uncomfortably. She was sure she had heard Zumbido tell the same joke to Johnny Carson on *The Tonight Show* in 1963, and it wasn't funny then either. It might have even been the same night he got into an on-air hair-pulling fight with latin songstress Charo and he gave up his dreams of fame in the States. He returned to Mexico where his fan base and nightclub were waiting for him.

"So anyway, that's enough of me talking about me. Why don't you talk about me for a while?" Zumbido sniggered. He went on to tell Diana about his new stereoscopic lounge album *Bejewelled, Blitzed and Bewildered*. He'd brought a copy for 105. The vinyl record had a trippy op-art cover that was once so common and seemed to be falling out of fashion in recent years. Stereo players were fairly common by now and albums with schmaltzy stereo effects were really not as novel as they once were. The title of the album seemed to capitalize on the fact that Zumbido occasionally guest-starred on a Mexican version of the show *Bewitched* called *Bruja Ha Ha*. He played a campy *brujo*, or warlock, who acted in a manner indistinguishable from the way he was now behaving. Diana wasn't sure that the role had constituted acting, aside from the freezing in place to allow the editing-in of dodgy stop-motion special effects.

She attempted again to start a conversation with Chago Serpiente. He was hulking and muscular, not unlike Señor 105, but his mask was an intimidating snake-skin affair. "So you're one of the Terrible Kings." He turned and glared at the red-haired art teacher. She should have been frightened of him, but somehow she wasn't afraid and arched a pointy peaked eyebrow at him.

Chago sneered down at her. "Have you ever met a Luchador other than our host?"

"Before arriving in Mexico City, no."

"My Grandfather was Hermano de la Serpiente." As she listened to Cago, Diana wondered if all the Terrible Kings had such Terrible Breath. "We are from the Yucatan, born on the site of the death of the dinosaurs, the Terrible Lizards. From their ashes, our family has risen to take its place as the new rulers of the world." His delivery started off strong, but had dipped into slight monotony, as if he has repeated this many times and couldn't quite be bothered to sell it absolutely.

"I see. I'm from Schenectady. Originally," shared Diana. She wondered if this guy could even read the books 105 had provided them with. She would be surprised if he had made it through *The Very Hungry Caterpillar*, much less the other more challenging selections from nineteen sixty-nine. She regretted the necessity of continuing the conversation, but she was desperate to avoid talking to Zumbido again. "So, you're from the 'snake' branch of the family, what are the other branches?"

Chago started to list them off by rote, "The 13 families are Serpiente, Rana, Lagarto, Pájaro, Salamannn...?" but he cut off suddenly, looking in surprise over Diana's shoulder.

She turned around to see 105 had just entered the room with some party supplies and talking to an Asian man wearing a bowler hat and a black suit. There was a red carnation in one of his buttonholes. Everyone was silent for a moment, wondering why the man had yellow eyes and fangs.

105 spoke. "Sorry to interrupt, please let me introduce you to our final guest to arrive. Jorge Zumbido, Chago Serpiente, Diana Gulbronson, meet Mr. Tea." The man stepped down the short steps into the study, swinging his umbrella seamlessly under his arm. He stretched out his hand, at the same time doffing his bowler.

"I say, how nice to meet you all." said the bizarre man, with an affectation of a clipped, precise British accent. Zumbido, Chago and Diana hesitated. "Oh. Oh, I do apologize, Señor 105 is accustomed to my altered appearance. He put me so at ease with his hospitality that I forgot. Please forgive me." He held onto his umbrella handle, closed his fearsome yellow eyes and concentrated. When he opened his eyes again, they were dark and almond shaped. His fangs were gone.

Zumbido was the first to speak, breaking the shocked silence. "Here kitty kitty!" he guffawed, taking it in stride. "Just kidding. My name is Zumbido, you might recognize me, I think they show *Bruja Ha Ha* in England."

"Lovely to meet you old chap. I'm afraid I'm from Tokyo, but as you can tell, I do love jolly old England!" The fact that this Japanese man was so obsessed with things English seemed suddenly more disturbing than the fact he had moments before been some sort of were-tiger.

Sheila appeared next to Mr. Tea. "It's fascinating the people you meet when you travel abroad, isn't it!" Zumbido, Chago and Diana suddenly shifted their attention from Mr. Tea to the yellow helium balloon floating next to him. The yellow helium balloon talking with a French accent. "Hello, I'm Sheila, it's so lovely to finally meet all of you." The yellow helium balloon talking with a French accent, whose name was apparently Sheila. "Who would like another drink before dinner?"

"ME!" shouted Zumbido, Chago and Diana in unison.

Everyone had their drinks and were over the shock of meeting Sheila. 105 looked around at the strange group he'd pulled together and grinned. "Not too many drinks, Chago, I wanted to play a fair game of pool with you."

Chago scowled threateningly from behind his mask. Then he laughed heartily. "Fine, I want to see you repeat that trick where you sink all the balls on the break. I still claim it was a fluke." He emphasised his words by tipping the mouth of his beer bottle in 105's direction. The two luchadors crossed to the pool table, and 105 manoeuvred an antique globe out of the way. They selected their cue sticks.

105 tossed something to Diana. She saw it was a Mexican coin. "Flip it for us. Chago, you call it, Eagle or Sun." Diana balanced the coin on her thumb and flicked it spinning up into the air. When the coin seemed to reach its zenith, Diana could have sworn it hung there spinning in place a few moments longer than it should have. No one else seemed to have noticed it.

Chago called *"Sol!"* as the coin plummeted to the green velvet surface of the pool table. Looking eagerly at the coin, he saw it landed eagle-side up and grumbled *"Aguila.* It's your break, 105."

105 gave an insincere sigh of resignation. "Ahh...If I must. If you're not happy with the coin toss, we could still do *'Pito, pito, gorgorito...'"*

Chago was scowling again. "Bah! Nonsense from Spain! Besides, as I said, I want to see you repeat your trick. Sink all the balls on the break."

105 was preparing to make his shot but Diana was distracted by a flash of light under the doors to the next room and missed what happened next. The cue ball struck the billiard balls, which went zooming around the table. If 105 had intended to guide them all to the pockets, then he was very disappointed, because none of them fell in. Chago was grinning triumphantly until he looked closer. The balls seemed to continue moving across the green felt surface longer than usual, colliding with each other and bouncing against the sides until they somehow slowly came to rest in their original positions, back in a perfect triangle.

Chago lost his temper and threw his cue stick down onto the table. "You are mocking me!" 105 seemed just as amazed as everyone else by the trick, but Chago was too angry to notice. He lunged at the older luchador, grabbing him by the lapels of his suit. He flipped 105 over his head and onto the pool table. 105's momentum slid him along the length of the table, the balls rolling him to the other side like a block of Egyptian limestone.

Mr. Tea's fangs were on show again and Zumbido was cowering behind him, laughing nervously, his hands holding on to his giant glasses. Sheila hovered excitedly near Diana, static electricity drawing in strands of her red hair.

105 jumped up and launched himself over the table to tackle the snake-faced Chago, the two of them knocking the globe off its base, which rolled away. Chago grabbed the lapels of 105's suit again and used his weight to flip him onto a nearby sofa. The piece of furniture tipped over, taking 105 with it.

105 poked his head up from behind the sofa. Sheila yelled a warning from

her new vantage point near the ceiling as Chago threw himself over the upturned furniture, almost knocking over Diana in the process.

Diana, regaining her balance, took in the scene, reminded of apes at the zoo; some fighting, some frightened, some confused. "STOP THAT!"

Chago turned to look at her. He was sitting on 105's chest, frozen in place holding a sugar skull high above his head, poised to smash it against their host's own cranium.

"Chago, I know you two are wrestlers, but calm yourself. And you, 105, you should know better than to get him riled up! You're both worse than a couple of Dadaists!"

Chago sheepishly withdrew and offered a hand to help 105 up.

"But Diana, I..." began 105, gesturing at the pool table, but didn't get any further.

"But nothing. I think we've had enough to drink, why don't we move on to dinner?" Embarrassed to have acted this way in front of a lady, 105 shook hands with Chago and both of them muttered apologies. 105 slunk off to do the final preparations for dinner.

105 dashed around the Map Room, arranging chairs and making minute adjustments to the objects on the altar. Normally he would relish the opportunity to show off his mask wall. However, he decided having his collection of over a hundred masks staring down from their cubbyholes would inhibit conversation, so he made sure they were locked away behind the large panels. His lonely little potted cactus, Fernando, had been moved to the mahogany end table. Sheila hated the thing and tried to convince him to get rid of it, for safety reasons.

He hit a few controls on the horizontal glass surface of his Zodiac jukebox and the lights within dimmed down to a minimum glow. Over the past year he had been tinkering with the machine's bizarre contents and he was still not ready to reveal his discovery to anyone. Especially not one of the Terrible Kings. If they knew of its existence, they'd be after it. He threw a drop cloth over it once he was satisfied that all processes were locked down. On this new surface, he arranged the books published in 1969 that the group would be discussing. *The Andromeda Strain, Slaughterhouse Five, The Edible Woman, The Beatle Man, The Very Hungry Caterpillar.* He had bought the last book for Rodrigo and included it on his reading list, just for fun.

105 took one last look in the mirror next to the doors to make sure his suit and tie looked presentable, and he ensured his mask was tight and flat, encasing his head. He stepped to the side and opened the double doors, inviting everyone into the

Map Room.

The guests shuffled past him and were all instantly drawn to the Day of the Dead altar. Zumbido, Diana, Chago and Mr. Tea stood in a row in front of the display and took everything in, reading all the book titles, looking carefully at the photos. Mr. Tea seemed especially fascinated by the sugar skulls.

"I painted those myself." 105 boasted. Sheila bumped against his shoulder with a little rubbery squeak. "...with Rodrigo's help."

Chago grunted. "Even the Terrible Kings have a sort of grudging respect for the Caretakers, but Viento in particular. She could hold her own in a fight with any member of the family, male or female. Are the Caretakers well known in the States, Diana? ...Diana?"

The art teacher was staring at the perfume bottle, sparkling in the light of the candles on the dinner table behind them. "Sorry, what?" Zumbido was fully absorbed by it as well. He seemed to be attracted to shiny objects; his sequined suit was a testament to that. He quickly snatched the bottle up and gave it a shake.

Annoyed, 105 took the bottle from Zumbido and diplomatically put it back in place. "Be careful please, that's fragile."

Chago waved his hand at the large leather book in the centre. "*Don Quixote!*" He thundered, sounding almost joyful for the first time since arriving at 105's house. "I'm glad there are some books written in Spanish present. Even if it is Spain's strange version of the language."

105 chuckled. He found himself warming to Chago Serpiente, which could actually be a dangerous thing to do. "Spain and Mexico are separated by a common tongue."

Mr. Tea opened his mouth to say something about England and English, but Diana was already talking. "Since we're here to discuss books, maybe we should have a warm up before dinner. What do you think of Quixote? He wanders around completely deluded, the butt of jokes and ends up a broken man."

"I pity the fool," said Mr. Tea, tapping his chin with the handle of his umbrella. "but I also admire him. He saw the world in a unique way, even if it was unusual to most people. He had a love for another time, another way of life. He was driven mad from reading books, you know."

Zumbido laughed loudly, to everyone's annoyance. "I know how he feels!"

At that moment, 105's house staff rolled a cart laden with dinner into the room and 105 invited everyone to pick a place around the table to sit. Finding his way to his seat, Mr. Tea found a map on the floor near the door. This was the map room, but he didn't see any other maps except for the ones put away neatly on the other end of the room. He poked it with his umbrella and lifted it up into the air. On closer inspection, the folded paper seemed to be blank and not a map at all. He asked if anyone had lost something. Chago claimed it and quickly pushed it into one of his suit pockets.

Diana commented on Chago's attire, noting the fine details, including his snakeskin boots. "Are they real snakeskin?" He confirmed they were. 105 started to look uneasy.

"Diana is a vegetarian." mentioned 105 meaningfully as the staff provided her with her special plate.

"That skin used to belong to a snake, and it's distasteful to see someone take something that isn't theirs simply because they can."

"The Terrible Kings are the inheritors of power. They take what they want and discard what is useless. Besides, I don't see you haranguing 105 for his leather masks."

"Actually, only a few of them are leather, most are lycra or other animal friendly materials." He tried to change the subject. "In fact, my Tantalum mask, number 73, was made of blue and red woven fibres for me by a group of Mongolians. I travelled there to watch some Mongolian wrestling, which is really quite interesting. They hand-made me a Tantalum mask, because that's one of the elements mined in their country. They even made me a matching jodag jacket, a pair of shuudag briefs and the gutal boots to go with it!"

Zumbido butted in. "Will somebody pass me the butter dish, I want to get started on one of these delightful rolls. Speaking of rolls, did anyone catch my role as Tio Arturo on *Bruja Ha...*" he trailed off as Diana and Chago both glared at him. "..ha.. heh heh...Oh look, tamales!"

Mr. Tea's stomach grumbled like a tiger's roar and Sheila hovered cautiously near 105's shoulder. Zumbido piped up again as various Mexican dishes were handed around the table. "So, Sheila...I think we're all very curious about you! Where are you from?"

"I am from Paris, but my family are wanderers. Gypsies."

"And are they..." Zumbido fiddled with his silverware. "Are they like you? You know... Are they all... as curvaceous as you?"

Sheila laughed lightly. "Oui, they are, Monsieur Zumbido. Unfortunately, I have lost contact with them and Señor 105 has allowed me to stay with him until we find them."

105 swallowed a bite of food and cleared his throat. "From what I understand, Sheila and her family are made from an isotope of sentient Helium."

Zumbido's eyebrows rose above the rims of his glasses, which was impressive considering their size. "As a musician, I'm very interested in sound... how do you speak?"

"I'm able to vibrate my molecules to create my voice." For a smooth, featureless yellow balloon, Sheila was very expressive in movement, swaying here and there, or bobbing up and down in excitement as she talked. "My family never really talked to me about where we are from, so it is 105 who helped me discover more about my true nature. And what better friend could the man of over 100 masks have than a living element?"

Zumbido smiled at the balloon. "Fascinating! You fit in at any party, don't you my dear?" Sheila noticed as he relaxed, he became more charming and less self centred.

105 was glad to see everyone was now getting along and dinner progressed without incident.

Señor 105 had intended to keep the dinner and discussion separate, but conversation naturally drifted towards the books everyone had read before arriving at his house. He was pleased to note that everyone seemed to have actually read and thought about the books and weren't just hoping to scrape by. His guests had taken their task very seriously, even Zumbido. The book-loving Viento would be proud.
What he wasn't anticipating was for people to pull parallels between the various books, which made for fascinating discussion. There were a lot of gender issues brought up in several of the novels, and feminist ideas of which he thought Viento would have approved.

Diana was discussing *Slaughterhouse Five*. "One character I'm not sure I liked was the disreputable harlot woman...". She searched for the name.

"Wildthyme" said 105 without thinking. Everyone turned to look at him. "I mean, Wildhack. Montana Wildhack."

"That's it! She isn't exactly portrayed as a paragon of virtue, is she."

"No," 105 grinned, "she certainly isn't."

"I'm glad you find the character so endearing, 105" Diana interrupted his thoughts with a smirk. "You know, now that I think about it, you are sometimes a bit like Quixote. Remember when we were running through the United Nations building construction zone and you put your cape down so I could walk across a puddle? Sometimes you're a little over-chivalrous."

"And you think this equates to sexism?"

"Possibly an undercurrent of sexism. It's possible you find weakness in a woman attractive, as it inflates your male ego. But the other books you chose would seem to indicate the opposite, the Edible Woman in particular, so I give you the benefit of the doubt. Maybe your parents just raised you correctly, after all."

105 evidently didn't have anything to share about his parents and a silence settled around the table. Diana noticed that Mr. Tea and Zumbido seemed very sleepy after the large meal and more drinks, but Chago sat stiffly, alert.

105 cleared this throat. "It's not about weakness, it's about being special. No man or woman is perfect. It's our flaws and quirks that make us unique. A book about perfect people would be incredibly boring."

Sheila floated back into the room. "That must be why no one has ever written a book about me!" She twirled, her string trailing in a curve. "It's getting late, Monsieur, the kitchen staff have a question for you before they leave."

"Thank you Sheila, perhaps the discussion has met its natural end for tonight in any case. I want to thank all of you. Viento was my mentor and largely responsible for me being the man that I am. She had a great love of reading, and your participation in this event honouring her makes me very proud. Sheila, could you possibly show our guests to their rooms?"

105 excused himself from the group and headed through the house to the distant kitchens. He thanked his staff for all their extra work and gave them envelopes with their week's salary in them. He told them to go home and get some rest; he would finish cleaning up before checking on his guests. After the last member of his staff left, he activated the security system, all lights glowing green. The house was secure.

After finishing the dishes, the Mexican wrestler removed the marigolds and replaced them with his normal gloves. Chewing some gum, he loosened his tie and the cuffs of his dress shirt. He left his suit jacket draped over the back of a chair and decided to check on his guests before they were settled in to their rooms. He double checked that the entrances to the other wings of the house were securely locked. The security system panel was green there as well.

As he was passing the hall that led to the greenhouse, he heard a distant noise. He paused in the dark, listening. A few moments later he hurried back to the Map Room. He quickly checked the jukebox to make sure it hadn't been tampered with. He grabbed one of the candles from the dinner/discussion table when something caught his eye. The spot where the perfume bottle had been sitting was now conspicuously empty. Had someone taken it?

Exiting the Map Room, he ran up the grand staircase that led to the next floor, holding his hand in front of the candle's flame to keep it from extinguishing. As he reached the landing, wild shadows played across his mask. To the left was his room and to the right were the rooms that had been prepared for his guests. He hurried to the right to check on them.

Pausing at the first door, the room Panda had stayed in, he listened. He heard a scuffle and sounds of conflict, objects hitting the floor. The door was locked, so 105 threw his shoulder against the wood. It was solid. Like much of this old house, it had been built to last. He saw a light under the door crack disappear. Once again the wrestler applied his massive bulk against the wood, which eventually gave way. 105 fell into a pitch black room.

As 105 retrieved his candle from the hallway, he saw his other guests started poking their heads out of their rooms wondering what was happening. Ignoring them, he hurried into the room and was met with the sight of Zumbido, spread out on the floor. He quickly knelt down by him, examining the body. Strangled. 105 quickly lit other candles that had been placed in the room just for decoration and knelt to examine Zumbido more closely.

He heard Diana and Mr. Tea enter the room behind him. "Oh, I say!" gasped Tea. Zumbido was definitely dead. Even by candle light, he looked battered and very clearly had been strangled.

Diana pushed in front of Tea. "105 what happened? Oh, Zumbido! And Sheila!!"

At the mention of Sheila, 105 looked around, panicked. There on the floor, a few feet away from Zumbido's body were fragments of a popped yellow balloon, still attached to a limp, motionless string!

"SHEILA!" yelled 105 and grabbed the string, lifting it. Shreds of torn latex dangled sickeningly from a knot. He held his head in his hand, feeling the number on his mask, his mind racing. Without her balloon, Sheila was lost. She would dissipate and die without an airtight vessel to contain her. Dropping the string, he felt through his pockets for a fresh balloon, but he had left his jacket in the kitchen.

"Tea! Tea, run to the first room on the other side of the landing. Somewhere in there, there is a small wooden box. I need it now. RUN!"

"Right-o!"

105 went through his trouser pockets desperately, finding no balloons, only pieces of gum. He had an idea. 105 yelled to the air. "Sheila! Are you there?? Sheila?!" He chomped his gum frantically, throwing a few more pieces in his mouth. Confident the gum was ready, he inhaled deeply. "Sheila! Are you there?" His voice had changed just slightly in pitch, indicating the presence of helium. Yes, she was there, thank goodness!

He doubted she could survive much longer, especially with candles burning everywhere. He inhaled as deeply as he could and tested his voice again. He was now squeaky and chipmunkish, and that meant Sheila was now filling his lungs. 105 blew the largest bubble he could with his gum, carefully and deliberately, knowing the chicle that Rodrigo sold him wasn't the best gum for blowing bubbles.

He started to feel dizzy from lack of oxygen just as Mr. Tea returned to the room with the box. "Is this it?" 105 nodded carefully and held out one of his massive hands to take it from him. Breathing through his nose and carefully maintaining the large pink bubble perched on his lips, he set the box down on the floor and opened it without looking. He took out a new balloon from the box and stretched it with his fingers, preparing it for Sheila. When he was sure it was ready, he held it in front of him, and made eye contact with Mr. Tea.

Looking cross-eyed at the bubble he mumbled emphatically. "You want me to pop it?"

Affirmative emphatic mumbling.

Tea jabbed the tip of his umbrella into the bubble and it collapsed backwards onto 105's face. With a *whooooooosh* the air slowly escaped from it and the balloon in 105's hand started to inflate itself, or rather, was inflated by Sheila's molecules. Soon the green balloon stopped growing. It was stretched full and trembled. 105, gasping for oxygen, his mask covered in sticky gum, quickly tied off the balloon. "Sheila? Sheila, are you okay? Speak to me!" Diana could hear the earnest concern in 105's still-squeaky voice. Chago had also arrived and was peering into the room to see what was happening.

Sheila felt like she'd been turned inside out. She'd almost died, but Señor 105 had rescued her just in time. "Who did this to you, Sheila? Who attacked you?" Her senses were muddy with pain... his voice sounded distorted. She could hear him asking about the body, but she felt too woozy and light to answer, as if she might just float away. She wanted to warn him so badly, but couldn't. It was up to Señor 105 to deduce things for himself, as Sheila drifted backwards into semi-consciousness.

"Was it Zumbido? Did he attack you?" 105 distinctly heard Sheila say "*Non*" before going completely unconscious. He knew she desperately needed rest and would be uncommunicative for a time. He relaxed for a moment, finally. Sheila was safe in her new balloon. 105 looked up from Zumbido's body to his three guests.

"I would watch each other carefully. Someone in this room is a murderer."

Everyone looked apprehensively at each other as 105 carefully moved Sheila to a place where she could safely recover. It was a few minutes before he returned and no one spoke until 105 returned.

Mr. Tea spoke up. "Couldn't it have been an intruder?"

"No, the security system is active. It had to be someone already inside the house. My staff always checks that the wings of the main part of the house are sealed off, and those sections also have their own security system. This just happened, so it has to be someone here."

He paused. "I heard noises from the hall before I barged in here." 105 looked around the room. There was Zumbido's body, he had been strangled, and Sheila had been stabbed. The remains of her old balloon were just as disturbing as the motionless corpse. The window was sealed. He'd seen light, he remembered that.

Mr. Tea spoke up again. "This is just like those British mysteries I'm so fond of reading. It's always the person least likely to have done it. So I bet it was Sheila! Who would suspect a balloon of murder? Or maybe it was the pacifist art teacher! Was it you, Diana?" He was grinning like a simpleton, his fangs glinting. Either the seriousness of the events hadn't sunk in with him or he wasn't in touch with reality. 105 wondered if the geneticist was trying to cover up for himself.

105 was getting a tension headache just thinking about it. "This isn't a game, Tea!" He examined the body. There were signs of a struggle; bruises and cuts on the wrists. "That's strange. Look at these scrapes and marks on his arms. They end suddenly in the middle of his forearm. That's extremely odd." Even if Zumbido had been wearing gloves, they wouldn't have protected him from such injuries, and besides, he wasn't wearing them now. He couldn't have worn them with all that gaudy jewellery on his fingers anyway. The line was so neat, so clean.

Then there were the marks on his neck. There were bruises that matched the jewellery on his hands. In particular, on the ring finger of Zumbido's right hand was a ring with three horizontal indentations. There were corresponding marks on his neck, but on the wrong side. Even if it were possible for someone to strangle themselves, which it wasn't, it was physically impossible for him to have gripped his own neck as the marks indicated. Was there some sort of evil double at work here? No, that was nonsense. Then he remembered the other strange events of the evening. The coin and the pool table. How did they factor in?

105 turned to take in the group, staring them down one by one. "We have more questions than answers. We're going to have to wait until Sheila is able to tell us what really happened. She's our primary witness." He made a point to look each of them directly in the eye. "I'd like to think I haven't offered my hospitality to a murderer. I'd like to think it was an intruder. But at the moment it seems likely that one of you did this."

Mr. Tea swallowed violently, his cat eyes looking worried, but Chago seemed unfazed by the accusation.

105 put a blanket over Zumbido's body. "I'm ashamed to treat my guests with suspicion, but I'm sure you'll understand. I suggest we return to the Map Room and

wait until Sheila can give us some answers."

Once back in the Map Room, 105 set the green balloon onto a couch cushion that looked comfortable. He sat by the motionless sphere, mothering it.

The group waited nervously. The atmosphere in the room as oppressive. They tended to stay as far from each other as possible, keeping a watchful eye. Suspicious glances filled the duration of silent waiting as time crept by at a snail's pace. An individual's smallest motion was caught by the entire group.

After about an hour, 105 stood to stretch, yawning. The waiting was getting to everyone. His boot caught on the blanket covering his jukebox and it slid off, all the books and other objects on top of it came crashing to the floor, making the most enormous commotion.

It was at that moment the lights went out.

After struggling to get a candle lit, 105 hurried to the circuit box and was working on getting the lights back on when there was a loud POP! Someone had struck again, just as he feared would happen!

He got the lights back on and rushed over to the sofa with the comfy cushion. There was a fork from dinner on the pillow next to the remnants of a green balloon. And there was a smaller salad fork in one of the outlets, which had tripped the house's ancient circuit-breakers.

Chago, Diana, Mr. Tea and 105 stood around the sofa looking at the fork, pillow and bits of popped balloon.

Diana was enraged by what she saw. "Who did this??" She stumbled backwards from the men on either side of her as if one of them were about to stuff a fork into her as well.

"Aren't you going to try to save her again, 105?!" cried out Mr. Tea.

105 stood stony faced, holding his chin in thought. "No... there's no point this time, Tea."

Chago took a step towards 105 and motioned back towards the sofa. "Then Sheila is lost! Now we'll never know what happened to Zumbido!" He quickly looked around the room as if searching for the easiest escape route. "I know you think I did it because I'm one of the Terrible Kings, but I assure you I had nothing to do with this." 105 moved to block the main doors, and turned to face his guests. "You know Chago, I may just believe you, but no one is leaving until we have our answers."

Chago crossed his massive muscular arms in front of him. "And how will we get them?"

105 tightened up his tie, pushing it back into its proper position, and grabbed

his suit jacket which he had retrieved from the kitchen. Dusting himself down, and certain that he once again looked immaculate, he stepped sideways and gestured dramatically at the doorway. From the darkness of the main hall, a familiar round shape bobbed into view, white string dangling underneath.

"You know, this is really not my colour." It was Sheila, green and healthy!

"Sorry, Sheila, that's the luck of the draw." grinned 105.

"Sheila! You're alive! But how?" asked Chago.

105 stepped next to Sheila and the two of them faced the three guests. "When I went to my room, I checked on Sheila, who was already recovering, to my great relief. Unfortunately, she hadn't seen her attacker. We needed a way to flush out the killer, so I found an ordinary balloon identical to the one Sheila is wearing and inflated it with normal air. I exaggerated how long it would take for her to recover so everyone would think she was still out of action."

"What's going on here? Is this a prank?" Diana had her hands on her hips. "Is Zumbido still alive too?" She looked over 105's shoulders as if she expected Zumbido to come walking out of the darkness.

Sheila, hovering near 105's shoulder, floated forward just a few inches. "You know he's not, Diana. You know because you killed him. I didn't see you attack us, but I saw you stick the fork in the wall when 105 'accidentally' created a convenient distraction hoping to draw out the killer."

105 cleared his throat. "Yes, I did that on purpose." He rocked back and forth on the balls of his feet. "Which made it possible for the very paranoid party guests to shift their attention away from you Diana, enabling you to kill the lights and attack the Sheila decoy under the cover of darkness."

The art teacher just laughed. "You're going to take the word of a balloon?"

Sheila swelled in anger, her accent more pronounced than usual. "You tried to *kill* me! In fact, you thought you'd succeeded."

Diana shot Sheila a murderous look. "105, you said yourself that the marks on the corpse indicate that he was strangled by someone with larger hands, wearing rings like his own. How could it have been me? Maybe it was you who suffocated him, Sheila, with your own helium. The marks on his neck are from his hands clutching his own throat, desperately trying to stop you, and he was able to pop your balloon in the struggle. You were locked in the room together alone, after all, with no other way out. And now you're lying about me popping the decoy, to cover for yourself. I'm a vegetarian for goodness sake. I'm an art teacher, why would I kill someone?"

105 was not concerned by Diana's accusations. While the events she described were technically possible, he could never suspect his friend of such a thing. "Sheila?"

"It's not true. I was there, she just came out of nowhere and attacked us." Sheila could see 105 believed her, but Tea and Chago were still suspicious. "I can't explain it, but it's true. For one thing I would never handle a fork, even if that was something I wanted to do. Horrible pointy things, I never use them."

105 was tracing the number on his forehead with his index finger, lost in thought. Certain details were annoying 105. "There are a lot of things that don't make sense about this, Sheila." He clenched his hand into a fist and tapped the knuckle of his curled-up index finger on his lip. Then he shook his fist once, neatly, in determination. "Everyone follow me." The entourage climbed the stairs and to the right, to the scene of Zumbido's murder.

The corpse was still there, underneath a sheet. 105 looked around the room, searching for something, but not finding it. "I want to try something."

He reached into his trousers and pulled out the same coin they'd used earlier that evening. "Diana, please flip the coin. Chago, I want you to call it, but not until I say so." Everyone looked confused, but did as he asked.

Diana positioned the coin on her bent thumb as she had done before. "Remember Chago, be ready to call it, but not until I say." 105 nodded to Diana and she flicked the coin into the air. It spun upwards, and reached its highest point. Chago was ready to call out "*Sol*" again, and waited for 105's cue, but he didn't give it. The coin, instead of falling down into Diana's hands, stayed suspended in the air, spinning madly.

"*Hijole!*" exclaimed 105. "I thought so! Turn off that light for a moment! Earlier when we flipped the coin, I thought I saw a flash of light. And again when I played the break on the pool table. Both are events impossible to predict. You were right, Chago, it was a fluke that I sunk all those balls the last time we met." Mr. Tea turned off his torch and 105 looked around the room. He was about to give up when he saw a flickering, a nearly invisible crack in the wall. He walked over to it.

"Call it now, Chago." Chago did and the coin finally plummeted down, ringing out in the darkness. The flickering crack of light also disappeared. When Mr. Tea turned the torch back on, 105 was forcing his fingers into a thin crack. A crack that widened, revealing a door leading into a passageway beyond. On the floor of the darkened hallway was the perfume bottle. "Look, the missing bottle. And the map you dropped earlier, Chago." He raised his eyebrow behind his mask.

"Actually, it's not really mine. It was Diana who dropped it. I pretended it was mine, because I thought it was familiar, and I was right. But how did you get it back?"

Diana threw her hair back over her shoulder in annoyance. "I don't know what you're talking about! Are all the Terrible Kings such terrible liars?"

105 wasn't sure who to believe. "The murderer came through this passageway, with that map and the perfume bottle. Zumbido and Sheila must have been caught by surprise when the murderer opened the passage at this end and that's when they were attacked."

Diana laughed. "But you admit Zumbido was strangled by his own hands!"

"But it doesn't quite add up, does it?" 105 then noticed Chago's snakeskin gloves. "Chago... remove your gloves."

Chago started to comply and 105 was almost sure that he was going to see copies of Zumbido's jewellery on his fingers, or something that would make sense of this situation. It seemed the only possible, although unlikely, explanation. But after Chago removed the gloves and handed them to 105, there were no marks, no hidden rings, nothing. Just his dark, hairy hands and forearms.

"Tea. Your hands, please." Nothing there. "And now you, Diana."

"Don't be silly" she argued, holding her hands out in front of her. "My hands are nothing like Zumbido's. I have dainty artisan's fingers and I don't wear jewellery."

"Turn them over." insisted 105 and Diana protested. When she refused, he grabbed her hands angrily and forced them around. There, on her forearms, were bruises and cuts that ended in a discrete line. They lined up directly with the bruises and cuts on Zumbido's wrists.

"I don't know how you did it, Diana, but somehow you strangled Zumbido with his own hands. He defended himself with yours!"

She laughed again incredulously. "Listen to what you're saying! I can't explain these marks, but I certainly didn't switch hands with the Mexican Liberace down there! It's impossible!"

"I see the impossible on a regular basis, Diana. Look at Sheila. Look at Mr. Tea's fangs. The rest of the world finds the Terrible Kings fairly unbelievable as well. The evidence is clear, Diana. You murdered Zumbido with his own hands, even if it's inexplicable how you did it. You're certainly a match for him physically; he doesn't have the same physique as Chago or I."

Chago cleared his throat. "105, I have a confession to make."

Everyone looked at him. Mr Tea wondered if 105 could be wrong? Maybe Chago really did do it?

"I came here under false pretences. The family offered me a chance to come back, despite my failures. They said they would forgive me if I betrayed my debt to you, and found something for them inside your house. Something they want."

Diana was getting frantic. "There, you see, he's confessing. Take him away!

He did it! We don't need to hear anything else from you, you disgusting snake!"
105 glared at Diana. "You will be silent."

    Chago continued. "When their informants learned of your invitation to me, they offered me my place back in the family if I used that map to find that passageway. And they described that bottle to me as well. The map is blank unless seen under the light from the bottle. They stole the map from Viento more than a decade back, and ever since then they've been trying to find a way to search your house for the bottle and passage."

    105 knew that the Terrible Kings had all sorts of knowledge and artefacts at their disposal. Their informant network was certainly capable of discovering his plans to invite Chago, and that bottle was probably only one of many rare items in his old house that they would love to get their reptilian hands on.

    Diana paced anxiously. "See? He's admitting it all! Tea, guard the door." Everyone ignored her. 105 urged Chago to continue.

    "I had no intention in helping them. It would be sacrificing my honour. I live now only because you protected me from the wrath of my brothers. And I don't want to be a part of a family that sees me as a pawn to do with as they wish. They left me to rot in prison because it suited their needs. I want nothing to do with them and I think they knew it. I did say I wouldn't interfere with anyone else they sent. There is no honour among thieves so...so I am no longer a part of that family." With these last words, Chago's hands moved behind his head and after a deep breath, he started unlacing his mask, slowly at first, but then with determination. Sheila gasped, hardly able to stay in one place. 105 covered his mouth with his hand in shock.

    Slowly, with just the slightest hint of a trembling hand, Chago slid the mask off his head. Keeping his face covered with his other hand, he held the mask in front of him. "I'm not revealing my face, but I'm no longer one of the Terrible Kings. Maybe you should wear this, Diana." He tossed it to her. "You're the one working for them." She threw it to the ground in disgust and protested as Mr. Tea and Señor 105 tied her to a chair. Chago continued. "Aside from 105, you hadn't met a Mexican wrestler. Until arriving in Mexico, you said. You met the Terrible Kings before arriving here. They contacted you and bribed you to do their dirty work."

    105 picked up Chago's mask. "This doesn't deserve to be dishonoured in such a way. Keep it as a reminder." The two of them stepped into the hallway and 105 pulled open a drawer, finding an old, featureless white mask for Chago to wear temporarily. Once Chago had it on, the two men shook hands firmly. "You can wear this until you decide what direction to go in next. It's a blank slate."

    Mr. Tea was still standing guard when the two of them returned to Zumbido's room. 105 put his arms on both of their shoulders. "We need to find out what the Terrible Kings were looking for, and how she switched hands with Zumbido in the way that she did. Perhaps she used some sort of strange technology, such as the kind the Terrible Kings are so obsessed with collecting."

They came back in the room to talk to Diana and she looked terrified at what they were going to do to her next. "Diana, we'll call the police and you'll get a fair trial. We don't want revenge, we just want to know why you..." 105 suddenly realised Diana wasn't looking at him.

She wasn't scared of *him*. She was looking past him. Zumbido was now standing up, his neck bent at an unnatural angle. His giant sparkly-rimmed glasses fell off his face to the floor and broke. A gush of air escaped his crushed windpipe, a sick parody of his trademark laugh.

"He's not dead!" yelled Chago, but everyone knew he was.

Zumbido went from being frozen in place to quickly and decisively rushing towards Diana. 105 threw himself across the room to tackle the strange Zumbido zombie but the creature casually swatted him aside with an unnatural strength.

Diana was hysterical. "All right, I admit it, I did it. I murdered him! I don't know what came over me, but I did it. I bashed him over the head with that damn bottle and then I strangled him... I... I..." She seemed confused, unable to remember events correctly, as confused as she was frightened. "Let me go, save me! He wants revenge!"

Before 105 could get to his feet, Zumbido put his dead, cold hands on both sides of Diana's head as if preparing to break her neck. But instead, in a clean, effortless motion, he ripped her head clean off her shoulders. Diana's body went limp.

Tea cried out loud, accidentally biting his lip with one of his fangs. 105 stood, blocking everyone else, urging them to slip out of the room quickly and carefully. Zumbido dropped the severed head clumsily, and it hit the floor with a sickening thud. 105 could see light burning from inside the secret passageway. The bottle was now positively incandescent, providing a surreal light show for what happened next. In a swift motion, the artist formerly known as Zumbido plucked off his own head and placed it on Diana's shoulders. Somehow it fit into place perfectly! His headless body then picked up Diana's head from the floor and placed it where his own had been. Both heads turned in unison towards the others, giving them a sickening grin. Never taking Diana's cloudy eyes off them, Zumbido's body pulled the hands off Diana's body one at a time and switched them with his own. This had the side effect of freeing Diana's arms from their bonds.

All three of the men swore, unable to comprehend what was going on or why.

Sheila sobbed slightly. "It's horrible."

Diana's dead eyes slowly turned in their sockets, searching. "The.... bottle....." 105 didn't quite understand what was happening, but he knew these creatures mustn't get their hands on anyone else and certainly not the bottle that seemed to have triggered these events.

"Chago, your assistance?" asked 105 and whispered something into his ear. 105 ran, grabbing Chago's arms who helped him flip in an arc through the air. He met his intended mark exactly and his feet struck Zumbido's body in the chest. Zumbido and Diana fell backwards in unison, hitting the door, slamming it shut, and closing off the most direct route to the bottle and map.

105 rushed his friends out of the room, but Chago was confused. "Didn't you want to force them into the passageway?"

"No, just the opposite." 105 pulled the hallway door shut with a loud crack. The lock was broken from being forced open, so he pulled on the doorknob, forcing the edges of the door to jam in place in the frame. "I want them trapped in that room so we can investigate the passageway from the other end! Quickly, to Diana's room, that's where the entrance should be."

Mr. Tea was wide eyed and fully fanged by this point. "I say! What's going on? What are those bloody zombies?"

"They must have something to do with what the Terrible Kings were trying to find in my house. They are steeped in secrets and old artefacts and forbidden information!" 105 felt like a fool not knowing his own house as well as they did. "Chago, did they tell you anything else?"

Chago scratched at his new white mask. "No, we didn't get that far. Once I made it clear I wasn't interested, they clammed up. I have a feeling they only let me walk out of there because they wanted me to distract you from Diana's snooping."

They burst into Diana's room, finding the secret passage entrance wide open. They ran down the passageway to the bottle, which was burning bright. The map was alive with lines and shapes that weren't there when Chago saw it. It showed a basic layout of the house and the secret passageways branching off. "Diana must have snuck back to the Map Room and checked the map with the help of the bottle."

Tea tapped the map with his finger. "That's how she knew which room to pick!"

105 nodded. "She must have had trouble reading the map when the bottle was hardly sparking, then took a wrong turn into Zumbido's room, catching him and Sheila by surprise. I had no idea she had the kind of instinct to attack instantly to protect her secrets. In fact, I would suspect she doesn't normally." The two luchadors

scanned the map, and determined the existence of a passage leading deep under the house. An area that was unfamiliar to 105. "This must be what she was looking for. Come on Sheila, Mr. Tea, we're... where's Mr. Tea?"

The two men and Sheila swung around to discover the creatures had gained entry to the passageway from Zumbido's room. Now there were three creatures, each a jumble of mismatched torsos, heads, hands and feet. One of the creatures had a tiger's head, the other two had a tiger's paw each. Mr. Tea had been disassembled and integrated, his bizarre DNA manifesting itself. 105 couldn't understand how body parts could just be pulled apart and re-attached so casually, like toy bricks. How could genes be so easily ripped to shreds and reassembled? This was almost magical technology.

The creatures started to advance on them, but froze in place when they heard the grandfather clock downstairs strike midnight.

"Why have they stopped?"

"I don't know Chago, but let's not waste the opportunity to find out what's going on. We need to get... here!" 105 thwacked a point on the map. "*Vamos!*" he bellowed as he ran down the dark corridor, holding the shining bottle out in front of them. He heard the last of the clock's chime ringing out and the sound of the creatures' footsteps begin again.

105 took up the rear to protect his friends if the creatures caught up with them. "It's November 2nd now. All Soul's Day. May our souls be protected and theirs be rescued."

Part 2: Day of the Dead - All Soul's Day

105 relied on Sheila and Chago to watch in front of them as they ran full pelt. This allowed him to read the map of the tunnels leading under his house. The map seemed old, almost as old as the house, although he wasn't actually sure how old his home was. He knew he was at least the fourth generation of wrestlers to live there. The history of the building went back further than that.

These tunnels led in a spiral, down much deeper than he thought possible. He was sure they were under the city by now. He stopped running for a moment. Under the city. The old city! He suspected that these tunnels would lead to Tenochtitlan. He caught up with Chago and Sheila who had stopped to look at the walls. The cement walls had become rougher stone, and now even larger blocks. These were Aztec constructions. He could see various markings that confirmed this. Chago was breathless. "The Aztecs! Your house is built on top of Aztec ruins!"

"The map ends here, there's just a little graphic of the bottle. I wonder if this was originally the map to find the bottle? But then why would the Terrible Kings want to come here if they knew the bottle wasn't here?" The passageway branched off in three directions at this point and 105 held the glowing bottle at arms length to get a glimpse of where they should go next. When he held the bottle to the left, it flared even brighter. "The map ends here because the bottle will lead the rest of the way. We go this way!"

Sheila could still hear the creatures sloshing down the hallway. Their mismatched body parts slowed them down, but they were making steady progress. The hallway eventually came to an apparent dead end with a deep indentation in the floor a few meters across. Chago pointed. "It's an inverted pyramid. Maybe we need to put the bottle there, in the middle?"

105 was no archaeologist but it was worth trying. Chago offered to slide down first and 105 gave him his hand in assistance, holding the bottle in the other. Something was wrong. "I'm falling?!" 105 felt Chago's entire weight pulling on him. "But how? It's a gentle slope down just a few metres!" 105 was losing his feet on the dusty stones and felt himself being pulled in too. It was a futile gesture, but Sheila wrapped her string around 105's arm in an attempt to help. Suddenly the three of them were sliding down the small slope, which seemed to be growing. The dimensions were all wrong, as if the three of them were shrinking as they slid. The walls fell away from each other in a manner opposite to the way that railroad tracks appear to converge in the distance. 105 realised it was an optical illusion. What appeared to be an inverted pyramid was a dimensionally distorted vertical shaft! This was parallax view made real.

Just as suddenly as they had started falling, the vertical shaft titled at a slight angle, then severely. All their momentum was gone and the three of them landed softly on the ground, which moments before they had perceived as the shaft wall. Behind them, the passageway appeared to be another recessed pyramid set into a wall! "Amazing!"

They could still hear the sounds of the creatures, at the other end, contemplating following them down. 105 could see his companions were uncertain about what to do next so he hurried them along.

Chago stopped abruptly. The bottle was shining brightly in his hand. "It's getting warm!"

Sheila was a few metres down the new tunnel and called back to them. "Look, the yellow stone turns into smooth grey metal."

105 rapped the material with his knuckles, but he wasn't sure he could identify it. The noise echoed down the hallway. As the trio continued their explorations, they

noted each section of the hallway was covered in different sized panels of varying colours and textures. The further they proceeded, the more extreme the panels became; fire engine red squares, ocean blue rectangles, smooth convex panels, sandpaper covered concave panels.

One section of wall covered in jagged points made 105 nervous for Sheila but she told him to stop fussing. "I may be delicate at times, but I do know how to take care of myself, Monsieur. By the way, have you noticed it's getting brighter? I can also feel a change in air pressure."

After about 15 minutes, they came around a beige bend in the tunnel. 105 pointed forward. "The passage widens and there's a gate!"

105 and Chago struggled across a slippery purple floor covered in bubbled tiles as Sheila glided ahead of them. "Hurry you two, you have to see!" The three of them emerged into what appeared to be daylight, despite being underneath at least two Mexican cities. Towering above them were the spires of a new city, full of buildings with wildly different styles and structures.

One thing each structure had in common with the rest was that each was adorned with the blades of windmills. Strangely, some were motionless while others whirled madly. Others even seemed to be spinning backwards. 105 didn't know how the windmills functioned or why they behaved the way they did, but he grinned up at them. "*Ellos son gigantes...*"

Chago rubbed his eyes, it was like looking through a kaleidoscope. The sky was not a sky at all, but a luminescent ceiling. He found it impossible to judge the distance.

Sheila lifted buoyantly into the air. "Look! There are people!" And indeed there were people everywhere along the streets of the city, on boats in the canals, on escalators and balconies. They all stood motionless, with their thumbs in the air. Each one of them was frozen in place in the act of flipping a coin.

Like everything else in this place, each person was a different colour. 105 inspected a woman close to him. She was oddly beautiful. The skin on her arms were blue and speckled like a robin's egg, but everywhere else she was a golden brown, the colour of beer held up to the light. Most striking of all, her face was yellow like the chest of an emperor penguin.

Chago and Sheila were inspecting a man on the other side of the woman. His limbs and torso were also a strange collection of colours. 105 walked over to them and joined their investigation. His attention turned to the coin, hovering above the man's yellow thumb.

The coin was square, with a circular hole in the middle. There were markings on the coin, unrecognizable shapes that could have been animals, continents or planets. Cautiously, 105 touched the coin. It was fixed in place as sure as if it had been glued to the pavement, except that it was in midair, presumably in the process of flipping. Every coin they tested was differently shaped with differently shaped holes or no holes at all. However, they were all just as immovable as the unusual people with funny coloured faces.

Chago jumped backwards as he saw a ball of blue energy forming in front of him. They watched as it solidified into a perfect sphere, which then popped. For a moment, an electronic box hovered in the air before gravity took hold and it plummeted to the ground. It smashed on the hard surface, pieces flying everywhere. Chago nudged the junk with the toe of his boot. It was a translucent box with bits of wires coming out of it. "It looks like some sort of scientific instrument? It's totally broken now."

Sheila pointed with her string. "There are more objects on the ground over there. Junk."

105 stepped over what looked like a smashed hourglass and picked up a familiar looking object. It was a toy monkey, holding a banana. The mouth was moulded so you could push the banana into the monkey's mouth and it would stay in place. He grinned at it, he had had one when he was young, named Mikey. "These things are not from this city, they're from the world above."

105 picked up a rectangular metal box with something inscribed on its surface. A series of letters and numbers were followed by *'Experiment Module 5: December 4959'*. 105 laughed, but stopped. He had seen movement out of the corner of his eye. He pivoted, taking an attack stance and heard a seam in his dress shirt rip. This adventure had not been kind to his expensive suit.

A feral growl echoed through the air and a pack of animals came rushing towards him. There were cats, dogs and the odd ferret. Some had wounds and mechanical attachments and others looked like they were pampered pets. 105 was worried they would attack, but they just weaved around them just as they had woven through the unmoving population of the city.

105 soon saw what the pack of animals were fleeing. A man, the first moving person they'd seen since arriving. "Annoying strays! Getting into our city!" He had yellow skin, but a contrasting green face. One of his feet was pink, matching one of his fingers, the rest of which were white as ice.

Glancing at the animals disappearing into the crowd 105 turned to the man. "I don't think you'll catch them now."

The green faced man caught his breath and exhaled it as a laugh. "I was talking about you! Normally I'd welcome you, but we aren't supposed to get visitors at all. Let's get you back home." He turned his attention to a flat tablet with characters dancing across it. "That's strange. I don't have a record of your arrival in la Ciudad."

The man appeared to be intelligent and not hostile, but clearly distressed. Despite his mismatched body parts, Sheila found him quite beautiful. One of his eyes was brown and the other was a sea green.

"La Ciudad?" queried 105. "That is the name of this city under the Aztec city?" The figured nodded and smiled a quick colourful smile. His tongue was pink. This normality suddenly seemed at odds with his otherwise unexpected colouring.

"Yes. Exactly, a city." The man was distracted. "La Ciudad." He was engrossed by his notes again. "I understand now. You entered through a spatial interface, not via the timewinds. You're flotsam, not jetsam." Sheila thought his mismatched face gave him the look of a masked wrestler. Startled, the man looked up from his tablet. "What are those doing here?"

The creatures from the house had emerged from the mouth of the tunnel. They were more mixed up than ever. It was hard to tell which parts belonged to whom. No longer possessing discrete features, the body parts of their friends had started to congeal into a large blob.

Not far away, a grey tabby cat, one of the unfortunate stray animals, sat licking at a copper coloured implant screwed into her paw. The poor puss had similar implants on her head. Deaf, she didn't hear the blob undulating up behind her. In a flash, the animal was absorbed into the mass.

The green faced man looked back to 105. "What are those sick creatures?" Then he caught sight of the bottle. "That. You shouldn't have brought that here! Not in la Ciudad!" He frantically checked his tablet again.

105 held out the bottle in front of him. "What do you know about this bottle? It isn't from here?"

"No. That... container and its contents do not belong here, though it... they...were once kept near here, geographically speaking. That bottle will impair the functioning of the city." He pointed vaguely towards the nearest windmill. He flipped through transparent sheets of paper that emerged from the side of the tablet. They were a shiny orangeish vellum. "In fact... it's in the city in its own personal timestream already! It really, *really* shouldn't be here!"

Before 105 could ask for clarification, the man held up a hand and the ground heaved in place, creating a hole that swallowed up the zombie blob. "That will divert the creatures until you can deal with them."

105 unbuttoned the cuffs of his dress shirt, trying to get more comfortable.

"Us? We don't know how to deal with them! What is la Ciudad, how long has it been here? Who are you?"

With distractions removed the man seemed much more composed and controlled. "I apologize. I am the main Administrator."

"I am Señor 105, and this is Chago and Sheila. It is nice to meet you." He extended his hand in greeting.

The Administrator gripped 105's hand in a firm handshake, then quickly removed and replaced 105's hand with his own. Chago cried out in shock and Sheila gasped. 105 wiggled his new ice-white fingers on his new yellow hand, dumbfounded. 105 tensed but kept himself calm and held his hand out in front of him. "Please. Can you put it back? The way it was." The Administrator shrugged and did so quickly and neatly. 105 relaxed. He had his hand back and it felt exactly as it did before it had been switched. He wiggled his fingers. "Amazing."

"Sorry, I was just trying to be friendly."

"That's how your people greet each other? You exchange body parts?"

"Yes, I forgot that's not the way you do things out there. I don't usually meet visitors to the city. As I said, we're not supposed to have any, but unfortunately, we've been having a lot of them. I just guide them back out."

"Out there? You mean in Mexico?"

"Out there, on Earth, in Time."

Chago looked like he was ready to break down in tears. "In time? You're saying we're outside of time? What's going on?" Everything had made a rough sort of sense to this point. There was a murder, and Sheila was a talking balloon. These things seemed ordinary and comforting at that moment.

105 put his hand on Chago's shoulder. "Please bear with me, amigo. I think we're close to answers."

The Administrator nodded. "You are in la Ciudad. This is a travelling city from another time and place. We have been moving from place to place since the first years after the creation of this universe. We have absolute mastery of the building blocks of creation. We periodically transfer our entire city from spacetime location to spacetime location." He pointed again at the nearest windmill. "Our time turbines gather energy from the passage of time. We divert your planet's time winds through our city and back out again."

Sheila bobbed up and down in place. "Wait... so to you, all matter, even living beings, are simply lego bricks? You can casually pull something apart and connect it to something else, even your own heads?"

"That's correct. We are the Modulars." The Administrator tapped his lip with his finger. "I'm surprised you don't know us, Sheila. May I say you're a lovely isotope of Helium? One of my favourites. There can't be very many Sentients around this far into the universe. I mean this far in time."

Sheila floated closer to the Administrator. "You know my people, Monsieur?" He nodded. "My wandering family doesn't know anything of our history. Tell me more about la Ciudad. How long have the Modulars been here?"

"We were here, on Earth that is, a few days of real time, but decided to move location again quickly. Once we got here, we realised there was some time complexity approaching and decided we had better get moving again before the storm hit. This planet has horrible time pollution. You should be embarrassed, really. It's all very irresponsible."

"How could your city be under the Aztec city, and have only been here a few days?"

"I'll explain. The city has been here for roughly 200,000 years, but frozen in time. We're not really here, we're in an indeterminate state. We are currently conserving the temporal energy of one million years in order to have fuel to travel to our next location. Still quite a ways until we reach that point. Not that any citizens will be aware of it, they're in temporal stasis. To them, it will pass in an eye blink. To me, it will pass in a matter of days."

105 tugged at his goatee. "You're converting time into energy?"

"That's right. I'm like a custodian, here on the edge of the city, I'll spend a day of real-time monitoring any situations that arise. Situations like the arrival of you three and those poor creatures. By coincidence, your race...I mean the human race, not yours, Sheila...the human race emerged about the time our city arrived. We took one look at you and knew you were going to be building time machines and causing trouble and decided to just leave you to it. And sure enough, your race is now swarming all over the city, all sorts of amateur time travellers loitering around the place!" He kicked at a pile of junk. "Your time experiments gumming up the works."

"The human race is 200,000 years old?" asked Chago.

The Administrator pointed to 105's hand. "That bottle thing, it's unearthly, it shouldn't be on your planet, much less in la Ciudad. You have to get it out of here. See how it's glowing? It's eating up the city's energy reserves for its own purposes!"

"But it just looks like a perfume bottle."

The Administrator took a perfect grey cube from out of his pocket and put it on the floor. Then he asked 105 to place the bottle on top of the tiny cube. The Administrator wiggled his fingers and the grey cube started to melt, dripping in an upwards direction like a bad stop-motion animation until the bottle was completely encased. "That will shield the bottle, and stop it from absorbing any more energy, but it will only last a short time. You have to get yourselves and your creatures out of here before that shielding decays."

"Our creatures? That's your technology, not ours!"

The Administrator considered this. "Perhaps the bottle did it, tapping not only into our energy, but also our technology. I suppose you're right, we need to do something about this." He walked to a nearby wall and pushed his palm against it slightly. It swung back, revealing a passageway. The four of them walked down stairs into more tunnels like the ones they'd traversed to arrive in la Ciudad.

The group stopped suddenly when the angry jumble creatures came around a corner.

The administrator quickly ran through a side alley. "Hurry. And be careful, these passages twist and turn in space and time, it's very easy to get lost. Whatever you do, don't let that bottle meet its twin!" When he turned around to make sure they were following him, they were nowhere in sight. "Drat."

105 had slipped on a discarded banana peel. In the chaos, he had run, but quickly lost sight of the Administrator. And everyone else. It was as though when you lost sight of someone in this temporally twisted town, you became irrevocably separated from them. The shifting blob made up of Zumbido, Diana and Mr. Tea was no longer chasing him, but he'd also lost his friends.

The side streets of the city were made of all the same unrecognizable materials but the walls had etchings on them. Sometimes he saw just a tiny circle here and there, and in other places giant chevrons zoomed up walls. Sculptures and alien plants were littered around the place. Long sheets of plastic, like stiff shower curtains, hung down from impossible heights, disappearing up into the darkness.

He could hear voices below him, so he descended a metal staircase and slid down a small curvy slide to the next level. It sounded like Sheila was right around the corner. He jogged right around to catch up with her and instead came face to face with a long haired woman.

Surprised by his mask, she fell, ungracefully, backwards onto the ground in front of him. 105 thought she might be a normal human. She was roughly the right colour, despite looking a bit ill.

Without taking her fearful eyes off 105, the woman called over her shoulder. "I found someone who isn't frozen in time. You better come to us." A voice called back, telling her, hopefully in a colloquial fashion, to keep her hair on.

That voice! 105 would recognize that coffee, cigarettes and gravel-laden birdsong anywhere. He felt his pulse race and he grinned so widely the muscles on the back of his neck ached. He didn't even have time to fix his tie, which was missing anyway. His dress shirt and trousers were ruined. He decided to stand as cool and collected as possible as the woman stepped out from behind a giant block of mechanical junk, muttering to herself and fussing with a pair of pink zebra-print opera gloves. When Iris Wildthyme was finally framed in his vision, he muttered breathlessly, "*Hijole!*"

She was pulling the gloves as tightly up her arms as she could manage. "Ridiculous things never stay up like they should, I've half a mind to..." Finally, mid-mumble and mid-glove-adjustment, with her right arm stretched to its limit, she noticed 105. Her jaw dropped and her left arm joined the outstretched right as she galloped to hug him. "Lovey!"

The younger woman was shocked to see them embrace, their faces so close they were going cross-eyed just trying to look at each other. Surprise turned into awkward discomfort and she cleared her throat. Without taking his eyes off Iris, 105 finally offered his gloved hand to her, helping the woman to her feet. He was asking Iris how they came to arrive in la Ciudad.

"Oh, chuck, I was in the neighbourhood and I was hoping to bump into you! And look at you, still just as ruggedly handsome as ever! I wasn't sure we'd see each other, considering the nature of this place...but I've had this funny feeling!"

"I know how you feel." said the woman, scanning the area for something. "We've definitely time travelled, Iris. I have that familiar sensation. Oh god."

"105, this is my old friend Jenny. We're here on a mission for MOOO." Iris saw 105's eyebrow raise through one of his mask's eyeholes.

Jenny nodded. "Yes, MOOO. The American branch of MIAOW, the Ministry of Incursions and Other Alien Wonders."

Iris rolled her eyes. "I still think an American version sounds like a blinkin' stupid idea."

Jenny ignored her. "Military Observation of Otherworldly Occurrences. And it's not stupid, Iris. It's perfectly sensible to have someone in North America checking into these sorts of things and coordinating with the UK. And I told you I've been assigned to come to Des Moines for a time, to offer my expertise until they get on their feet."

Iris dropped her purse to the ground roughly and made a noise of disgust. "They're got a bloody secret base under the Pappajohn Sculpture Garden! But they're not needed! America has Señor 105 and the rest, the whatsits, the Caretakers of the Unknown! They've taken care of things in this part of the world for donkeys without anyone's help!"

Jenny fanned her face with her hand. "Oh yes, I remember now. MOOO has files on your quaint little third world operation. Why don't you just take care of the chupacabra or the Cactus Men or whatever, and we'll take care of the big problems." Suddenly Jenny clutched her stomach and doubled over in pain. Calling her 'Señorita Henny', 105 asked if he could help. Jenny ignored him. "Iris, it's worse than it's ever been."

Somewhat unsympathetically, Iris pulled a bleeping box out of her handbag and theatrically pointed it in various directions. "That means it's coming!" she declared as Jenny rushed off somewhere.

"What's coming, Señora?"

"No time to explain." Iris shushed 105. "I need information about the cosmic ether in this part of the world. Tell me about your jukebox, the Zodiac Machine. I know it's not just a jukebox." He looked sheepish about attempting to keep this information from her. "Tell me how it works. It might be important."

"The jukebox is an amalgamation of parts I've found. Leftover bits of technology that I've acquired on my travels. It seems to have the ability to absorb them and integrate them into its functioning. While it can be used as a normal jukebox, repaired with parts I found in a pub in Maine, it's also an incredibly compact supercomputer and a teleportation device, rigged up with parts I found in the Chixhulub crater."

Iris bit her lip as she fought with the noisy electronic device in her hands, but encouraged him to continue talking about his strange machine. "And what happens when you use the 'porter thingy?"

"On my test flights, as when Rodrigo and I went to Paris, I've found myself thrown into a strange whiteness. It's soft and warm... but clean, like a fresh towel. Or new sheets."

"Oh! That could be the Very Fabric! That helps!" said Iris. She adjusted some of the controls on her device. "I've never experienced it quite like that, though."

Iris' device squawked, then blooped. "That's done it! I've locked on to his signal! Here he comes!" A blue energy bubble appeared, like the one 105 had seen when he first arrived in the city. It was full of swirling shapes which finally solidified into a familiar black and white figure. The very serious face of an intellectual and somewhat snooty panda who was not at all amused.

"Panda!" cried Iris. The bubble burst and he plopped down into her arms. She gave him a crushing hug despite his protests.

He was indignant. "Iris? Where am I? Last thing I knew I was being squished into that dratted machine by a large, insane Scandinavian! Then I heard this sort of odd sound..."

"Sven Tollefsen, Head of MOOO. He's going to get what's coming to him, Panda. Don't you worry. He'll wish he'd never left Finland!"

Panda was indignant. "Leave to you to get mixed up with an organization like MOOO, you ridiculous woman!"

Jenny had returned, but still looked ill. She started digging through Iris' handbag. "Do you still carry those pink tablets? And Sven is Norwegian, not Finnish, Iris. A lot of Americans in the upper midwest are of Norwegian descent."

"I don't care what he is! He's big and mad and used my best friend as his time machine guinea-panda just because he was the only one that would fit in the machine! What kind of monster would do that? It was quite a gamble he took that I would be able to track Panda to this place, where all sorts of time clutter accumulates!" She kicked at some detritus at her feet that looked suspiciously like a six pack of Pepsi Blue. Since waking that morning, 105 had hosted a book discussion group, fought in a pool-hall style brawl, solved a murder/mystery, and was caught in a chase with a zombie blob in an ancient city frozen in time, populated by people who could exchange body parts as if they were made of biological Duplo. But somehow bumping into Iris and Panda was by far the most confusing and emotional part of his day.

"Iris! Listen to me for a moment. I want nothing more than to stay and talk to you, but... my friends are in danger. I have to find them and help them."

"Sorry chuck, things seem even crazier than normal right now. We have to go and stop MOOO's insane experiments. I'm happy to see you, I really am." She sighed and her giant hat seemed to droop in sympathy. "Tell you what! Contact me when you're done with your adventure. We'll have a date!"

"But how? I have gone a year without having a way to contact you."

"That's easy, ducky! If you ever need to contact me, just punch the letters I. W. into your jukebox!" Iris poked her fingers at empty air, miming button-punching.

"I. W.? Ah, for Iris Wildthyme! You did something to my jukebox?"

"I noticed you were working on it. And while I wasn't sure what those bits and bobs were, I could tell they weren't all jukebox parts. That's not technology from any race I've ever met and I've met a bundle! I get around, chuck. And I don't mean like that." Behind her Panda laughed a solitary, haughty "HA!"

Head tilted, 105 tugged at his goatee with his fingers. "So while you were staying with me, you made some modifications to the jukebox so I could contact you? Why didn't you tell me? I've...thought about you often, Señora."

"Didn't I? Silly me, I thought for sure I did, or put a note on the front of your fridge." Iris noted more wrestler eyebrow-raising and finally relented. "Oh fine. I didn't tell you because...I didn't want you to feel pressured, ducky. Pressured to call me." She fussed, picking at an invisible stain on the back of her hand. "Mind, I also didn't want you to *not* call me."

'*How wonderfully like a woman*' thought 105, but caught himself from saying so, especially to a strong, independent, intelligent woman like Iris. "So why are you telling me this now?"

Iris grinned coyly. Her teeth reminded 105 of a slightly off-white picket fence with small gaps in it. A picket fence that is a welcome sight because it means you're home. Perfectly imperfect, and comforting. He wondered how to describe the combination of comforting familiarity and the excitement of the unknown that he felt for Iris.

Iris pulled something out of her purse and handed it to him. He smiled broadly. It was a 7-inch record sleeve. "Here's some 'liquorice pizza' for you. If you have trouble contacting me via your jukebox, put this record in the appropriate slot. It should boost the power to reach me wherever I am!"

105 looked in the envelope and saw tiny pieces of a broken record. He could still read the label. "Little Shirley Beans?"

Iris looked up in alarm. "Not that one! That was meant to be your birthday present!" She grabbed it back from him and shoved it in her handbag. "Shame on you for peeking! I meant to give you this one."

This 45 was intact and in a glossy, yet foldy-cornered, four colour sleeve. Emblazoned on it was the singer's name and slogan, which 105 read aloud excitedly. "Brenda Soobie: The First Lady of Infinity!" Señor 105's exclamation made Iris jump. "I saw her perform in Vegas in '63! The second half of the show was cancelled, I didn't even get to meet her."

Iris smirked knowingly. "You don't say! So, what did you think of her?"

"Simply amazing. I haven't been able to find any of her singles. It's almost as if she disappeared from the face of the Earth! It's a shame, I'd love to see her perform again. She was so lovely."

"Oh really?" Iris smiled proudly for a moment, but then suddenly frowned and crossed her arms. "Oh *really*."

105 sensed the tension and realised he was being thoughtless, talking about the loveliness of another woman.! He tried to do some damage control. "Oh yes, she was very... talented." Iris seemed content with this. "In fact, she probably retired, she was starting to look a bit haggard by the time I caught her show".

He was completely sidelined when Iris seemed angry again. "Oh really?!" Unable to understand the complexity of the female psyche, he quickly changed the subject. "So, what is special about this record?"

"It's temporally charged. It's a bit of an anachronism, songs from the future, recorded before they were written, remixed in the future! It's practically sparking with time energy, with some cracking tunes to boot!" She pointed at the back of the sleeve. "The A-side is *Poker Face*. They loved that one in Vegas! It's a Brenda Soobie original! It got stolen by some bloomin' copycat, became a hit forty years later! The little tramp took off with half my wardrobe too! I bet Kylie wouldn't have done that!"

105 smiled. Sometimes when Iris was talking, it was a beautiful babble of nonsense, like a dozen exotic birds. Iris continued. "The B-side is the Vegas lounge version of *Walking on a Dream*."

They both looked up in surprise as a blue glow started to envelope the mass of metal from which Iris had first emerged. 105 suddenly realised that it wasn't abstract metal shapes; he could see axles and wheels. It was the bottom of Iris' bus! "Oh lovey, we have to go! La Ciudad's time technology is pushing my bus out and back to Des Moines in the future!" Jenny and Panda were already climbing up onto the overturned vehicle. "I've done some bad parking jobs before, but I don't think I've ever landed her on her side before! Give us a leg up, you big lug!"

105 folded his hands into a step for Iris. As she put her weight onto that spot and pulled herself up, she leaned over, quickly smooching him on the cheek. She scrambled to a safe position on top of the quickly fading bus. He couldn't hear her any more, but could read her lips spelling out "*I.W.*" and her fingers punching pretend buttons.

He nodded to her and smiled. Just as the bus, Jenny and Panda faded from view he saw Iris wink at him and blow a kiss. As if she were extinguishing a candle with that burst of breath, they were gone.

Sheila and Chago were running through the frozen crowd as the liquid blob of shifting shapes poured down the street and around the inert coin-flipping citizens of la Ciudad. Sheila heard a yip as the blob absorbed another unfortunate animal, this time a rat terrier. The poor creatures were used as experiments in time machine tests and then found themselves trapped in the city. She knew what it felt like be lost and alone in a strange city.

Chago pointed a snakeskin glove at the base of an orange windmill. He'd spotted the Administrator who was waving them down. They hurriedly climbed up the structure, which was easier for Sheila than Chago. She could float up at will, but was then at the mercy of stronger winds at higher elevations. Chago held her string tight once they reached a safe height.

The Administrator asked if they knew where 105 was. Unfortunately, they had no idea where he could be. The angry blob swirled around the base of the structure, unable to create enough of a cohesive shape to climb, but it was learning. If 105 was here, he would have found it fascinating.

The Administrator was engrossed in the undulating mass. "That is definitely la Ciudad technology being used, but it's amateur work. Whatever is in that bottle doesn't know what it's doing. Sheila, could this be one of your people?"

Sheila hovered near the bottle in Chago's hand. "I don't think so. You seem to know more about my people than I do."

The administrator frowned. "The Modulars knew the Sentients. Sentient elements. Consciousness is one of the fundamental forces of nature, after all. It spreads from elements to molecules to simple organisms, more complex organisms, complex organisms' machines, clusters of bio-organic machines communication systems becoming gestalt consciousnesses, that sort of thing." The Administrator pulled a thought from Chago's head. "The birds and the bees."

"It really is exciting to meet a Sentient after all this time. The Sentients and the Modulars were neighbours in the days when the Multiverse was recently cooled. The Sentients, the Modulars, the Clockworks, the Recursives, the Binaries... and more. We were all friends...in the beginning." The administrator trailed off lost in thought, but then shook himself out of it, chuckling softly. "Your people, Sheila, they were about all about being pure and ours were all for messy mixing. The Sentients weren't all superior about their purity or anything, it was just a chemical sort of purity. It's a shame we lost contact. They were a lot of fun. You might say their parties were a real gas!" The Administrator laughed at his own joke.

Chago groaned. "You just reminded me of Zumbido. May he rest in peace."

"Peace? You mean pieces, don't you? He's not dead, he's just jumbled up and under the influence of that bootleg technology. I don't know where that bottle came from, but it must have been here before to learn those tricks. And it's power-mad."

"What kind of energy is the bottle taking from your city? Where does la Ciudad get its power?"

"Temporal energy. It turns our time-windmills, which feeds into our main generator." He showed Sheila a screen set into a small device. An image of a gigantic stone cube rolled in place, like a die on a craps table, glowing orange. Unlike a die, this cube didn't come to a rest. It just kept spinning, as if it didn't want to choose a result. It was hard to see, but the cube was split into nine smaller cubes, which rotated into different positions, as well as rotating on their own axis. These cubes split yet again into nine smaller cubes each. Chago blinked and shook away his disorientation, it gave him a headache.

"This is our probability generator. It's all powered by the indeterminate quantum particles generated when probability is denied. Like when a coin is flipped, but hasn't yet landed." Sheila remembered the spinning coin and other odd happenings back at the house.

The Administrator sighed. "The time streams flow in, powering our probability generator. It's really quite simple when it runs smoothly."

Chago peered down to the base of the windmill. The howling blob showed no sign of giving up trying to reach them, so he continued the conversation. "Why are things such a mess here?"

The guardian removed his forearm and used it to scratch his back. Chago couldn't help but shudder slightly at the casual dismemberment. "In this era, the planet is a convoluted mess! Time travel is rampant! Human technology, alien technology! The planet flickers. It's constantly being destroyed, replaced, removed from history, alternate histories cancelling each other out. But somehow it always stabilises."

Chago knew about some of those things from his involvement with the Terrible King's experiments with found technology. "And you met my ancestors... the Aztecs."

Struck by a sudden thought, Sheila asked about Modular procreation. The Administrator laughed. "It's different." He removed his left foot. "We split. We shuffle. We exchange. We gradually become new people through this process. Humans create their offspring's bodies from available material, which they ingest and re-route. Our parts are immortal, but always mixing, evolving, changing."

"Uh... Administrator... I think the blob is learning. It's already halfway up the windmill!"

Sheila was worried for her friends. She could probably escape easily, but they couldn't just fly across to another structure like she could. Looking around for a way for them to escape she spotted 105 down on the ground.

He was holding a brick under his chin like a shot put. He spun around gracefully and powerfully a few times before launching the heavy piece of stone into the air. It landed short of the creature. 105 frowned. "It looked so easy in the Olympics." However poor his aim, he'd gotten the blob's attention and it started to swirl towards him. The administrator yelled to 105, instructing him to lead it toward the centre of the city.

105 ripped off his tattered shirt, threw it into the air and ran away as fast as he could. The dark swirling cloud absorbed the shirt as it fell and chased after its owner.

As 105 neared the centre of the city, he could see a giant cube, spinning and grinding in place. The tiny cubes that comprised it seemed to be rotating through every possible combination at once. The blue time bubbles were forming, popping and reforming everywhere around him. Baffled time travellers and their bizarre machines were arriving and disappearing at random.

The cloud seemed unwilling to come too close to the cube or the time activity happening around it. 105 took the opportunity to catch his breath. He nodded to a blond man in a sharp grey suit who registered no surprise at all. Presumably, this was another time traveller drawn into la Ciudad. 105 stared into the cube and tried to start a conversation with the man. "I like the orange glow, but not the irritating noises."

At that moment, the Administrator, Chago and Sheila joined 105 in the safe zone. He was happy to have everyone together. The Administrator said hello to the man in the suit and his friend; a woman wearing a blue dress. The two of them stared back, expressionlessly. The two then looked knowingly at each other, wordlessly deciding to leave. They disappeared into the crowd.

The Administrator sighed. "Wood and Stone. They keep appearing in la Ciudad, but won't speak to me. It's as if they're just observing. Sometimes there's a third with them. For some reason they really don't like la Ciudad or what it represents." Sheila bobbed up and down anxiously. "The creature, where did it go?" No one could see it in all the chaos.

105 was getting impatient. "Administrator, there's too much going on, I can't concentrate. Can't you do something?" The green faced man nodded and made some calculations on his clipboard. Suddenly the space emptied except for the four of them and the sound of the grinding cube. The blue time bubbles stopped forming.

"I can't clear away the creature in the same way because it's tapped into the city's technology, but I can hold back the time incursions for the moment. But I need to concentrate on it." He scribbled wildly on his notes. Reaching into his robes, the Administrator gave 105 a hand held device that looked like an Etch-a-sketch. "The cube can restore the people and objects that comprise the cloud into their proper shape. Use this to steer the cube towards the creature."

With his pencil, he pointed to the bottle in Chago's hand. The yellow coating was bubbling and flaking. "You need to get this vessel out of the city and soon. But first, use it as bait to lure the creature into the path of the cube. Whatever you do, don't let the creature touch the bottle. If it does, it may gain full access to la Ciudad's power. We have to prevent that at all costs." Chago looked unsure, but Sheila promised she would help him. The two of them ran away from the cube, yelling to get the creature's attention.

105 struggled with the ridiculous controls. It was almost impossible to direct the cube's path with any degree of accuracy. The horizontal and vertical controls were separate and no path could be plotted smoothly. He winced when he almost sent it trampling right over Chago and Sheila.

He twirled the controls again, and panicked when he almost ran over a different man. Almost a blur as he leapt out of the way, he did a flip and landed on his feet, clutching something to his chest. The cube swerved and 105 lost sight of the mysterious figure.

He caught sight of the cloud creature approaching the man's previous location. It seemed to be sniffing the area. 105 quickly aimed the giant cube towards it, but the cloud narrowly escaped being absorbed by the lumbering shape. He cursed, wishing that he could just wrestle the damn thing and make it admit defeat. Failing that, he wished his hands were free so he could dig in his pockets for some fresh chewing gum.

105 gasped when he saw Chago trip and drop the bottle, which rolled a distance away. The cloud engulfed him and he screamed in agony as it paused to absorb him. His very atoms were being shorn off his body. Through the pain, he struggled to yell to Sheila. "Get the bottle... away.. aaAAAHHHHHH!" Sheila sniffled as she saw Chago torn to shreds as if he had been caught in a dust storm.

She hovered above the horrible perfume bottle with disgust. All this death because of this ridiculous object. She didn't care what it really was, or where it came from, but she knew she wouldn't let the creature have it. She sighed deeply, gathering inner reserves of strength. What did the Administrator say? Her family was old and powerful and could do amazing things. She could do this. She felt a new energy in her molecules.

Wrapping her string around the neck of the bottle, she floated up as hard as she could manage. By sheer force of will she could almost make the object lift up off the ground. The cloud, finished digesting Chago, was now rushing towards her. She could see 105 working the controls of the cube frantically. The creature was now directly between her and the rapidly approaching cube.

105 yelled for Sheila to get to safety, but she couldn't let the creature gain control of the bottle for even a moment, and by extension, la Ciudad. She thought of her new friends that were lost in that twirling mass of horror. She thought of the new lease of life that 105 and Rodrigo had given her. She'd give anything to free her friends from this creature. Somehow, unbelievably, she felt the bottle rise into the air with her. She attempted to take it high enough to keep it from the creature, luring it into place so 105 could crush it with the cube.

She was doing it! String taut with strain, she and the bottle were high above the cloud. It snarled, snapping at her non-existent heels with its non-existent fangs. If she could just hold on, the cube was almost there. It was about to crush the creature when she felt herself slipping. Her newfound strength was suddenly gone and the bottle pulled Sheila down into the whirlwind of particles, just as the cube crushed everything.

105 cried out in despair. "Sheila!" He threw the etch-a-sketch thing to the ground. It smashed into plastic chunks. His hands covered his face in disbelief. He told himself that if anyone had faced this foe physically, it should have been him. Not poor, defenceless Sheila, so playful and alive. The drops of sweat that had been gathering on his bare shoulders slid down his back, icy cold. He heard laughter and was enraged that someone would find amusement at the death of his friend. It was the Administrator.

"How dare you? She sacrificed her very atoms to stop that creature!"

"Don't you see? You got them! You got them!" He pointed at the cube which was twirling in place, flashing in brilliants colours. "It's searching through all the possibilities, trying to find the correct combination of matter and energy! It's solving the puzzle, it's putting your friends back together!" 105 allowed himself to feel a carefully reserved amount of hope.

The cube continued to spin and flash, the light becoming blinding. The cube was spinning so rapidly that it was turning the stone floors into dust. A cloud quickly filled the chamber. This wasn't a malevolent cloud, it was simply dust, filled with the flashing light that was once the cube. It had now completely transformed into a ball of energy while it did the job of reconstruction.

105 and the Administrator both cheered when Sheila came floating out of the dust and zoomed directly over to them. She wasn't so defenceless and vulnerable after all! 105 found it amusing that she sounded like she was out of breath when she was literally made out of air.

She giggled euphorically that she was still alive. "Monsieur 105! I did it!" 105 hugged her eagerly. "Yes, Sheila, you did it. You did it! Our friends are broken down into their elementary states and are being reassembled by the power of la Ciudad. The cube will pick the correct combination of particles. Combinations are what it does best!"

It was at that moment that Diana, Chago and Mr. Tea came flying out of the ball of light. They looked confused as they got to their feet and dusted themselves off, coughing. The Administrator laughed at their confusion. Chago was holding the bottle which barely had any protective coating left.

Using the power reclaimed from the bottle, the Administrator opened a time-vent portal to Mexico City and 105 hurried his restored friends into it. He was becoming concerned that maybe their last friend didn't make it. Maybe the Mexican nightclub owner was really dead after all. But no, there! A sparkle in the dust! A gaudy rhinestone covered jacket! Hot pink wingtip shoes! "Zumbido lives!"

Holding a cat with metal ears, Zumbido laughed, perplexed. "My glasses... where are my glasses? I can't see a damn thing without my god damned glasses!" He patted down his jacket and found a spare pair in his pocket. "That's better. These don't match my jacket, though. Where the hell are we?"

Sheila zoomed over to him and urged him to follow her to the portal. "Zumbido, hurry! We have to get out of here!"

Taking in the bizarre surroundings, Zumbido laughed. "You don't have to tell me twice, you loony balloony!" Everyone ran except for 105.

"Goodbye Administrator! Thanks for your help. When I get back home, I'll seal off the tunnels in my house so that no one else wanders into your city through conventional means." The Administrator thanked him just as the ball of energy imploded and was once again a spinning cube.

105 stepped through the portal which closed behind him. The Administrator sighed, relieved it was over. Blue bubbles started forming again, bringing with them strange time travellers asking annoying questions, this time an elevator full of department store employees; somehow whisked away through time. He sighed and got back to work cleaning up the mess as best he could. He grinned. If there's one thing a Modular loves, it's a big confusing mess. That, along with scaring the shit out of people by pulling their hands off. That never gets old.

105 slammed the heavy front doors to his house and leaned back against them, as if now that his guests were finally gone they were going to try to force their way back inside. After they'd escaped the timeless city below the ancient city, the entire bunch had been exhausted. The portal sealed itself behind them, and everyone fell asleep where they landed.

Zumbido didn't remember anything, and Diana proclaimed her innocence. 105 had to admit it was a probability that the bottle had influenced her. He had to grudgingly take her word for it and let her go. She had been working for the Terrible Kings, that much was certain. Bitter that her art career had never taken off, she had sold out her old friend for the chance at becoming rich.

He warned the art teacher never to cross his path again and she left in a hurry. The rest of his guests - Chago, Mr. Tea, Zumbido and his new pet, a deaf cat from the future, said their goodbyes not long after that, climbing into a taxi together.

He would talk to them again and soon, but not right now.

Clad in fresh attire, a very comfortable Hawaiian shirt, khaki shorts, flip flops and his Californium mask, 105 strode back into the Map Room. He paused to look at the Day of the Dead altar again. Viento's smiling photo was right where he'd left it. She would have approved of how lively the house had been last night, almost like it had been back in the 30s and 40s. He would have to take a photographic portrait of himself and Sheila soon and find a bit of blank wall somewhere to hang it. Maybe Rodrigo would be interested in helping to develop the film? Surely the boy's time could be better spent learning, instead of scrounging on the streets. It was time to breathe life into this house again. But first, 105 had to do something.

Sheila was not surprised to find 105 tinkering with the jukebox. He shut the top, locking the horizontal glass surface back into place. He took a coin out his pocket and flipped it into the air. It fell to the ground without incident, eagle side up. He picked it up and pushed it into the coin slot of the jukebox and listened to it clunk down into the workings of the machine.

Making sure he was ready, he punched the button for the letter *'I'*. It stayed in for a few seconds, ticking, then popped back out with a *ker-chunk*. His finger hovered over the *'W'* button, then decisively poked it. *Tick, tick, tick, ker-chunk!* Whirring emanated from inside the machine, mechanisms were set in motion, gears turning and slots rotating. He heard a scrape and a click as a mechanical arm put the Brenda Soobie record into place. The needle dropped into the groove. A gentle crackle filled the time until the music started.

105, arms folded across his chest, tapped his foot to the beat and glanced over at Sheila. "Not bad, right?" Sheila bobbed up and down in time to the music, her string dancing below her.

With a happy hum, a button lit up on the display panel of the Zodiac machine. It was a simple green circle. He pressed it and a red circle appeared on the horizontal surface of the jukebox with the simple phrase *'Place message here'*. 105 had been expecting some sort of audio/visual communication and was caught off guard.

He set the bottle down and reached for a pen and started scribbling on the back of a handy envelope. Upon having the bottle placed on it, the circle turned yellow and an insistent beeping ensued. It beeped faster and faster indicating 105 only had a short amount of time to add his note. Just as he was about to place the envelope next to the perfume bottle, the circle turned green. With a *zweeeeoop!* the bottle disappeared, transmitted through the space-time Maelstrom to an unsuspecting Iris Wildthyme. 105 cursed himself for his reflexes not being fast enough.

Pressing *'I.W.'* a second time didn't reactivate the message system. Sheila suggested that perhaps the record had to recharge between uses. 105 admitted that could be possible. At any rate, he had faith that Iris would recognize the bottle's true nature. She was an experienced traveller of the cosmos. Surely she wouldn't simply take the bottle at face value and assume he was sending her perfume. Would she?

He was sick of thinking about that bottle and decided to put it out of his mind for now. He could do some tests on the samples he'd collected later. He smiled at Sheila who was still dancing to Poker Face. "Sheila? I'm very proud of you."

"I'm proud of me, mon ami! I've had people look at me and dismiss me just because I'm a petite balloon. They don't know I'm a molecular being composed of pure, sentient Helium! They're always mistaking my outer shell for what I am."

105 nodded. "That's true for all of us, Sheila." The song faded out as the needle trailed into the run-out groove. After a few moments of gentle crackling, the needle lifted and the mechanisms of the jukebox became still and silent once again.

105 enjoyed having someone around with whom he could share his record collection. He grinned through his mask.

"Want to listen to the B-Side?"

The Shape of Things
By Stuart Douglas

It's far too simplistic to say 'start at the beginning' like that. For one thing, who's to say what the beginning is? Ask two people to tell the same tale and they will struggle to agree on identical iterations of even 'Once Upon a Time'. How much more difficult, therefore, to expect one person to choose a single starting point from the many available. I could choose one of a dozen places to begin and the story which followed would bend and deform itself as a result. Even fact can be made as flexible as fiction and, that being the case, perhaps it would be better to pick a beginning which satisfies dramatically rather than that which most slavishly follows fact?

In any case, I had best make a start. I can see the Inspector is impatient to be scribbling things down, positively salivating at the thought of the terrible truths I have to tell, and I have no wish to disappoint him.

Besides, I'm completely gagging on for a drink.

Detective Inspector Bailey cupped his hands round a match and lit his cigarette expertly in the face of the biting wind. He flicked the match high into the air and the wind caught and swirled it quickly into the distance, well away from the crime scene.

'Let's go over this again then, Markham' he said to the young Constable at his side. 'The phone call from the kidnapper said Mrs Hunter could be picked up at noon today, so long as we followed the directions in the map delivered by that lady.'

Bailey's look managed to convey both awe and revulsion as he extended his neck in the direction of a most peculiar pair of onlookers.

The lady in question was a woman, about fifty, smoking a pink cigarette in the shelter of a Police van. As Markham turned to look at her, she was pulling a ratty fur coat down at the hem in an obvious attempt to protect her legs, purple leggings being no match for the flesh stripping fury of a gale force wind coming off the Forth.

If this vision in fox fur was likely to cause the raising of an eyebrow or two at the local Police Association Annual Ball, her companion would undoubtedly cause the Chief Constable to call in the doctors from the Royal Edinburgh loony bin.

For a start, he was only 10 inches tall. And he was stark naked. Or, Bailey conceded (for he prided himself that he was a fair man), as naked as a panda could ever be, with the plush magnificence of his fur putting the tatty state of his friend's to shame. And the paisley patterned cravat.

Some kind of clever oriental toy, he reckoned. His daughter Alison wanted something very like the panda for Christmas – a giraffe you could buy outfits for, he thought she'd said, so maybe the panda was in the same set. There was always a set of these things.

Though he didn't remember Ally mentioning the giraffe being able to talk.

'Come on then, Markham' he said, 'Let's get this over with.'

The first few flakes of the promised snow had begun to fall as he shouted 'MS WILDTHYME! COME HERE PLEASE!' and, Markham in his wake, strode to the edge of the muddy field which stretched in front of him.

The field was large and scrubby, a mix of sleet and slush covered mud, frozen in choppy ridges, and thin, patchy waist high grass, like the sparse hair of a balding man grown pathetically, foolishly long. It stretched for perhaps half a mile, ending in a small incline which sloped down to the water itself. The only substantial structures in sight were two grey electricity pylons, spaced a few hundred yards apart, and at the water's edge, part of a derelict house, reduced by decades of wind, rain and general exposure to little more than two half collapsed walls and a green wooden door, plastered with faded bill posters for long forgotten shows.

Bailey felt the presence of Iris behind him long before she spoke. Truth be told, he'd never met anyone with a personality as big as hers before, and that personality seemed not to follow her around so much as precede her at a distance of about two hundred yards, waving flags and beeping loud horns to announce her arrival.

She smacked him hard on the shoulder and before he could react, snatched the map out of his hands.

'Right then love' she said, her accent broad Lancashire he thought, though she claimed to be from much further away than Manchester or Bury. 'According to the map that Panda and me brought you, the girl should be tied up eighty five paces that way, then twenty seven paces to the left. Why don't we go and get her, then we can head back to the station for a drink and a chinwag about the dirty bugger who pinched her in the first place?'

She strode into the field as though she owned it, counting 'ONE, TWO, THREE...' at the top of her voice, but Bailey had decided enough was enough.

'Give me that!' he said, jogging after her and grabbing the map. 'FOUR' he said as he took one large, careful stride into the long grass, Iris trailing indignantly in his wake.

'FIVE, SIX, SEVEN, EIGHT...' he continued all the way to eighty five, then stopped and took his bearings.

'This way' said Iris, heading east, in parallel with the shoreline. 'ONE' she said pointedly, but acquiesced with a wide grin when Bailey resumed his own count.

As he approached twenty seven, Bailey trod more carefully, scanning the ground to the front and side of him, alert to the smallest sign of the girl. Iris too seemed altogether more sober and serious now, her eyes narrowed in thought, the cold forgotten as her fur coat flapped and fluttered in the freezing, sleet-laden wind.
'Where is she?' Bailey asked her, the question only partially rhetorical. She might look a bit weird and her need to cart an electronic panda around with her was plain peculiar, but she'd demonstrated several times even during their brief acquaintance that she was, as they said on the telly, one smart cookie.

'How would I know!' Iris snapped back. 'I'm not a bloody mind reader! I was sure she'd be right here, and if she's not then she could be bloody anywhere.'

Bailey was inclined to agree, which made their discovery of the girl's naked and dead body a couple of hundred yards inland all the more unexpected and shocking.

Bailey was, he knew, a difficult man to love. The fact he was merely an Inspector after twenty five years in the Police Force, and in spite of several successful and high visibility cases, attested to that. He suffered from too independent a mind, according to various evaluations and reports – committee speak, he mentally translated to himself when feeling particularly unappreciated, for intelligent but mouthy.

Which was fair enough, really. He was self-aware enough to know that he was best suited at his current level and no higher. 'If you climb too high up the tree you can become dizzy and fall', he was fond of telling Markham. 'And besides', he almost never continued, 'the tops of trees tend to be where the monkeys congregate'.

Still, he wondered if his intelligence was playing him false this time. Iris Wildthyme was proving something of a puzzle, and if he'd judged her incorrectly a woman had paid for that with her life.

She'd rolled up (literally, in a red double decker bus of all things) at the station the day before yesterday. He'd been having a quick cigarette out the back when he'd heard the commotion and coming through to see what was going on, had been confronted by the sight of Iris battering her fist off the counter and declaring loudly that she needed to speak to whoever was in charge. The fact she'd placed a small stuffed bear on the counter beside her failed to register until he'd invited her into his office and she'd picked it up as she allowed him to lead the way.

Now, forty eight hours later, standing over a body lying under a white sheet in the clinical surroundings of the mortuary, he wasn't sure whether he'd done the right thing in not simply throwing her back out into the street.

But there was something about her, something almost tangible, that made him, if not trust her, at least believe that she could help.

She'd discovered the map and instructions after all. Though perhaps 'supplied' was a better way of putting it?

'Don't you worry yourself, love' she'd said before he'd even had a chance to ask her to sit down. 'Now that Auntie Iris is here you can relax.' She paused and frowned. 'Well maybe not relax so much as have a bit of a breather.'

She reached down into her bag and pulled out a thin packet of Sobranie cigarettes. She lit one and sat back in the chair, gesturing for him to sit down in his. He should have thrown her out then, he realised in retrospect.

And he might well have done, had not a cultured voice come from nowhere to say 'Oh for God's sake Iris, put that bloody ciggy out, and show the man the map.' And now a somewhat different voice cut into his reverie and jerked him back to the present.

'Are you even listening, Inspector?' it said shrilly, and with obvious annoyance. Bailey jerked forward guiltily.

'I already know all this', he snapped, wondering again where the map had come from and why he'd been quite so trusting of a woman who'd led him straight to a dead body. 'I was there, remember? Although given the fact that you appear to have changed your physical appearance completely in your brief absence, I only have your word that you were.'

'We don't have time for your narrow-mindedness, Inspector! You were happy enough to accept a ten inch tall talking Panda back when we first got here and we were helping you solve your case, so exactly why a simple matter of bodily regenera...'

'Perhaps if I recap what I do know and you can fill in the rest?' Bailey interrupted. 'We found the body and you said something about it being odd, and then we examined the corpse and...let's see,' he flicked open his notebook, 'I noted down the fact that death appeared to have been caused by over a hundred individual blows to the legs and lower half of the torso.'

The detective inhaled deeply on his cigarette and glared across the table. 'Soon after that the two of you announced that you'd received a very important message from an old friend – a 'great mad, dashing, gorgeous bastard' according to my notes – and that you both had to leave without delay. Which,' he finished accusingly, 'you did.'

Through the haze of cigarette smoke, Bailey saw what he realised he was now beginning to think of as 'the suspect' lean forward to speak.

'Well, it was important...'

'But why has Senor 105 sent you this bottle?' Panda asked for the fiftieth time as Iris threw the collected detritus of a two month stay in Edinburgh into the Bus. 'There must be a reason!'

If he was being completely honest, he found the whole situation a bit suspicious and not a little unnerving. 105 snaps his castanets and Iris comes running! And sending a bottle of cheap perfume too, as though Iris were some conchita he'd picked up in a Guadalajara street market! It wouldn't surprise Panda in the slightest if the swine intended to ruin the poor sweet girl, trample on her fair innocence like a... well, that was perhaps taking things a bit too far. It was Iris he was talking about after all.

Still, he didn't like the way in which Iris had so quickly accepted this present from the masked Mexican wrestler. It wasn't like her. Though, to be fair, getting bored of being a policewoman and deciding to bugger off at a moment's notice was entirely in keeping with the Iris he knew and...hmm, tolerated.

He belatedly realised that Iris was talking to him. 'I told you, you daft Panda – 105 used the secret code on his jukebox to send me that beautiful little bottle. Stands to reason it must be important. The fate of the Universe probably hangs in the balance, with planets in perfect alignment and once in a million year conjunctions and whatnot. We have to leave.'

She picked up the little yellow bottle of scent once again, and turned it thoughtfully in her fingers. 'And he probably wants me to put a splash on, too. Get things rolling, as it were.'

She pulled, then twisted the lid of the bottle with no obvious effect. 'It's...a...bit...stiff!' she gasped as the tiny object slithered in her fingers, the glass strangely slippery and difficult to get a grip on.

'Oh for God's sake woman, give it here!' said Panda in exasperation. If they did have to shoot off across time and space at the beck and call of a man who thought a lilac face mask was the ideal accompaniment to full evening wear, then it was best they got it over with as quickly as possible.

He beckoned with one paw towards Iris, but with a muttered 'and what are you going to do with no fingers?' she turned her back on him and began hunting through the cutlery drawer.

'This'll do the trick,' she crowed as she emerged with the bottle in one hand and a sharp knife in the other. She wedged the top of the blade under the rim of the bottle lid and gave the base of the knife a hard thwack with her palm. This caused the knife to skitter off the smooth metal of the lid, deflect itself at an angle of 45 degrees and narrowly miss cutting a large chunk out of Iris' hand. The air turned a blue so deep as to be almost purple as Iris cursed, kicked and condemned bottles, wrestlers and knives in equal measure.

Panda picked up his paper and went back to the crossword as Iris stomped upstairs, still muttering dire imprecations under her breath.

'Five across. Foul mouthed, time travelling drunk with an eye for flowers, four letters,' he said to himself with a small smile.

An hour or so later, Panda had finished the puzzle and was lightly dozing in his favourite wicker chair, pillows piled up on either side of him and his tartan shawl thrown over his legs. He was dreaming that a beautiful young woman was calling him her 'great big hero' as she sat at his feet in adoration, so it came as something of a shock to be rudely awoken by Iris poking him with a long stick and shouting 'wotcha' at him.

He opened his eyes slowly, fearing the worst. Everything seemed as it should however. True, there was some sort of laser gun affair mounted on a steel tripod in the centre of the floor, and Iris was wearing orange protective goggles that covered nearly all of her face. But other than the Bus appeared unchanged from the moment he'd fallen asleep.

He stretched and shook off his rug, then braced himself to jump down from the chair.

'DON'T MOVE!'

Panda had thrown himself back in his chair before Iris has managed to scream the second word. Years of travelling with her had taught him that when she bellowed it was best to listen.

'For God's sake, Iris, what's the problem now?' he asked testily. He followed Iris' silently pointed finger as it angled towards the floor and was shocked into silence himself as he (rather vertiginously) came to terms with the fact that virtually all of the floor of the Bus was missing, and he could clearly see the Maelstrom swirling malevolently directly under his chair.

Iris, he now saw, was standing on a small patch of carpet entirely surrounded by deadly Maelstrom gubbins, with the laser occupying a similarly reduced patch of floor alongside her. Other than the section underneath his own chair and another small section connected to it along the front of the Welsh Dresser that Iris kept all her good china in, there was not a safe spot anywhere else on the lower deck.

'I see,' said Panda calmly. He felt round underneath himself and located the biro he'd used for his crossword. 'So what happens...' he began as he dropped the pen into the void where it burned for a moment in a bright verdigris flame before disappearing into ashes. 'Ah, I see,' he concluded.

'Will you stop saying that?' snapped Iris, 'It's not helping.'

Panda frowned. 'Might I at least be allowed to ask what you've done?'.

Iris looked apologetic, and shrugged. 'I was trying to use the laser to blow the lid off that damned perfume. But the beam reflected on the glass, bounced right off my pill box collection and before I knew it we were running well short of floor space. If I hadn't shot the bloody thing with my little pink gun it'd have killed us both.' She slumped against the laser. 'God, I need a drink!'

'First things first,' said Panda. 'Before we have even the merest hint of the juniper berry we need to get the floor back. Apart from anything else, the drinks cabinet is way over there, well beyond my reach.'

Iris grinned, her confidence evidently returning. 'Oh, that's a doddle. All we need to do is generate enough additional power to give the thingamajig circuit a boost and it'll fill in the gaps in the Bus' infrastructure in a jiffy.'

Panda looked doubtful. 'And how, pray tell, do we do that?'

'Can you reach the bottom cupboard in the dresser? Iris asked unexpectedly.

"What, the cupboard you said was full of old pairs of tights?"

"That's the one!"

"The tights you said you were going to tear up one day to use for dusters?"

"Yes," Iris said testily, "that one."

Panda looked at Iris over his half moon glasses. "I know I'll regret this but I have I ask. Why would I want to reach that cupboard?'

Iris stood up, took two steps forwards then jumped in the direction of the cupboard. "Never mind," she said as she landed, "I'll bloody well do it myself!"

She threw open the two small wooden doors and Panda felt a huge wash of heat engulf him and throw him back in his seat. As he squinted through the heat haze he could just about make out a very bright yellow light filling the cupboard completely.

His ears were ringing, and though Iris was evidently speaking he couldn't make out a single word she said.

"That isn't like any kind of nylons I've ever seen," he thought as the yellow light faded to orange, then brown, then finally black as, to his surprise and minor embarrassment, he fainted.

When Panda came to a few minutes later, he was unsurprisingly miffed.

"It's a sun," said Iris before he could say a word, affecting a degree of insouciance which fooled no-one, least of all Panda.

"Is it? Is it really?' he said, witheringly. "My my. Fancy me not thinking of that, what with the talk of tights and dusters and whatnot. I mean I'm aware you suffer from the delusion that the sun shines out of your gusset, but still, that did come as a tiny surprise I must say."

He dusted himself down, idly rubbing at a slightly scorched spot on his white front.

"AND WHAT WITH IT BEING INSIDE A SMALL CUPBOARD UNDER A TABLE INSIDE A SODDING BUS, YOU GIN ADDLED OLD HARPY!'

Iris shrugged, anger and embarrassment evidently battling for command of her temper.

Predictably, anger won.

"Well, without being indelicate, you ungrateful, mardy bear, you're mainly made up of cheap acrylics and knock off stuffing which, let's be honest, would never get an EU Fire Safety Kite Mark. And inside that cupboard, through a miracle of Clockworks' technology, is a full sized sun artificially moved into a separate dimension in which it is both very, very big and yet also very, very small. It's best the two of you don't meet. It could get a bit fiery. That's why it's only when you're out that I can leave the door open and warm my feet. It doubles up lovely as a stand in for a Calor gas heater, it really does.'"

She smiled in a conciliatory manner at Panda, then leaped across the room as her small friend approached the cupboard with his newspaper in his paw.

"What are you doing?" she shouted, "Are you completely mental?!?"

"I was just going to throw this into the cupboard and watch it burn, like I used to do with that Aga your artist friend had on that farm in Devon!" Panda replied, indignantly.

Iris sighed. "Yes, but if you throw that in there, it'll instantly grow to about a million times its size as it leaves the Bus and the Universe tries to make it fit the scale of the real sun! Plus the spurt of energy provided by a newspaper the size of Brazil burning up would overload dozens of the Bus' delicate insides."

She sighed again, and shook her head. "What we need to do is throw in these...eh, let's see..these..eh..yeah, these roast chicken flavour crisps I keep on the carpet for just these kind of occasions. They'll puff up to about ten miles wide and the burst of power can be used to power the laser in the front cab. Ooh, that'll fill in the missing floor, no bother!"

She smiled in triumph. Panda pulled his blanket over his head as she scooped up the bits of fragmented crisp. Best to leave her to it when she was in one these kinds of moods.

Later, some time after the floor had been repaired and some time before Iris had fixed the singed bits in her hair, Panda examined the little bottle through his jeweller's eyepiece.

It was quite a plain object when you looked closely, he realised. The dull yellow was, as he'd expected, only gold leaf and where it had chipped away some sort of clear glass could be seen underneath. Inscribed around the middle were half a dozen characters, presumably letters, but in no language known to Panda.

He pressed a nail under the lid and slid it round the circumference, but it was sealed tight. He checked that Iris was still busy with the scissors and flicked the side with a finger. The bottle gave a deep, hollow ringing sound.

It's not even bloody full, he thought indignantly, and was about to point this out to Iris when, utterly unexpectedly, the bottle rang out once more – only this time he hadn't touched it.

Again he was on the verge of calling Iris over, but curiosity – and a certain degree of continued irritation at the place 105 obviously held in Iris' heart – made him stop. Perhaps he should investigate a little further himself before he involved Iris and her undoubted attempts to make excuses for the tight-fisted wrestler?

Turning himself round in his chair, so that he was almost entirely hidden by the runkles and ruffles of his blanket, Panda rested the bottle on its side and leaned in as close as he could, eyeglass in place, to peer through one of the tiny chinks of exposed glass.

At first he could see nothing at all but he rubbed a paw hard over the glass' grubby surface and when he looked again, he swore he could make out a shape moving about inside the bottle!

It was impossible to be sure, though, and suddenly he desperately wanted to know what the bottle contained.

'Needs must', he thought with a grimace. 'Brave heart, Panda.'

With one final furtive peek over the blanket, he braced himself, popped the bottle in his mouth and sucked hard at the encrusted dirt and grime. It tasted vile. He could feel bits of grit sticking to the top of his mouth, and saliva softened mud sliding down the back of his throat. He closed his eyes in determination and sucked harder than ever.

Nearly there!

'What the blinkin' flip are you up to, Panda?' Iris asked as she pulled back the blanket at the exact moment he finally got enough dirt off the bottle to get a good clear look at the figure inside.

'Fine. I get it. There was some odd behaviour on your Bus. Odder than usual that is.' Bailey was rapidly running out of patience. He'd stopped writing about ten minutes before and was seriously considering terminating the interview and charging every unhelpful, story telling idiot in the station with wasting police time. And to think he'd once thought Iris a smart cookie. Though, admittedly, the Iris of today and the Iris of a few days before were quite different people.

'What's that to do with my dead body?' he asked. 'And how on Earth does any of this enable you to turn up here, out of the blue, looking completely different to the way you looked two days ago, and claiming you know who did it and how?'

'Patience, patience. I'm getting to it...'

'Up to? UP TO?' Panda boomed indignantly. 'You have the effrontery to ask what I'm up to?'

He stood up in his chair, bottle still clasped in one paw, and glared at Iris.

'I must say, it's come to a pretty pass when one is incapable of so much as enjoying a fine piece of glassware without accusations being thrown about the place like so much poisonous confetti!' He jumped down. 'I won't say I'm not wounded Iris, because I am. To the core. Perhaps it would be better if we spent a small period of time apart.'

So saying, he turned on his heel and headed upstairs, where Iris heard the sound of his door slamming and the snib being firmly pulled across.

That Panda is getting stranger by the day, she thought with a shrug.

In his room, Panda sat on the edge of his bed and peered through the gap in the grime which otherwise coated the bottle.

Inside, swooping and gliding through the tiny yellow ocean, a smudge of black and grey grew larger and larger as it approached the side of the bottle, until it finally coalesced in front of Panda's eyes.

He couldn't believe what he was seeing.

At one end, a long dark torso ended in a pair of strong flippers, which gently rippled from side to side as the creature kept itself in place in the liquid. She (for it was evidently a female) had her two paws pressed against the inside of the glass, and for all that the murky perfume prevented him from being absolutely certain, her face seemed to be fur covered and...Panda-like.

No, more than that. It seemed to Panda that her face was perfection itself. From the tips of the upturned arches that were her ears, down to the broad curve of her chin, she was everything he had always dreamed of.

He craned his neck to see further and confirmed to his delight that she was a female. He had been known to dream about that sort of thing too at times.

He hardly dared think it, but could she be one of his own people? Admittedly the mermaid's tail was unexpected, as was the fact she was about half an inch long, but still - was he no longer Last of the Pandas?

Panda's antecedents were, in some respects, even more mysterious than Iris' own. True, Tom had once said that he'd found Panda in a raffia basket in a corner of Platform 7 of Kings Cross Station, but Panda himself had always thought that a bare-faced lie, brought about by a surfeit of Harry Potter movies and cheap drink.

Other than that dubious anecdote, however, Panda knew nothing about where he came from. He remembered the moment he'd first laid eyes on Tom, sitting at one end of O'Malley's Bar while Tom sat at the other, the two of them the only ones drinking Bombay Sapphire with a twist of lemon in a bar full of off duty Irish policemen sipping Jamesons and Bushmills. Before that, nothing. Though he had the very faintest ghost of a memory of a garden full of roses and, improbably, bicycles.

He'd come to accept the fact that he was alone. He had Iris, of course, but nowhere the two of them had gone had he ever come across the slightest suggestion of another Panda like himself. Not in the Clockworks, or in the Pseudo Obverse or even in the terrifying Mirror Universe where Mirror Iris had threatened to have him turned into a glove puppet by the simple application of her right hand. Every lead they'd followed back in the early days, every clue they'd unearthed, each had led exactly nowhere until finally, sick to death of the entire thing, he'd convinced Iris that he wasn't really all that bothered.

A lie, of course, but not a complete one. He didn't really care where he came from, but he did sometimes wish that there was someone else like him. Just one other ten inch tall, sentient, talking, stuffing filled Panda.

Panda's room was a reflection of his character – or so he described it to the occasional visitor he allowed over the threshold. Neat and tidy to the point of having a condition named after it, he sometimes liked to sit on the bed and look out over the little corner of sanity he'd managed to salvage from the chaos of the Bus.

Along the wall opposite his bed, bookcases covered the entire area from floor to ceiling, stuffed full of tattered paperback mystery novels, dog-eared travel guides and immaculate copies of the classics. Memory crystals, Betamax videos and neural implants lay in carefully constructed piles on the floor to his left and to his right there was a large wooden desk on which sat an ancient Earth computer, the chunky monitor for which partially obscured the signed copy of the script to 'Carry on Camping' hanging behind it. A very small russet coloured teddy bear sat slumped disconsolately on the desk.

The object he was looking for, however, was nowhere in sight. Panda had to jump down and scramble under his bed, pushing aside anything which got in his way, until he reached the skirting board at the back. Working by touch alone in the dark, he found a small raised point on its surface, and pushed.

There was a barely audible click, followed by a slightly louder purring sound and a hidden drawer popped out in front of him.
Panda gingerly poked a paw into the drawer, grabbed the only thing inside and hurriedly backed his way out from underneath the bed.

An hour later Panda was still considering the object in his hand, twisting and turning it in the light, unsure what to do next. It was about four inches long and cylindrical, a dull white in colour and featureless save for a jack at one tapered end and three buttons at the other.

Had Iris walked in she would immediately have recognised the pale, thin tube as a Hylon Time Vibrator and, judging by its unusually short length, the more powerful Mark 20 at that. Designed to cause time and space to vibrate unsympathetically with one another, she had picked it up from a MAIOW operative in Leeds back in the nineties, intending to use it to fix the embarrassing problem of the Bus' interior being smaller than its exterior.

Because its main use was to change the size of things.

Panda came to a decision and twisted the bottom of the Vibrator ninety degrees, causing it to hum gently. He'd never actually seen Iris use the thing, since she'd quickly realised that a bigger interior meant more surface area to clean, but it seemed fairly intuitive. Turn the knob one way to make things bigger and the other to make them smaller. Then point it at something, press the button and watch in amazement as it shrunk or swelled in size.

He moved back over to the desk on which the perfume bottle sat and moved it very slightly for the tenth time, then stepped back and aimed.
He closed his eyes, muttered a short prayer, and fired...

'...and it turns out I was holding it the wrong way round. So that's why I'm a little taller than the first time we met,' Panda concluded, leaning forward in his seat as though daring Bailey to make a comment.

Not for the first time, Bailey wondered if he was going insane. Why should it seem odder that Panda was now six foot tall and 200 pounds rather than, say, the fact he was sitting at a desk, chatting away as though that were the most normal thing in the world? Really, wasn't big and heavy at least the way pandas were supposed to be? He stubbed out his cigarette, pushed his chair back and stood up. He wasn't a small man but Panda was now a good couple of inches taller. In fact as Bailey watched him slump back into his chair and pull the peak of his baseball cap down over the big dark circles round his eyes, he reckoned that Panda could pass in a dim light for the sort of surly teenager he often saw in interview rooms.

'So,' he said, clapping his hands together in mock enthusiasm, just as he would if one of those self-same goth glue sniffers had turned up at the station, 'what say we go and see if Iris has confirmed your story and if you really have solved my case for me!'

He pushed open the door and moved back, gesturing for Panda to step through. Panda scraped his chair back along the floor and with a polite nod to Bailey moved slowly into the corridor where a slightly tattered Iris was arguing with a policewoman standing behind what he assumed was the reception desk.

Iris was clearly in the middle of a protracted rant. 'What do you mean 'No Fixed Abode?I'll have you know, young woman, that Panda and I live on my Bus, the only one of its kind in the multiverse! Though,' she trailed off reflectively, 'it isn't actually fixed to any one time or place, so you might have a point there.'

Having convinced herself that no insult to her beloved Bus had been intended, Iris looked around with her usual keen interest in surroundings. 'PANDA!' she shouted, as she spotted him emerging from the interview room, 'Come over here, love, and let the fox see the rabbit!'

She strode over and enveloped him in a hug which squeezed the air from his lungs. 'Are you still feeling all mega intelligent then?' she whispered in his ear in mid-embrace. 'No other weird side effects from being super sized? Purple wee or spots before your eyes? Nothing...homicidal?'

Panda flexed his upper arms and broke Iris' grip. 'I can assure you Iris, that I have never felt better. It's as though I've been sleepwalking all my life, and only now I've woken up. Suddenly everything seems so clear to me. For a start, I know who killed that poor unfortunate girl. So let us dispense with the pleasantries and take Inspector Bailey to, as I believe they say, get his man.'

With that, he turned on his heel, grabbed a rain coat from a nearby coat stand, and swept out of the Police Station, Iris and Bailey belatedly following at his heels.

'It's simplicity itself,' said Panda.

He was standing in the shelter of the ruined hut in the same freezing cold field in which they'd found the body. On the wall of the hut he'd drawn a map in chalk, with the position of the body marked out with a cross, and two thin white lines, numbered '85' and '27', forming a reversed right angle alongside and past it. Inside this dog-leg he'd drawn two further lines in red, also numbered '85' and '27', but in this case ending exactly on top of the cross.

'The issue we had when last we were here was that the killer appeared to have given us bad directions; to have directed us to the body but then, for indecipherable reasons of his own amusement, to have had us wander past it and only in fact find it by pure chance.'

He pointed to the white lines. 'Eighty five paces north, followed by twenty seven paces west. Like the man said.'

He paused dramatically as though expecting someone to say something, but when the silence stretched for more than a minute, he sighed and continued, 'Unless it wasn't a man at all!'

Again, he allowed a moment to pass and was about to continue when Iris, who was sitting on her coat on the damp grass, flicked away her cigarette and whooped 'What if it was a woman!' She jumped to her feet and grinned hugely. 'Ooh, you are a clever Panda now you're big, chuck!'

She took a couple of steps towards him, intent on another crushing embrace, but skidded to a halt as Panda held up one imperious paw.

'Not quite Iris,' he said, with a slight shake of the head. 'I suggest to you in fact that the murderer was in fact...a performing midget.'

For a third time he paused dramatically.

Bailey shot Iris a look of disgust, and shook his head. 'You got us all the way out here to announce that?' He could feel the anger building up inside him, a rare occasion in itself but justified in this instance, when a dead woman seemed to be a source of amusement to Iris and her bear. 'A woman is dead!' he all but shouted, 'Stabbed to death and dumped in this field, and all you can do is mock!' The last word was delivered in a shower of spit as he took a step towards the panda, his hands coming up involuntarily, forming fists.

Without looking, Panda reached out a paw and tore a yellowing flyer from the collection pasted and pinned to the hut. Even through the staining and weather beaten discolouration, a drawing of an elephant standing on a ball could clearly be seen and, in the background, a large tent with a wide, open entrance. The words 'Czech National Circus' were printed across the top in letters now faded to pink but once obviously an enticing and inviting red.

'Twenty years ago,' he said, ignoring both Bailey's words and actions, 'an east European circus played here for a period of two weeks. Amongst the circus people employed at that time were a young girl of eighteen named Irina and a midget (or whatever the correct term is nowadays) who went by the unlikely soubriquet of Tiny Tomsk.' Panda held up a paw. 'I took the time to check the local council records to see who had ever used this field and telephoned the circus myself this morning. The owners are the same now as then, and they remembered both Irina and Tomsk. Indeed, they were worried about both of them.'

He passed the faded poster to Bailey, then continued 'Worried about Irina only in a vague unfocused sort of way, granted, for they'd seen neither hide nor hair of her since she disappeared one night in Scotland twenty years before. But worried about Tomsk in the here and now, for he is the only son of the owners and he too has disappeared – though in his case only last week. Disappeared, I would suggest, to this very location. Looking, I would hazard, for the woman who scorned him all those years ago, who preferred to run away from everything she knew rather than be with him. Looking for her in order, I believe, to kill her.'

Panda spoke for the next ten minutes, carefully constructing his tale, laying out the facts as he knew them and demonstrating exactly how each matched up with the next to make a complete picture of a man, twisted in both mind and body, who searched for years for the girl who rejected him. He pulled from his pockets photographs of a tiny, middle aged man arriving at Edinburgh Airport the week before. He thrust birth certificates, passport photos and signed affidavits into the Inspector's hand. He explained how the killer had never intended the woman to be found alive, how the map they had obtained had always been intended as a final mocking gesture, to be delivered only after the little man had left the country and returned home. He showed them the crushed grass where someone had dragged a heavy object, a dead weight, from the hut. Finally, he described the victim's wounds and demonstrated that only a person of far below average height could have inflicted them.

Only once he was certain that he could see belief in the eyes of every person there, did he take out a piece of paper and a pen and, in a careful, measured hand write an address down. He passed the piece of paper to Inspector Bailey.

'You'll find Tiny Tomsk staying here, under the name of Petrovich,' he said, pulling his overcoat closer around him as the wind picked up again. 'Shall we go, Iris? There are other mysteries my newly magnified brain can help unravel, other cases I can solve. I am needed, Iris!'

Iris wasn't sure she cared much for this new super confident and pushy Panda, but she followed him, with a wave of goodbye to the dumbstruck Inspector.

Manchester, March 14, 2004

'It's perfectly straight-forward, Superintendent. You know the direction that the bullet hit by dint of the angle of the wound and hence you know from which direction the shot came. This city has a CCTV feed of one sort or the other every three and a half feet. Simply take a map and draw a line running back from the wound, reversing the direction the shot must have taken, and then look at every bit of CCTV footage you have along that path at the appropriate time of day. I hazard that at some point along that line you will find the man who shot your fashion designer chap.'

Panda pushed through the crowds of fascinated onlookers – really, wasn't it a bit early in the new century for grown men to go out dressed up like eighties fashion victims? – and shouted for Iris to hurry up with the umbrella, he could feel his fur getting damp in the mist.

Hong Kong, January 28, 2021

Panda felt right at home in the palatial surroundings of the corporate headquarters of Sun Lo Finances Ltd. He'd been particularly struck by some rather exquisite Ming vases in the boardroom and was thinking of asking for one – no, two – in payment for solving this case.

He turned back to the tall, red-headed policeman standing in front of the collection of tacky tourist miniatures of medieval Hong Kong harbour.
'...and striking just here cracks the ceramic exterior and reveals within the undamaged statue of the Jade Pagoda. Really, Inspector Potts, I'm surprised you never though of that yourself. Tut tut...'

He must remember and send Iris back to the Bus to pick up some packing materials, he thought. It wouldn't do to damage the vases in transit.

The Expanse, Date Unknown
Iris stood in the background, bored. She wasn't allowed to smoke, she had no-one to talk to and Panda was, as usual nowadays, showing off.

'It goes without saying that only a species which is capable of flight could have perpetrated this outrage, Pro-Consul. Which, I think, narrows things down to the Insectoids of Planet X or the Bird People of The Planet of Cascading Light. Throw in the presence of feathers, three newly laid eggs at the scene and some millet...well, need I say more? No? I thought not.'

He adjusted his silver cape and waved imperiously in Iris' direction. 'Case closed. Time to go before the autograph hunters arrived and ruin my entire day. Chop chop, Iris.'

I'll swing for that little bugger if he doesn't snap out of it soon, Iris thought as she trudged slowly after him.

London, November 3 1888
Panda, for the first time since he had (as he thought of it) Come into his Size, was a little uneasy as he waited for his eleven am appointment to arrive. Not about the case, of course. True, it was possibly the most famous series of unsolved murders in history, and the person he was about to meet was certainly the most famous private detective ever, but neither of those facts bothered him in the slightest. The solution would have been child's play to a...well, to a child, with the only mystery being the fact no-one else had suggested it before now. As for the Great Detective, he expected a decent mind at best, blown out of all proportion by the narrative talents of his biographer and sidekick.

No, what was bothering him was the way in which thoughts of a certain little yellow bottle kept bubbling to the surface of his mind.

He thought he'd gotten over that brief obsession when he'd had his growth spurt, literally out-growing the tiny Panda he thought he might have seen inside the viscous liquid. For a month or more neither the little Panda or the bottle in which she lived has crossed his mind. Then, little by little, she'd crept back into his thoughts. When he'd been embroiled in that investigation into the stolen Greek antiquities, he thought he'd seen an amphora identical to Iris' bottle but it had been a trick of the light and, viewed close up, the two had nothing in common. But it had brought the bottle to mind again and he now found himself sitting in bed each night staring through the glassy gap, willing the tiny furry face to reappear.

He pulled the bottle out of the pocket of his overcoat, unsurprised to discover that he had picked it up that morning even though he had no recollection of doing so. He held it up to his eye and stared at a few lazy bubbles working their way through the liquid. He could hear her voice now too, sultry and seductive, calling his name and promising him love eternal once they were together. But he could see no sign of her. He started guiltily at a noise behind him and quickly stuffed the bottle back in his pocket. Turning, a smile fixed on his face, he held out a paw in greeting as Iris escorted Sherlock Holmes and John Watson into the room.

As he gestured for the two men to sit, Panda was already considering how to handle this interview to best advantage for himself – and Iris, obviously. If rumour was to be believed, the two men had recently been involved in some way with a scandal in the horse racing fraternity, so it might perhaps be best to break the ice with a little joke. Wasn't one of the horses reputed to be involved named Iris?

He was about to remark on the fact when Holmes beat him to the punch and spoke first.

'So this is the gentleman of whom I have heard so much from my friend, Lestrade. I must admit to knowing little about you, Mr Panda, other than what the good Inspector has told me. That, and the obvious facts that you spend much of your time in a larger version of one of those new vehicles which the Germans call a Moterwagen, have a fondness for good quality gin, have recently purchased something called FHM from somewhere called Forbuoys and, of course, that you are a time traveller.'

Holmes turned to Watson, with the faintest of smiles on his lips. 'You know my methods, Watson. Perhaps you would do me the kindness of explaining my simple reasoning to Mr Panda?'

Watson flushed very slightly, but was evidently used to being called upon by Holmes in this manner, for he cleared his throat and replied at once.

'I'm afraid I have no idea what the Germans or anyone else might call a...what did you say, Holmes...motor wagon?' he said, with a shake of the head. 'But I think I can account for the fondness for good gin. There was a very slight odour of gin on your breath as we shook hands just now and from the exquisite tailoring of your suit and your presence in this luxurious suite, you would hardly be expected to drink the gut rot which passes for gin in the poorer sections of the city. As for the peculiarly named FHM – you have dropped a piece of paper on the floor with what seem to be typewritten details of just such a purchase. I would, I think, be safe in further hazarding that this FHM is an object of a some size or value, given that it appears to have cost you only a shilling less than four pounds.

His recitation over, Watson beamed at the assembled company and made to sit down, pausing only briefly to say 'And as for the time traveller, I can only assume

Holmes is making an ill-judged attempt at humour.'

'Not at all, Watson,' Holmes replied before Panda could get a word in. 'But before that, the trifling matter of the moterwagen. I was fortunate enough to be permitted to take a tour of the Benz factory in Germany earlier this year, where I was shown an entirely new form of transport being created by our Teutonic cousins. This moterwagen is a carriage which replaces the horse with a form of internal mechanical engine somewhat akin to that present in a train, only far smaller. One side effect of this engine is the presence of black oil on the hands of everyone who comes within touching distance of it. The same sort of oil as I observed on Mr Panda's thumb when he shook our hands just now. And as we entered the hotel today I also observed a large red vehicle situated just around the corner and smelled the same – you will excuse me, Mr Panda, Miss Wildthyme – dirty, oily odour as I had in the Benz works.'
He smiled again, more widely this time, in the direction of Panda and continued.

'As to the matter of time travel. In the first instance, Mr Panda is clearly not a "person" in any sense recognised by Her Majesty's government and laws and is, in fact, a type of creature the creation of which is far beyond the capabilities of even our English scientists. I would hazard that he is an automaton, a mechanical man made in the shape of a Chinese Panda, and controlled by his companion, the inestimable Miss Wildthyme.' He bowed once, briefly but clearly, to Iris. 'This leads me to conjecture that he is the product either of a civilisation not of this world, or from this planet's own future.'

'But,' Watson interrupted, obviously believing he had found a flaw in Holmes' reasoning, 'what made you plump for time traveller over space traveller, Holmes? Either seems equally improbable to me.'

Holmes reached down and picked up a rectangle of white paper from the floor. 'One thing you missed in your otherwise not entirely inaccurate analysis of Mr Panda's piece of paper, my dear Watson, and another that you noticed but misconstrued. The latter is an understandable mistake to make – that nearly four pounds in price necessarily indicates that the item purchased is one of some value. But as you are aware, everything costs a great deal more today than it did a century ago, and it seems reasonable to hypothesise that the same will hold true of one hundred years from now. That being the case, it further might be reasonable to hypothesise that time travel, rather than existing only in the minds of fantasists and the insane, is a genuine possibility.'

He smiled a final time, real pleasure in his thin face. 'The other indicator is, however, enough to convince even the most hardened of sceptics. There is a date on this bill of sale – '24/02/21'. And while those final two digits may refer to 1821, the type-written (if that is, indeed, what it is) nature of the document strongly indicates otherwise. I would suggest rather that it refers to the year 1921, or possibly a century later than that.'

He too sat down and with the merest hint of a nod indicated that Panda now had the floor. Iris, all but forgotten at the back of the room, had a worried look on her face as she glanced, uncharacteristically nervously, between the two figures.

'Very good, Mr Holmes,' said Panda, showing no sign – if any such feeling existed – of discomfiture at the detective's analysis. 'Very good indeed. Dr Watson's accounts of your abilities did not flatter to deceive, it appears. I might even go so far as to say that yours is the second greatest mind I have encountered in all my many years of travel around the multiverse. After my own, of course.'

This statement proved too much for Watson, who stood up and turned to confront Iris. 'This is outrageous behaviour, madam. My friend may believe that you are travellers in time, but I hold to my initial belief that you are no better than a common con artiste, and this companion of yours merely a man, cunningly disguised to take advantage of the unwary. As I will now demonstrate.'

He took two steps forward as he finished speaking and swung his walking cane in a wide arc, striking Panda hard across the side of the head.

'Oooowwww!' said Panda, pressing a paw to the point of impact while Iris came thundering towards Watson with fury in her eyes.

'Don't you dare harm a hair on his head, you big bloody bully!' she roared, swinging her handbag like a mace at the doctor's head while raking one stilettoed heel down his defenceless shin. 'Let's see how you like it!'

There was a confused moment in which Watson wondered both why a man in a bear suit would bleed so copiously through the suit, and where exactly Miss Wildthyme had learned to fight in so unladylike a manner. Then the pain of his ruined shin flooded over him and he was forced to retreat back to his seat in disarray.

Throughout the brief furore Holmes had remained seated. Now he rose to his feet.

'Do remain calm, Watson! And please accept my apology on behalf of both Dr Watson and myself for his recent, most precipitous actions.' He turned solicitously to Panda. 'Are you hurt, Mr Panda? Watson can strike quite a heavy blow at times.'

Iris nodded, not placated but prepared to call a temporary truce. She took Panda by the elbow and lowered him onto a nearby sofa. 'Do you want a drink, lovey? A glass of water maybe?'

'WATER!' Panda recoiled in mock horror, 'It's a stiff drink I want, Iris, not a bloody wash!'

For a moment, to Iris' delight, he seemed like his old self, but then his face shifted and he continued, 'I'm fine thank you Iris, now perhaps you could unhand me so that I may be allowed to speak?'

Iris couldn't help but look hurt, but she let go of his arm and took a few steps back, leaving Panda alone again in centre stage. He, meanwhile, shot his cuffs and minutely re-arranged his cravat, then grasped a lapel in each hand and prepared to speak.

'The issue as I see it,' he began confidently, 'is that Jack the Ripper, the name most often given to the perpetrator of these vile crimes, is a name which has all but eradicated an earlier, far more useful label, that of "Leather Apron". This is particuraril...'

He stuttered and appeared to stumble over a word, paused for a second, then took another turn at it.

"Particularly galling in that this initial nickname offers us a vital clue in the quest for the killer's genuine identity. In fact I would go so far as to say that this nomencal...nomencat...nomenla...'

Everyone in the room could see that something was wrong. Panda was swaying on his feet, his paws clenching and unclenching spasmodically. One of his eyes was twitching erratically but very visibly. He opened his mouth and closed it again without saying another word, then shook his head repeatedly as though in an effort to clear some obstruction. He closed his eyes and held up a paw intending, it seemed, that no-one should move.

'Have you ever seen the movie Fight Club, Mr Holmes?' he finally asked in a voice wholly unlike his own. He giggled. 'The one with Brad Pitt and Meatloaf with pendulous manboobs? That's what the Ripper is, you know; it's a Fight Club gone too far!' He was laughing now, short, sharp hyperventilating laughs punctuated by sudden whooping intakes of breath. 'A Victorian Flight Club for girls where everyone tries to cut the other girl's guts out and the winner gets a beautiful bonnet and a handy leather apron. A beautiful bonnet for a beautiful girl. A beautiful, beautiful girl...'

His voice trailed off. He turned to face Iris.

'Oh my God! What's that!' he shouted, gesturing over her shoulder. As she turned, he grabbed a heavy ashtray from the table and cracked her across the back of the head.

Before she even hit the ground, he was out the door, knocking a servant flying on the way, and had disappeared into the crowds and fog of Victorian London.

Panda had some explaining to do if he didn't want to be unceremoniously dumped on his backside at the nearest branch of Toys R Us.

She'd come round to discover Dr Watson waving what smelled like a bottle of distilled Pure Evil under her nose. Holmes had filled her in on what had happened and had been able to point her in the direction in which Panda had fled. He had even volunteered himself and Watson to help in finding Panda, but Iris had turned him down. She knew where he had gone as soon as she realised that the perfume bottle was missing from her handbag.

He's a homebody at heart, is Panda. He'll be heading back to the Bus.
But why had he bolted like that? And what was it with him and that damn perfume in the first place?

He'd never shown any great interest in scent before and if he did like to knock out those daft articles on art and whatnot for the Sundays, it'd never led him to go round stealing other people's perfume bottles before.

She sighed in exasperation and sat down heavily. It was all very strange. She'd have a fag, she decided, then go back to the Bus and kick his arse for him.

An hour and a half later and Iris still hadn't found him. And she was really, really getting sick of playing Hide and go Seek.

He'd definitely been back to the Bus – he'd left the bloody doors wide open – but in spite of turning the entire place upside down, neither he nor the perfume bottle were anywhere to be seen. She'd opened every drawer, shone torches in every cupboard, peered into unused spaces and caught her knee a nasty knock on an inlaid occasional table.

She was now officially annoyed with Panda. When she got her hands on the little...

In fact, while she was stomping around the Bus in the highest of dudgeons, kicking random objects, poking sticks into corners and generally combining the maximum amount of grumpy bad temper with the minimum amount of useful searching, Panda was watching from a somewhat cramped storage cupboard which, before he'd grown to nearly six foot tall, he'd occasionally hidden in when seeking a little peace and quiet.

He had the little yellow bottle clasped tightly in one paw, the remote controls for the laser in the other, and a song of the purest joy in his little fabric heart.

No longer alone!

It took all his self-control not to scream that fact out loud. After all this time, he was alone no more! No longer Last of the Pandas! Finally...finally...he had found another one of his people!

Shrunk down inside a tiny bottle, granted. Which was unusual, granted, but she'd explained all about the evil race of conquerors who had enslaved her people, shrunk them down and imprisoned them in these glass prisons. It was very Superman II, he'd said, but she'd looked blank.

It would be foolish to complain about so minor an issue (both the size and the lack of knowledge of Richard Donner movies) in light of the beautiful, fur covered black and white face he had glimpsed staring coquettishly out through the glass. No, worse than foolish – positively churlish.

Especially when he had the means of bringing them together literally to hand. Watson's blow to his head had jerked everything into place, and now he knew exactly what to do!

He risked a glimpse through a crack in the door frame and caught sight of Iris disappearing through the Bus doors, obviously intent on checking outside.

This was the moment he had been waiting for!

He jumped up from his hiding place and quickly ran to a spot six feet or so in front of the laser. He carefully lowered the bottle onto the floor, sighting back from there to the tip of the laser's firing element and doing the necessary calculations in his head.

Perfect.

With one last tiny adjustment to the position of the bottle and a hurried prayer to the ghost of Larry "Buster" Crabbe, he headed back to his hiding place, where he ducked down and prepared to press the button on the remote which would fire the laser. If his amended version of Iris' calculations was correct then the laser would shear right through the top of the bottle, releasing the gorgeous little Panda inside.

Here goes nothing, he thought, and pressed the button.

The next few minutes were confused.

There was a bright light from the spot at which the laser hit the bottle and an unexpected noise very like the sound of a small elephant being forced through a mangle. Panda thought for a moment he heard the words 'hell doing stupid' on the wind but he was distracted by a great black cloud coming towards him and was never sure later if he had just imagined them. He leaped to his feet to avoid the oncoming storm, banged his head off the bottom of the shelf above him, staggered forward in a daze and, as he simultaneously tried to duck underneath the arms of the angry cloud and have a little lie down until his head stopped spinning, tripped and threw the remote control directly into the path of the laser beam.

There was an extremely loud BANG and, as quickly as it had begun, all the noise and lights stopped and the Bus returned to normal.

Panda rubbed the sore spot on the top of his head and smiled sheepishly at Iris, who was standing alongside the gently smoking ruin of the laser.

'Sorry about that, my dear' he said. 'I thought I might have a bash at getting the lid off for you.' He shrugged helplessly. 'It didn't entirely work out. So how about a tiny tincture and then I'll clear up this mess.'

He was smiling his most winning smile and counting on the fact that Iris was a big softie at heart, so it was doubly unfortunate that it was at that point that all the rivets on the walls of the Bus started popping out and whizzing dangerously across the room, to be followed by thin, high pressure jets of what looked and smelled suspiciously like pale yellow perfume.

'What have you done, you dozy bear?' Iris shouted. She sprinted along the aisle of the now wildly rocking Bus, headed for the driver's seat. As she ran, the windows cracked horrifically, spidery lines spreading willy-nilly across the glass. A cabinet fell forward and struck her a glancing blow across her back, knocking her briefly to her knees – but no sooner did she stumble than she was back up, throwing herself forward and wrenching open the door to the driver's section.

Panda meanwhile hadn't moved. He stood, speechless, and stared at the nearest window, which was bowed inwards like a soap bubble, the usual view of iridescent void matter replaced by a solid wall of yellow liquid, broken here and there by chains of tiny bubbles spiralling upwards. For a moment he thought he saw something moving outside, then he was certain as a dark shape came barrelling towards him, before coming to a halt directly in front of the deformed glass.

The vision presenting itself directly in front of him was covered in what he was sure must be the softest of soft fur, a mix of deepest black and most pristine white, with two tiny, sparkling eyes set deep in a perfectly round face.

'Oh my' he said and reached out with one nervous paw.

As the window in front of him finally gave way to the pressure of the sea of liquid outside and shattered into a million shining, deadly pieces of glass, each of which speared through the air towards Panda.

And stopped.

The shards twisted and struggled in the air, for all the world as though alive and vindictive and desperate to drive themselves into Panda. As the light of Iris' standing lamps caught the edges of the glass fragments, it reflected like tiny beams of sunlight, brightening the sullen reflected yellow gloom of the Bus interior and glinting in the beads of Panda's eyes.

'How's that for timing then?' Iris shouted with a grin as she strode back up the aisle. 'You shrunk us down and zapped us along the laser beam, straight into that bloody bottle. And the pressure of the perfume was about to squish us flat when I put a force-fie…Panda? Love?'

She reached a hand up to her head and wiped blood away from her eyes. Tentatively – far more tentatively than Iris ever usually did anything – she prodded Panda in the side with one finger. 'Panda?' she said again, quietly. 'I've saved the day, chuck. Turned the Bus windows into a force-field. Brilliant, eh?'

She glanced round the Bus, taking in the damage over and above that caused to the window now vibrating in razor sharp splinters in front of Panda.

Three other windows were in pieces, one gone entirely, replaced by a wall of frozen yellow ice. Elsewhere the very walls of the Bus had buckled and cracked, arcs of perfume reaching into the room like thin, nicotine stained fingers. Even the door had concertinaed back on itself with gallons of perfume turned solid across a large portion of the floor.

And then there was Panda. Iris ran a hand across the top of his head, smoothing out a tiny knot in his fur and unconsciously making small, soothing noises at the back of her throat.

'Oh Panda,' she whispered, 'what have we done?'

"I don't know what to do, Panda love, it's as simple as that. Your old Auntie Iris is out of tricks. Stuck inside a bottle, of all things. Ironic, really. Iris Wildthyme trapped inside some cheap splash. That's not going to stop her, is it? Not the transtemporal adventuress. A shimmy here, a swivel there, press the red button, pull the silver lever – 1, 2, 3 and off we go. Escaping into the big wide Universe again and just in time for Sloe Gins at Raffles and a bag of chips with loads of vinegar from the Kingfisher! Brown sauce for you, though. Because vinegar smells like a public urinal in Inverness on a Friday night, you said, but I know it's because it gives you a rash.

Iris Wildthyme's Eleventh Law of Time and Space, that is – always make sure you've got plenty of gin, and money for chips.

Get a bit tipsy and eat a lovely big bag of burning hot chips. Maybe a pickled onion and a bottle of pineapple juice. Just the two of us, off together on some fantastic, improbable adventure.

But we won't be doing that again, will we Panda love? Not now. Because the only way I can get us out of this mess is by turning off the force field for a few seconds.

And if I do that the perfume will flood the Bus and that'll be that.

Look on the bright side, though. That means you don't need to blame yourself. Even if you weren't frozen in front of all that glass, only a beat of your little heart from it cutting you to tiny cloth pieces, even if you were sitting here beside me, sharing this – what the hell's it say on the label? – this Aquavit, even then there's all those other smashed windows and the pressure of all that buggering perfume on the walls, ready to crush us flat in a second. There's not even enough booze in the perfume to make it worth trying to drink our way out.

Remind me to thank 105 for the present will you, Panda?

What about that 105, eh? I never did find out his real name. That's the story of my life though, isn't it? Bombing about the place in a mad rush, never stopping long enough to get to know anyone, not really know them. Then off to somewhere new. New planet, new time, new people. Sometimes I sit at night when you're asleep and I feel dog tired, deep in my bones, like I just want to stop moving and sit down in my Bus and wait for miracles to come to me.

Not that we can sit here until something miraculous happens though. I don't know if your little eyes are working but I can see the way that everything's still moving, only ever so slowly. Those bits of glass are half an inch closer to you than they were a couple of hours ago and that puddle of perfume is a teensy bit bigger. Three hours I reckon, no more than that, and then it'll all be finished for us. You like a novelty glass holder and me and the Bus flat as one of Jenny's parties.

Funny how she turned out, eh? Delhi Belly Jenny, with the time trots propelling her across the known multiverse. She knew the location of every Portaloo and pub toilet from here to Swindon, you know. Swindon, the planet, that is. Always getting things wrong and needing me to come and rescue her. I remember once she got herself trapped in what she thought was the belly of a killer robot and she sent me this terrified video message saying she was being slowly digested. Turned out to be one of those sentient elevators that were right in fashion on Aridis at the time and the 'stomach acid' she was being coated with was just a spray designed to keep the pot plants moist. And now look at her. Swanning around Darlington with MIAOW and that creepy bugger Alucard.

I never liked him much. Still don't, if truth be told. That anagram got right on my nerves, for a start. Taking the mickey if you ask me. Even Barbara figured it out and, Lord love her, she had no more brains than a minor Royal. And that flashy cape and the way he leered! Poncey bugger. Fancied himself a bit too much, if you want my opinion.

Not like Noel. Now there was a gentleman! And Tom. He was lovely too. Remember his smile, Panda? I miss his smile. And Flossie and Fritter the poodle, and

Captain whatsisname, the one that married a wolf. And whatever happened to Harriet, eh?

Companions, people used to call them, as though I were a rich old posh bird and they were impoverished youngsters being paid to take walks with me and read me improving books. Iris and her companions, they used to say. And I suppose they were, at that. Not proper friends, really, but not just lodgers on the bus either. Somewhere in between, like people you meet on holiday. You kick about together, meeting every morning at breakfast and spending the day nattering by the pool, ordering four bottles of cold beer at a time, and getting rat arsed every night. But it only lasts a wee while, and even if you meet up when you get back home it's not the same and by the time the next holiday comes round you're struggling to remember their names. That's what it's like having companions.

But not you and me, Panda. You and me are pals. Friends. Proper friends that you can't leave behind, no matter what. That's us.

But never mind all that! I need another drink! Better than all this moping around. How about you, love? A teeny weeny gin?

No, I suppose not.

Maybe it's best you can't see what's out there anyway. I can, and it's not very nice. A minute ago I got a glimpse of a long tooth and a scaly hide as whatever they are swam too close to the window. They look a right shower of ugly buggers. Can't think why on earth you wanted to go and visit them.

Anyhow, no point in sitting here pining. I'll just finish this glass of whatsitsname, I think. I feel a bit dizzy to be honest. And the blood keeps getting in my eyes. And I've got such a pain in my back.

All I need to do is turn off the force field. How about I tidy myself up a bit, sit down there, right beside you, my little...well, not so little now...pal, and we'll get this over with?

I'll do my hair first, I think. If I can keep myself upright for long enough...and it's not even the drink for once. I do feel a bit funny, Panda, I'll not lie to you...maybe I'll have a sit down first...

Later, Panda often asked Iris to explain how they'd ever managed to escape from so vexatious a conundrum. It was her favourite story and Panda, for all his occasional sulks and huffs, was her friend and he did like to make her happy.

'There I was, lovey,' she always began, 'ready to chuck in the towel and lay down and die. You were standing there doing sod all, there was perfume everywhere, I was bruised and battered and bleeding and, if I'm being totally honest, I'd had a bit of a drink. I didn't know what to do.'

Depending on how much gin she'd had at that point in telling the story, she would then either sigh melodramatically and allow a tear or two to slide down her face, or cackle madly and shout 'Oi, Manuel! More sangria over here!' at the nearest barman.

'Things looked black, Panda,' she would invariably continue, 'they really did. And not just because I was reduced to drinking all those odd bottles in foreign that people leave at parties! I was all for sitting down beside you in me best frock and spiffy hair-do and letting the perfume do its worst. I'd even got as far as shifting my chair over beside you, you know. And I'd have done it too if it hadn't been for your paper jabbing me a nasty one in the ribs as I sat down. You must have gone and stuffed it down the side of the cushion after you'd done the crossword, you lazy sod.'

At this point, Iris always grinned widely. 'And lucky for us both that you had because it gave me a brilliant idea! What we needed was something focused enough to make the Bus bigger than the bottle and powerful enough to move it away from the bloody thing at the same time. Something that you had been going to throw your paper in not so long ago!'

The triumph was writ large across her face by this point, sober or not. 'All I had to do was materialise the Bus inside the Bus! Well, inside the cupboard with the mini-sun in it to be exact. And then throw one of my cans of hairspray out the window. It was a bugger to figure out exactly how long the Bus could stay inside its own insides before the Universe noticed and it was an even bigger pain in the bum to decide between hairsprays, but I can be bloomin' clever when I need to be. Five minutes of mental arithmetic, a couple of quick ones for the road and I started the engine. Ooh, but I felt dizzy as anything. All I could see out the side windows was cheap plywood veneer and I couldn't see a damn thing out the front except ruddy great wall of flame. I wasn't sure we were going to make it for a minute, I don't mind telling you, and when I bunged out the hairspray and it expanded to three miles long well...lucky for us both that the explosion knocked the Bus about twenty light years away from the sun and not towards it. I hadn't considered that, between you and me. Anyway, once I picked myself off the floor, all I had to do was dematerialise - and ten minutes after that we were in a London back street in 1985, windows knackered, door hanging off and the whole place stinking of cheap splash and ozone. But alive! And you were back to your normal compact self! I tell you Panda love, that were definitely one of my more brilliant ideas!'

'Oi. Manuel!' she nearly always concluded, 'More sangria over here!'

Gingerly pushing the remains of the Bus doors to one side, Iris stepped down from the battered remains of her combined home and means of transport, and took a walk round its outside to check the full extent of the damage.

The door could be pulled back into shape and the various dents and bumps in the metalwork bashed out by some brawny Kwik-Fit lad, but three windows needed replaced and both front headlights had disappeared entirely.

Still, not too high a price to pay for escaping certain death, she decided. She'd need to have a long chat with Panda, now that he was back to his more familiar size, concerning the danger of playing with high energy laser beams. And get to the bottom of what about the bottle had...

The bottle! She'd forgotten all about that! That was a present from Senor 105, the big softie, and she was damned if she was losing it just because Panda had gone a bit mental.

She'd need to get the windows fixed and the door kicked back into sha...

For the second time in as many minutes, Iris found her train of thought derailed. She'd been walking as she was thinking, circling the Bus, mentally making notes of the damage, assessing what needed replaced and what could be left temporarily as it was while she went and recovered Senor 105's gift. She's been concentrating so hard that she'd almost not noticed the man who'd stepped out from the shadows and was now pointing a gun at her.

He was medium height and build, maybe five eight or nine, with longish blond hair, obviously dyed and styled in a familiar looking wave cum side parting across his deeply tanned face. Carefully cultivated two day stubble and sparklingly white teeth combined with tight blue jeans and a pastel jumper to complete what passed for his look.

'You're the dead spit of George Michael!' Iris burst out laughing, then as suddenly stopped. 'Here! You're not him, are you?'

'No,' the man said, looking straight at Iris and causing her to shiver. 'I am not George Michael.'

Standing up slightly straighter, he shook himself and air shimmered. His clothing, his body, even his head appeared to morph and shift like coloured sand rearranging itself in a child's toy. The very skin of his face twisted into one shape after another, one or two familiar enough for Iris to give a tiny start of recognition. The air began to ripple like a wave and for a moment she could only make out a vague, molten shape where he stood, as though viewing him through an imperfect piece of glass, filled with bubbles and bends. Then everything was still and a naked man stood there, taller, with flat, black eyes and odd tattoos ('markings' Iris thought, 'not tattoos') covering every inch of his skin. The gun remained firmly held in his right hand.

'My name is Dove Davies,' he said simply.

'Please to meet you I'm sure' Iris replied, trying desperately not to stare anywhere embarrassing. There was a long silence, then 'So, you're a shape shifter are you?'

Dove Davies tilted his head to one side. 'I can change form, yes,' he said with a puzzled look. 'But you ask as though that one simple thing should be enough in itself to define who I am. It is not. Would you, for instance, be content to describe yourself as primarily someone who bends at the waist?'

His lips curled into a tiny smile as he spoke and Iris found herself thinking that he was actually quite dishy for a naked, tattooed blue and orange guy.

'Fair dos' she said. 'What can we do to help you then?'

'You have something of mine. Something deadly.' He held out his left hand. 'The bottle, please,' he said.

'What bottle?' asked Iris in what she considered an innocent tone of voice. 'I haven't seen a bottle for...ooh, years. Not much call for them round here. No, sir. Not for BOTTLES,' she ended with a shout.

'What's that you say?' asked Panda, as he popped his head round the ruined door of the Bus. 'No bottles? What are you talking about? There's a lovely bottle of house red decanting even now, you silly old mare.' He noticed Davies for the first time. 'Oh hello there,' he said.

Davies turned round to cover this new target with his gun, which allowed Iris to lash out with all her might at another unprotected target altogether. As Davies crumpled to the ground, she kicked the gun away and ran into the Bus, heaving the door closed through sheer panic-driven strength.

'We'll just have to take off with no windows' she shouted to Panda. 'Strap yourself to something solid, preferably in the middle of the Bus and close your eyes. We're only moving through time and not space, so it should only be for a few seconds but you really don't want to be looking at the Maelstrom as close up as we're about to get.'

She headed off to the driving compartment while Panda secured himself in place. He screwed his eyes shut as he heard the familiar sound of the Bus dematerialising.

Watson crouched over the servant's body and gently closed his eyes. 'I've no explanation for it, Holmes. But I've no explanation for any number of things which have occurred today.'

He straightened up and was in the process of putting his jacket back on when, with a clatter of high heels, Iris shot into the room.

It didn't require Holmes' magnificent mind to tell that in some way everything had changed in the few minutes Miss Wildthyme had been gone from the room. Somehow she had contrived to become bruised and filthy. There was blood caked above her eye and in her hair, and her clothing was ripped – thankfully not indecorously – in several places. Of Mr Panda there was no sight, though she was carrying a small toy bear under one arm. Mr Panda's child perhaps? Or some form of doll designed for use in voodoo, the savage religion practised by Her Majesty's less civilised subjects, in the jungles and mountains of the Empire?

'We came back for the bottle,' Iris said, breathlessly, 'but when we got to the street outside there was a great bloody crowd and we couldn't get near the spot where we used to be parked, so we thought we'd duck in here and see if you know anything about it?'

She placed the bear on a table. Holmes was secretly rather pleased with himself that when the creature suddenly spoke he managed to maintain an air of nonchalance.

'There's a body on the floor, Iris,' it said, tilting its head stiffly downwards.

Iris knelt and took a closer look at the dead man. 'Isn't that the lad you knocked arse over...well, knocked over anyway, on your way out of here?'

She reached up and helped the bear down. 'He's dead. And his face has gone all withered and horrible looking, like Goldie Hawn with her make up off.'

It was difficult to make out facial expressions on the tiny mannequin, but Holmes could hear the horror in his voice as it whispered 'Do you think I killed him, Iris?'

'The poor chap was knocked over and he was like that before he hit the ground,' Watson interjected. 'I can't explain it.'

'He said that the bottle was deadly.' Iris was almost speaking to herself. 'That Dove Davies said it was deadly, and now we know just how deadly it is.' She stood up, lifting the bear as she did so. 'It's not your fault, Panda love,' she said, 'but we need to find the bottle before that bugger Davies does. God knows what he intends to do with it – nothing good, I'll bet. Let's go!'

And with that, she ran out of the room, and the last Holmes saw of either was a pair of black paws wriggling under an arm and a plaintive voice saying 'At least stick me in your bag, woman, I'm starting to feel sick...'

It's one of the useful peculiarities of the temporal traveller, especially the less than rigorously moral one, that no matter how long you take to do one thing or how many attempts you have at fixing the other, there's always more time, always another chance.

So it proved now with Iris and Panda as they sped across the multiverse in search of the little bottle of perfume.
Iris had spoken to Senor 105 and had the whole story of its tangled history from him, complete with the most dire of warnings.

'Ah, Iris, rather would I have died myself than put you in danger! Too late, my tests indicated the bottle is of extra-terrestrial origin, and that there is a thin coating of an element I do not know round its surface. That I cannot put a name to the element is bad enough, but there is far, far worse news. In the hands of any normal man or woman the element is inert and harmless, the cause of a small itch at worst. But in the hands of one who has travelled through time? Then it turns that person into a máquina de la muerte – a machine of death! His most light touch will kill instantly. Everywhere he turns...death!'

'Calm yourself lovey, and stop worrying. Me and Panda are on the case now. Soon have it back from that Davies bloke, if he's got it. But first I think we should take a wander back a bit in time, see if we can't pick it up before it even gets to you, or me, or him...'

So it was that the two travellers had taken the Bus, now fixed up and back to normal, to England at the turn of the century where they'd searched a country house from top to bottom and attempted to rob a tomb, and from there to the London home of Lord John Roxton, who had blanched at the very mention of the bottle, but could shed no light on its whereabouts. Enquiries in back alleyway jewellers and dodgy pool halls the multiverse over produced equally disappointing results, but they kept looking, giving themselves three hours in each location, then looping back on themselves temporally and trying somewhere else.

But it got them nowhere. They'd failed. No matter where they looked or who they spoke to no-one knew anything about Mr Davies or the Bottle.

Iris sat in a desolate Wotherspoon's and pushed a half-empty glass around the table. She was dog-tired after days of constant searching and unlike Panda, who she could hear snoring loudly in her bag, she couldn't even seem to drown her sorrows in drink. She flipped open her cigarettes with one nail and hooked a long thin Sobranie out between thumb and forefinger. She was just about to raise it to her lips when the teenage barmaid caught her eye and nodded at one of several identical signs on the wall. No Smoking.

'Bloody hell, this is getting us nowhere,' she said to the air. 'What we need is a gang. Me and Panda and Sherlock, maybe even that crook Dorrington, and 105 and MIAOW. Maybe Brenda and...'

She trailed off and stared silently for a few moments into the middle distance. '105 and MIAOW,' she finally said, then repeated the words while giving her bag a firm shake. 'Wake up, you lazy sod – it's time we went hunting in an invisible city!'

'...and then it came to me, like ones of those epiphanies you hear about!' Iris explained as the Bus rattled through the Maelstrom. 'I'd seen that Mr Davies before but I never made the connection until just now. In La Ciudad that time Jenny and I were trying to find our way back to the Bus after that first MOOO affair, well one of the. faces that I saw Davies face change into, I saw the same face in La Ciudad. He was there, Panda! And we can catch him!'

She happily flicked ash out the window of the Bus and Panda watched with fascination as it sparked into tiny flames. He couldn't help worrying that Dove Davies would be able to snuff them out with equal ease, should they ever catch up with him. Still, there was no point in saying any such thing. Iris, he could see, had swung round to her usual wild self-confidence and in that mood anything negative he said would simply be ignored. Really, sometimes he wondered why he even bothered speaking at all. He might as well sit in dumb silence for all the attention Iris paid to him. Just sit there and say nothing and let her blunder from one disaster into another.

'Iris!' he snapped at her, just as she flicked a switch and the Bus materialised in front of La Ciudad. 'I think we should have a proper think before we go marching in there. What if this Dove Davies can turn into anything he wants? What if he turns into a dragon? Or a dinosaur? Or the little girl in red from Don't Look Now? You know how much that gives you the willies.'

Iris just grinned and stuffed him into her bag. 'Let's go get ourselves a shape-shifting, perfume stealing nudist!' she said as she opened the Bus' doors and headed for the city entrance.

Inside was a scene as chaotic as anything Panda had ever witnessed. Aliens he'd never even dreamed existed - and a few which qualified as Actual Nightmares – flapped, slithered and slapped through the myriad corridors and levels of the city. Every few seconds there would be a loud pop and another confused looking creature would suddenly appear as if by magic. Here and there Panda could see animals running around and in the middle distance he could swear he could just make out a colony of monkeys. The noise was unbelievable. The smell wasn't much better.

He reached up and pulled at Iris' sleeve. 'For pity's sake Iris, can we get this over with? If I don't go deaf the stench in here will kill me.'

'It won't take a minute, pet,' she said, shading her eyes with her palm. 'I just need to get my bearings. It's been a while, but we can always ask the Administrator if we can't find...ah, there you go!'

Panda pulled his opera glasses out and peered through them in the direction she was pointing. He could see another Iris talking with Senor 105 on a raised balcony. A young woman, obviously part of the group, was gesticulating at the two of them but she had her back to him and he couldn't tell who she was. In front of them a balloon was floating towards a giant, spinning cube. 'There he is!' Iris hissed in triumph, pointing at the figure of a man who had just leapt to one side to avoid being crushed by the cube. 'I'd recognise that thieving bugger anywhere! Let's go!'

Panda was forced over the next several minutes to concede that there was a surprising amount of both strength and agility in Iris' deceptively relaxed frame. With liberal use of her elbows and handbag, she cleared a path through the crowds of time travellers until she and Panda were only a few feet away from their quarry.

Davies in this form was a tall black man with a neatly trimmed beard, dressed in a simple, yet expensive, black suit. He was obviously well built and at his hip Panda could make a weapon of some sort, loosely clipped to his belt. It looked as though it were intended to be easy to take out quickly, Panda thought nervously.

'So what's the plan then?' he whispered. 'I hope it's something foolproof and really, really clever because he doesn't look like the type to play games.'

'Watch,' said Iris, 'and learn.'

She tightened her grip on her bag, put one hand in her coat pocket and ran forward, shoulder charging the hairy, one eyed creature directly in front of her straight into Davies. Caught off guard, he stumbled backwards and tripped over a small, golden robot which had been standing, immobile, behind him. Iris took two quick steps and, before he could do anything, reached into the inside pocket of his jacket and grabbed the little Bottle. She turned quickly and began the bruising process of making her way back to the entrance and, from there, to the Bus.

Davies, it was clear, was determined to get the Bottle back. He jumped to his feet, throwing the golden robot off him, and set off in pursuit.

For half a dozen steps Iris thought she was going to make it. But then, within sight of the doorway, she felt Davies' hand on the hood of her coat. She spun in a circle, letting each fall arm out of the jacket in turn, but in spinning she'd moved away from the door and straight into a cul-de-sac, the exit to which Davies now blocked. He held out his hand. 'The Bottle please, Iris.'

Iris' shoulder slumped. Panda, looking out from her bag, was suddenly acutely aware of just how tired she looked. The cut above her eye had opened again and blood was slicked across her forehead. Her hair hung in rats tails down either side of her face. Her clothes were dirty and torn. He could see her cigarettes lying crushed underfoot on the ground, where they must have fallen. She looks beaten, he thought, and felt an unfamiliar pain in the pit of his stomach.

As Iris opened her hand and showed Davies the little yellow bottle in her palm, Panda was briefly reminded of the lady panda trapped inside, but that all seemed terribly unreal and unimportant to him now, when his friend was so utterly abject.

Davies reached forward and gently took the Bottle out of her hand. 'Why?' she asked as he slipped it into the pocket of his jacket. 'Just who are you?'

The man has been in the process of turning away, but he stopped and turned back. 'I suppose it can do no harm now. I am...I think the closest analogy you would understand is... a policeman, though as with shapeshifter the word is both too small and too specific to have very much genuine utility,' he said. 'I come from a time long after you, Iris. Long after everyone you can see around you now. You and your people will be dust and legends before the ancestors of my people are even born. I can name very single star still burning in my Universe, and every race still living. Have you ever been that far, Iris? To the Last Planets, where the sky at night is full of the corpses of galaxies and dark as pitch? You should go one day, and see what delights the final gutterings of this Universe have to offer. Fly through the Fields of Universes, or visit the Boulevard of Brutalities, designed by the Faction and built by the Carpathians, a million mile street lined with alternate realities gone rogue, used as a prison and a dumping ground by a thousand races through the long years of forever.'

'Been there, it was rubbish,' Iris interrupted with a flash of irritation, 'We don't need the five dollar sales pitch, just get on with it.'

Davies showed no sign of offence or surprise, but continued smoothly, 'And the creatures within this bottle come from that time: my time. For thousands of years I have been searching for them. I had them once, long ago, in the city which once sat above this peculiar place. But I was chased and I fell and I lost them and could not reclaim them, though I came close once or twice. You must understand, Iris, that they are criminals and murderers, and far, far worse. They are able like me to take on any form they desire, but unlike me they use that ability to woo the unwary and snare the less advanced. A long, long time ago they were sentenced for their crimes to be shrunk down and enclosed in this glass prison, then cast adrift on the time winds. But they are able to call out to the minds of others, requesting aid, offering the heart's most secret desires in return. They destroyed an entire race to obtain enough of the time displacing element to coat their ship and escape from the Maelstrom.' He gestured at the bulge in his jacket. 'But there is no escape and there is always justice.'

He turned again to leave, but Iris grabbed the tail of his jacket. 'Wait just a minute, Inspector Morse,' she said, some of her old vigour in her voice. 'What's going to happen to them now?'

Davies appeared puzzled for the first time. 'I am not an Inspector,' he said finally, 'I am a Dove, as I told you when we first met. As for these criminals, they will be tried and, if found guilty of their latest crimes, destroyed.' He held up a hand, forestalling Iris' protest. 'There are not enough resources left for any to be wasted on the likes of these. We are just, but we are rarely merciful.'

And then he walked away, leaving Iris to sink to the ground, her back against the wall of the City.

The trek back to the Bus seemed far longer than it had on the way in. Panda tried once or twice to speak to Iris, but each time she shook her head and kept walking. All the life seemed to have drained out of her, leaving her almost physically changed. She trudged heavily towards the red expanse of the Bus, barely managing to lift her feet off the ground and instead dragging them listlessly across the smooth floor. Once or twice Panda thought he heard her sniff back a tear and as she pushed open the Bus door and stumbled inside he couldn't help but fear that something had broken inside her.

He jumped down and immediately headed for the drinks cabinet. A spot of the hard stuff would put some fizz back in her glass. He poured two generous gin and tonics and...

'GET IN!'

Iris was literally jumping with excitement, hoping from foot to foot as though on a griddle, and swinging her arms around her head like the most drunken of revellers at a seventies New York disco.

'Quick!' she shouted at Panda, grabbing a gin and knocking it back in one. 'Grab a seat, we need to get out of here before he realises!'

She opened her hand and with a 'catch!' threw a small yellow bottle to Panda. 'The old switcheroo, chuck, it's a classic! Buy a cheap bit of tat that looks the same from some back alley jeweller and then give that to the bad guy instead of the real thing! Works every time!'

She threw the Bus into gear. 'We need to get a move on now though. We need to go back to the city which used to be up above us and put the bottle in place for Dove Davies to steal and then lose. Trap them in a never ending loop. They can't hurt anyone else, they serve their time and they don't get squished by what sounds to me like a right kangaroo court. And then we can go and get absolutely plastered!'

Outside, a tall black man watched from the shadows as, in a cloud of exhaust smoke, the Bus vanished. 'I think that is acceptable, Iris,' he said quietly, tossing a small yellow bottle from one hand to the other and then dropping it to the ground where it smashed. The air was filled with the sickly stench of cheap perfume. 'Justice and mercy need not always be strictly binary.'

He pushed a finger into a small box he pulled from his pocket, which then unfolded to a flat wooden square. A faint smell of jasmine drifted across the air and had anyone walked by at that precise moment they might well have unexpectedly found themselves thinking that the smell was at one and the same time the sound of new snow underfoot and the texture of rough blankets. Dove bent his arms back on themselves and quite clearly said 'One', then disappeared.

will return